CINDERELLA AND THE MARINE

San Diego Social Scene Book #4

Tess Summers

Seasons Press LLC

Published: 2018

ISBN: 9781723823664

Published by Seasons Press LLC.

Copyright © 2018, Tess Summers.

Edited by Sandy Ebel, Personal Touch Editing

Cover by OliviaProDesign

This is a work of fiction. The characters, incidents, and dialogues in this book are of the author's imagination and are not to be construed as real. Any resemblance to actual events or persons, living or dead, is completely coincidental.

This book is for mature readers. It contains sexually explicit scenes and graphic language that may be considered offensive by some.

All sexually active characters in this work are eighteen years of age or older.

Cinderella and the Marine

One night. No strings attached. What could go wrong?

Cooper

I was pretty happy living the carefree life of a successful bachelor. Money to spend, a revolving door of women, no commitment, no relationship troubles—it was perfect. At least, that's what I thought until I held my friends' newborn baby in my arms, and she smiled at me.

That was the moment I realized what life was all about. That was also the moment it occurred to me I needed a baby mama—stat.

So... the hunt is on for the perfect candidate. But first, I might have to have one last fling—you know, go out with a bang. Literally.

Kate

Thanks to making a few wrong decisions along the way, I'm now busting my ass waiting tables while putting myself through college. It's not ideal, but I'm determined to stand on my own two feet and take care of my responsibilities the best I can.

But I'm still a woman. I have needs. I just don't have the time for any kind of commitment. Naturally, when a smoldering hot Marine offers me a no-strings-attached one-night stand, I'm all on board.

Turns out... he wants more than I'm willing to give.

Dedication

This book is dedicated to the men and women in uniform who help keep us safe. Thank you for your service to our country.

Acknowledgments

Mr. Summers: Thanks for being such a good sport when I tell you to get the hell out so I can write. You're kind of awesome.

Summers children: Thanks for leaving me alone so I can write, and to Oldest and Middle Kid for taking care of the dogs when I'm in Michigan writing.

Bad Girls' Club–expanded version: I simply love you guys. You're the best.

Sandy Ebel: Thank you for everything you did to make this book better.

Janece Ellers: Thank for your fast feedback every single time I send you anything. I loved brainstorming on the boat and discussing the cum on the face issue. LOL

To the writing community: I am still amazed at how supportive and generous you are. Thank you for everything.

All my friends on social media: Thank you for your continued support of my writing. It means a lot.

My real-life friends: Wow. You've been amazing how you've backed me in this chapter in my life. Thank you.

My extended family: Best. Family. Ever.

Lastly, to my readers: Thank you for continuing to enjoy my stories as much as I love writing them. I remain in awe that I get to share my work with others.

Table of Contents

Chapter One

Cooper

He walked out of the building's automatic sliding doors, deep in thought, not noticing the ambulance as it approached.

The honk of the vehicle's horn snapped him back to reality, and he stopped abruptly on the sidewalk to let it pass before stepping into the crosswalk.

Cassie and Luke Rivas' brand new daughter was so tiny. The Marine captain didn't realize human beings could be that small, and there was something about holding the little creature in his arms, her teeny fingers gripping just one of his that had him unsettled.

His thirty-fifth birthday was coming up in a few months, and he'd never even had the slightest desire to have a child. Little Sofia Claire Rivas' cooing response as he spoke softly to her had just changed all that.

That might be a problem since he didn't even have a steady girlfriend. He was what one might call a *perpetual bachelor.* The buffet of women in Southern California was too tempting to pick just one entrée—variety being the spice of life and all that.

But that baby, man, he wanted one of those.

Cooper noticed the neon sign of the diner across from the hospital and decided to stop in for an early lunch before heading back to the base.

The bell on the door jingled as he pushed it open, and he surveyed the restaurant with the pink vinyl seating and fake wood linoleum tables in need of updating. The sign by the door indicated he should seat himself, so he decided on one of the counter seats available at the huge square in the middle of the eatery. Picking up a stray laminated menu from a few seats to his right, he flipped his ivory coffee mug to indicate he'd like a cup, getting lost in thought again as he looked the menu over.

Maybe he should start thinking about settling down and starting a family. His promotion to Major was right around the corner—the timing made sense. He'd gotten serious with a few girls over the last ten years, but it was always short-lived, and the last woman who'd held his attention for more than a day just gave birth to another man's daughter, so his prospects for a lasting relationship weren't exactly lining up at his door.

No, the line at his door was more of a revolving one—enter at night, leave in the morning. You want to come in again? Go to the back of the line.

Cassie once told him he should try going on ten dates with a girl before sleeping with her; it would give him the opportunity to get to know her as a person. He'd scoffed when she said it, but now he thought she might have been onto something. It might be his best bet at finding his future bride and mother of his children. It had apparently worked for Cassie and Luke.

Looking up at the sweet sound of a woman's voice, he was eye level with a pair of perky tits that were spilling out of a tight grey waitress uniform and decided, *next week*.

Chapter Two

Kate

She was running late as usual and pulled her hair up in a ponytail as she scurried through the parking lot to the staff entrance of the diner, punching her timecard just before the clock turned 11:01.

"Cutting it close again, Katie," the diner's curmudgeonly owner chastised as he walked by with a tray of dirty dishes.

"I know, Frank, I'm sorry! This instructor likes to teach right until the end of class. Then sometimes I hit traffic," she called after him as she washed her hands at the staff sink.

"I could always schedule you to start later," he suggested as he walked by again, a stack of clean dishes in his hands this time.

"No, don't do that. I'll just drive faster."

She knew he was only trying to be helpful—as surly as he pretended to be, he had a soft spot for the twenty-five-year-old brunette, but Kate needed all the hours she could get. This being a grown-up thing was kind of expensive; it didn't help that she'd lost all her scholarships, so her career and path to bigger bucks was delayed. Even taking just two classes at a time to try to finish her degree without going into debt was a struggle on top of all her other bills.

Yeah, adulting was not what it was advertised.

"You've got customers," Frank called as she tied her apron around the uniform that was a little too snug on her now. It was the one she'd worn the first time she had this job when she was a senior in high school. Since it still sort of fit, she didn't see the point in spending the money on a new one when Frank hired her back when she came home, tail between her legs. Besides, she noticed she got better tips now that she had a hard time containing her boobs.

Her late development in the chest area was one of two things about her adult life she didn't curse.

"I'm on it, chief!" she teased with a mock salute as she backed out of the swinging double doors into the dining area. Turning around, she was relieved to see she was working with Carol today. They always had a fun shift when they were together. The redheaded woman was in her forties and took absolutely no shit, but she had taken Kate under her wing when Kate returned to work at the diner, a little more vulnerable and beaten down than she'd been in her cocky high school days.

"There you are!" Carol tucked her pen behind her ear as she greeted the younger woman. "Check out Mr. Hot Pants in your section. I was hoping you'd get here in time to wait on him."

Kate glanced over at the counter where she was serving today. Sure enough, a blonde Adonis in a grey Henley was busy looking at the menu.

"Wow," she murmured.

"Wow is right. Get your cute butt over there and pour on the charm."

Kate smirked and shook her head as she made her way to the pit. Carol was always trying to fix her up with any halfway decent looking man who walked into the diner alone.

She took the step into the pit and did a quick survey of the number of open spaces versus the supply of silverware and dishes in stock. Kate never understood why they called the area in the middle of the counters *the pit* since it was actually raised, so the servers stood above the customers. She grabbed the coffee pot and made her way to fill Adonis' coffee mug.

"Do you need cream and sugar?" she asked the man sweetly as she began to pour.

The sound of her voice made him look up from the menu he was perusing, his gaze lingering at her chest before he looked up at her face and smiled.

"Both, please."

Several thoughts bombarded her at once. First and foremost—*he's even better looking up close.* Second—*what a jerk for staring at my chest,* and third—*his smile is so beautiful, he must have had braces when he was a kid.* And finally—*braces. Ugh.* She wondered how much those were going to cost. Hopefully, Adonis was at least a good tipper. Usually, the guys who came in alone were.

His attempt at chatting her up wasn't unusual, a lot of her customers did. What was strange was how self-conscious she was while talking to him.

He watched her every move, almost scrutinizing her with a thoughtful expression and an occasional smirk as they bantered back and forth. Their exchange bordered on flirting, and she was ashamed to say, her other customers may have suffered from the service they received from her that morning.

Kate served him his All-American meal—cheeseburger, fries, and a chocolate shake, pausing to ask if he needed anything else.

"This looks really good... Katie." He glanced at her nametag before saying her name—she'd meant to ask Frank for one that had her grown-up moniker. Once again, Adonis paused to stare at her boobs.

"Eyes up here," she scolded with a laugh although a secret part of her liked that he seemed to appreciate her assets. She certainly appreciated what she could see of his—muscular chest, defined arms, blue eyes that stood out from his golden tan, and blonde hair she could almost picture running her fingers through.

Oh geez, Katie Connelly, get a grip. Even *she* scolded herself like a child.

He was an older man, probably with an established career and a sophisticated girlfriend or wife although she noticed there was no ring on his finger, so probably a girlfriend. She had absolutely nothing to offer someone like him. He was just having fun and passing the time flirting with her.

That's okay, that's really all she was doing too because even if he was interested in her, she could never date him. She had too many things to do to let someone like Adonis sidetrack her. She snuck a glance at his handsome face and concluded, boy, could he have the potential to throw her off course.

Never again. She remembered what happened the last time she let a good-looking man turn her world upside down.

When she noticed he'd finished his meal, she went back one last time to check on him. Standing before the sexy stranger, she was poised with her pen hovering on the notepad of green checks where she'd written his order.

"Anything else?"

"Your phone number?" he asked with a grin.

His cockiness caused the corners of her mouth to turn up, in spite of herself. She ripped his tab from her stack, flipping it over in front of him.

"Have a nice day. Thanks for coming in," she said with a coy smile, then walked away.

She was a little disappointed when she saw him walk out the door without another word. *If he were really interested, he would have at least tried asking again.*

Carol had a knowing smirk when she brought Kate the tip he'd left her when paying his tab. It was twenty dollars. His bill was nine.

"Seems someone liked his service," the redhead mused.

Kate looked down with a blush. "I guess so."

Then a pang of regret hit her. Maybe she should have given him her phone number after all. Or at least gotten his name.

It was probably better she hadn't, the angel on her shoulder advised.

Still, their playful exchange at the counter was going to be enough to keep her smiling until she went home—and she was working a double today.

Chapter Three

Cooper

He found himself thinking about that little waitress, Katie and her amazing tits all afternoon. She'd flat out turned him down; he couldn't remember the last time a woman didn't give him her number when he'd asked for it. Hell, chicks were usually slipping him their digits, even if he was out with another woman.

His pride should be hurt. Instead, he was thinking about going back to the diner and proving to her how charming he really was so she'd be begging for his number. He chuckled and shook his head, still in disbelief over being rejected.

He did love a challenge.

Her sexy little body and adorable face might also have something to do with his reluctance to accept defeat so easily. He wondered how often she worked and how late her shift ran today. Too bad he had a shitload of work to do at the base, or he'd be back before she left for the day.

Tomorrow, he appeased his libido. He definitely wanted to visit Cassie's baby one more time before they left the hospital, and it just-so-happened, visiting the diner across the street would be a convenient place to have lunch after he did.

Thankfully, a mini-crisis landed on his desk that managed to occupy his thoughts until he left late that evening. He decided to skip meeting the guys for drinks and headed home, Kaytits—his new nickname for her—occupying his mind the whole drive.

The things he wanted to do between her boobs... and to them, with them, for them. His dick started to get hard in his pants at the thought.

Yeah, one could say Cooper Johnson was a tits man, so he could say with authority, hers were fucking awesome. He wanted to see them naked, feel how heavy they were in his hands, and what her nipples looked like. His fingers itched just thinking about fondling them.

He went to bed that night with a hard-on and had some pretty weird dreams involving boobs smothering him everywhere he went. Death by titties... what a way to go.

Cooper woke up determined to get Kaytits' phone number today so he could take her out. Show her a good time. Fuck her senseless. Send her home with a smile.

She'd be his last hurrah before getting serious and settling down. He needed to do that soon if he really wanted to have a baby. The idea of being sixty when his kid graduated high school was not appealing.

Then again, maybe he'd visit little Miss Sophia Claire today and decide the baby thing wasn't really all it was cracked up to be after all.

Yeah, no, that didn't happen.

He stared into her perfect little face, her bright eyes expressive as her sweet, bow lips puckered and smiled at him, and he was gone. He didn't even mind that she puked on him, that's how smitten he was.

Cassie watched him holding her daughter and grinned knowingly. "I wondered why you came back here for a second day in a row. Here I thought maybe you were secretly in love with me. Turns out, you're just using me for your baby fix."

Cooper tickled Sofia's chin, not looking up when he confessed. "I didn't even know I needed one until I met her yesterday."

Cassie's husband, Luke chuckled from where he was sitting in the grey pleather chair by the window. Holding his oldest in his lap while the boy studied a new book he'd received for becoming an older brother, Luke warned, "Be careful. There's only one cure for baby fever."

"Fuck, I want one," Cooper sighed as he stared at the tiny baby in his arms, then grimaced. "Sorry, didn't mean to curse in front of the littles."

"It's a work in progress for all of us," Luke admitted.

Cassie looked at Cooper thoughtfully, tilting her head. "Do you have anyone in mind to help you with that?"

"Not at the moment."

"Don't rush things for the sake of having a child, Cooper. That has disaster written all over it. And when you do find someone, remember the ten-date rule."

"Yeah, cuz that worked so well for us," Luke snorted from the corner.

"You shush," his wife scolded with a smile. "We're talking about Cooper, not us."

"Kind of a do-as-I-say, not as-I-do sorta thing?" her husband teased.

"Exactly. Besides, the premise was good. And it did help us get to know each other, regardless, so again, shush."

Cooper had been wrong about his initial assessment of these two. He used to think he'd be a better match for Cassie, but watching them together now, even in their teasing banter, he realized Luke and Cassie were perfect for each other.

And they made a perfect little human together.

He wanted what they had.

But first, he needed to sow some wild oats by means of a little waitress with a pair of perky tits. Then, he'd worry about getting that.

****

Kate

She arrived at the diner at three o'clock, in time to prepare for the early bird dinner rush that would be starting in an hour. Fridays were always her busiest but most lucrative shift, and she was ready to lay on the charm—her rent was due next week, and she was still a little short.

She knew her landlord, Mrs. Neal would graciously give her a few days extra to pay if she needed it, but Kate hated to ask that, especially given how much the beautiful French widow already helped her. She rented the older woman's upstairs apartment when she returned to town four years ago after her world was turned upside down, and Mrs. Neal quickly ingrained herself into Kate's life, acting as both a friendly neighbor and mother figure. Kate knew she wouldn't be where she was—living independently and working toward her degree—without the French woman's help.

No, she'd be living at home and hearing every damn day about how she threw away her future.

Fuck that. God, what a miserable existence.

She owed Mrs. Neal a lot, which is why Kate agreed to go to some military ball with the woman's nephew next Saturday night when she asked.

"Strictly platonic," she'd said in her French accent. Kate loved listening to her talk. Even at fifty-seven, the woman was sexy as hell—her accent was just the icing on the cake.

"Do you even know what that word means? I don't want you to say it got lost in translation," the younger girl scolded with a laugh, suspicious of her landlord's intentions.

"Yes, of course. It means no amorous feelings."

"And your nephew is aware of this?" she asked, looking for Mrs. Neal's loophole.

"Yes. He just needs a date with a nice girl because he's trying to make a good impression with his superiors. He's up for a promotion and thinks having a date will make him look more stable, not footloose and fancy-free like he really is. I told him I knew the perfect girl."

Kate had been skeptical, but like she said, she owed Mrs. Neal a lot, so she agreed. Of course, Carol had been delighted when she learned the news Kate was going to a ball.

"Maybe you'll be like Cinderella and find your handsome prince at the ball," she'd said wistfully.

"I found a dress today," she teased Carol as she walked by.

The older woman was carrying a large tray of food on her shoulder, but that didn't keep her from calling after Kate, "Do you have pictures?"

"You know it," she replied, then walked into the waitress station to grab a tray of silverware to roll into napkins while she sat at the counter in case any early, early birders or late lunchers came in.

Her redheaded co-worker joined her at the counter, asking to see the pictures of her dress.

"Oh, I like the color. Is it royal blue or purple, I can't tell," Carol asked when Kate produced the selfies she'd shot in the dressing room.

"Purple. Do you think that's okay?"

"Oh, yes," Carol said authoritatively. "Very regal. It will look great with your skin tone. Are you going with dark or natural makeup?"

Kate thought about it for a second, finally replying, "I think darker will go better with the dress."

The older woman nodded in agreement before breaking out into a sing-song voice. "Guess who came in for lunch today and asked for you?"

Since she'd been dress shopping today for her date with Mrs. Neal's nephew that was who she guessed. "Trevor Neal."

Carol scowled. "Who the hell is that?"

"My date for the military ball."

That, apparently, was an acceptable deduction because her co-worker's frown disappeared, and she replied, "Oh. Well, no, not him. Someone better."

Kate furrowed her eyebrows. "Who?"

"Mr. Big Tipper from yesterday."

Adonis came back for lunch and asked about her? No way.

"Well, what did you tell him?"

"That you'd be in at three and off at ten," Carol said with a wide, conspiring grin. "He said he'd be back for a late dinner."

Ohmygod. Her stomach was doing cartwheels, but she tried to act impervious. "Oh, well, hopefully, he leaves another good tip, my rent is due on Monday."

"Oh, he wants to give you more than the tip," Carol cackled.

They both started giggling just as the bell above the door started to jingle in repetition. Her grey-haired dinner crowd was arriving—time to smile pretty and get the decaf brewing.

Friday night's dinner rush was steady all the way until after eight. Then, it was time to clean up the aftermath in between serving the stragglers. Frank let the less-tenured girls go home, but only after asking Carol and Kate if they wanted to leave. Both women decided to stay. Her paltry hourly wage wasn't much, but combined with just the two women manning the restaurant for the late crowd, it was worth it to stay. She needed every cent.

Staying had nothing to do with the possibility of Adonis coming in later.

Nothing!

As the clock got closer to nine, she wasn't feeling optimistic about his appearance. Not that it mattered, she couldn't date him even if he did show. It was just nice to be wanted. She was a little curvier than she'd like these days, so her ego appreciated it.

"He'll be here," Carol told her confidently when she noticed Kate looking at the clock again.

"Who?"

Her co-worker smirked. "Gee, I wonder."

"Even if he does show up, it's not like I can go out with him."

"Who says you have to date him? Just fuck him."

"Carol!"

"What? It's true. Baby girl, you need to get laid. You work too much and have too many responsibilities not to have a little fun when a gorgeous man comes calling."

"Well, I doubt he's even going to show up. I'm flattered he even asked about me at lunch."

Except the pit of disappointment settling in her stomach was calling her a liar. She would not be satisfied with him simply asking about her.

She was replenishing the supply of cups in one of the server stations when Carol appeared, whispering excitedly, "You have a customer at the counter."

She smoothed her ponytail and pressed her lips together to try to redistribute the lip gloss she'd been applying and reapplying all night.

Her lips were chapped that's all!

"You look great, but fix your boobs," the older waitress advised.

Kate stood facing the wall, leaned forward, and pushed her boobs toward the middle of her chest, instantly creating more cleavage.

"Wait, why am I doing this?" she wondered out loud.

"To get laid," her coworker hissed and shoved her out of the station.

She tried to compose herself as she stumbled out of the closet-sized area, smoothing her apron while she surveyed the restaurant. Adonis was in a bright-blue button-down that matched his eyes, sitting where he sat yesterday with his coffee cup overturned. She picked up the coffee pot and put a little extra sway in her hips as she sauntered toward him with a smile.

"Coffee at this hour?" she teased as she filled his mug.

"I plan on staying up late tonight," he said with a wink.

She glanced at the big clock on the wall. "I guess the bar scene doesn't start for another hour or so."

He shook his head with a smirk. "I'm not going to the bar."

"Oh? Why not?"

"Well, I guess we can go to the bar if you want. I was hoping we could have a quieter setting."

Kate grinned in spite of herself.

"I don't date."

"Customers? Because I don't ever have to come in here again," he teased.

"No, at all. I don't date—period."

He shrugged. "Okay," but she knew by the twinkle in his eyes the matter was far from closed.

Chapter Four

Cooper

His little Kaytits looked hot, hotter than yesterday if that were possible.

She'd just told him she didn't date—little did she know he wasn't giving up that easily.

"So what do you do when you're not working here?"

She seemed flustered trying to come up with an answer and finally sputtered, "Normal stuff, I guess. I'm going to school, so I study a lot or am doing homework. I also take care of... things at home, do a little volunteer work, hang out with friends... Just regular stuff."

"But you don't have time to date? Too busy watching *Game of Thrones*?" he teased.

She shot him a look equivalent to *puh-lease*. "I've never even seen one episode. Trust me, I'm not sitting at home watching television. I don't even have cable or any streaming devices. That's not why I don't date."

He cocked his head, "Why don't you then?"

"I have things I want to do with my life. Getting involved with someone would just get me off track."

"What if it was just for one night? Would that still get you off track?" he asked with a dirty grin.

Her nipples pebbled through her uniform.

Oh, sweet Kaytits, you're coming home with me tonight, and you don't even know it yet.

She gulped, then stammered, "Let, let me, let me go check on your food," and whirled around to make her escape.

"I'll be right here," he assured her, chuckling to himself while staring at her ass as she scampered toward the kitchen. *She was fucking hot—coming and going.*

She was shaking when she set his dinner plate down in front of him.

"Do you need anything else right now?" she asked in a voice higher pitched than usual.

He liked that he was getting under her skin.

"Just your company, Katie."

"Oh, well, I—I have some side work I need to do, but I'll be back to check on you soon."

"Don't be too long," he teased with a wink.

He was the last customer in the diner, and he was pretty sure the two waitresses were unaware he could hear their conversation in the server's station from his seat since the restaurant was so quiet.

"I think he just propositioned me for a one-night stand!" she hissed, trying to sound scandalized instead of tempted.

"So? Go home with him!" came the other voice.

He liked her friend.

"I don't even know his name. I'm not that slutty."

"Katie, my sweet young friend, let me tell you something. If you don't let that gorgeous man take you home and violate you seven ways til Sunday, when you're old and married like me, you'll look back on tonight with regret instead of a smile. And by the looks of him, he is more than capable of putting a smile on your face, probably multiple times."

"I don't know," Katie whined. "I have to get home. Mrs. Neal will be wondering where I am."

"So call her and tell her you have a date. She'll understand, and I'm sure won't be bothered in the least. If it is a problem, call me. I'll come over."

"I don't know," she repeated.

"Honey, you need to get laid."

"I can't believe you're encouraging me to go home with a complete stranger. Do you know how dangerous that is?" the younger girl admonished.

"I'll take a picture of his ID before you leave, how's that?"

"A lot of good that'll do me when I'm lying dead in a ditch somewhere off of I-5."

Remorse filled the other waitress' voice. "I'm sorry. I shouldn't be trying to talk you into something you don't feel comfortable doing."

Fuck! For a minute there, he thought he had red on his side.

It's okay. He could put the time in and prove he was trustworthy. He liked the food here, so it wouldn't be like it was a hardship to make the effort. He was determined to get Kaytits in his bed for his last hurrah.

She came back to check on him.

He had finished his chicken pot pie and threw his napkin on his plate, looking up at her with a friendly smile. "I'm Cooper Johnson, by the way." There, got that box checked, now she knew his name.

The corners of her glossy, rosebud lips turned up. "Well, you already know I'm Katie, but I'll let you in on a secret—I usually go by Kate now, it's more grown-up. It's nice to meet you, Cooper Johnson."

He liked Katie better. "I'll take the check whenever you're ready, *Katie.*"

For a second, it seemed like she was disappointed at his blunt request, but quickly regained her composure and smiled as she laid his check face down on the counter next to him.

"Just let me know when you want to pay, and I'll meet you at the register."

"I'm ready." He waited for her to come down from her station in the middle of the square and walked with her toward the register.

"So, are you working the dinner shift again tomorrow?" he asked, trying to come off as innocuous as possible.

She shook her head. "No, just lunch tomorrow, then off Sunday and Monday."

He pleasantly noted she was volunteering her schedule to him.

"Twelve seventy-two," she told him as she totaled his bill on the cash register.

He handed her two twenties and winked. "Keep the change." The corners of his mouth turned up when she gasped and murmured, "Thank you so much."

He grabbed a toothpick from the complimentary dispenser at the register and slipped it into his mouth. "See you tomorrow," he said with a grin, then walked out the door before she could reply.

He could hear her squeals from the parking lot and laughed out loud.

Yeah, she was going home with him. Not tonight, but soon. It'd be a fair bet to say she was starting to realize it.

Patience, grasshopper. He had a feeling this last fling was going to be worth the wait.

****

Kate

Oh, Cooper Johnson, thank you for pushing my tip total over the amount I needed to make rent this month.

In addition to being an amazing tipper, he really was charming, not to mention hot, and there was definitely chemistry going on between them.

Once Kate told her his name, Carol was on her phone doing a Google search and flashed her phone at Kate, showing she'd found his social media accounts.

"Well, he's got a lot of pictures of himself at the beach with his friends," she said as she repeatedly swiped her finger across the screen.

"Does it say if he has a girlfriend or is married?" Kate anxiously asked, standing on her tiptoes, trying to look over her friend's shoulder.

"No, it says he's single. There's a couple of pictures with women, but they're in a group, so you can't tell if he's with any of them."

Well, that was a good sign. No obvious photographic evidence to suggest he was in a relationship.

"Does it say what he does?"

Carol shook his head. "No, there're no details of anything other than where he and his friends have visited. He does have a cool car though."

"Can I see?"

Kate didn't have an online presence, so she was relegated to relying on Carol when she wanted to know about anything social media related. The people Kate wanted knowing about her life already knew what they needed, and if they were curious for more, they knew where to find her. Besides, she remembered what a time-sucker it was when she was younger. To quote an old internet fad, "Ain't nobody got time for that." Not to mention, a data plan for her phone that would allow her the luxury to surf the internet and waste time on social media was too expensive, anyway.

Once Carol handed her the phone, Kate pushed on his face on the screen and spread her fingers to enlarge one of the photos. It was of him laughing; he really had a beautiful smile—like toothpaste commercial worthy.

With a sigh, she lamented if maybe she'd met him ten years from now, she'd have more to offer than sex. Right now though, she knew he couldn't be interested in anything but sleeping with her—she didn't have much to bring to the table in the remarkable department. Not to mention her baggage would be too much for a man like him. Judging by his pictures, he liked to have a good time, and she no longer had that luxury.

She blew up another photo of him where he was shirtless, in just a pair of board shorts next to his surfboard, and she felt her lady parts tingle. Carol was right, she needed to get laid, and Mr. Cooper Johnson, a.k.a. Adonis might be just the man to help her with that. If he really came back a third time, there was a good chance she'd be going home with him—at least for a couple of hours of fun.

Chapter Five

Cooper

As he drove to Frank's Diner for the fourth time in three days, he considered whether he was coming off as persistent or desperate.

He didn't lack for female company. He could have any number of women in his bed within the hour with a simple text, but he only wanted the little waitress he was on his way to see.

There was something about her that had him intrigued, more than just her sumptuous tits and ass or her adorable laugh. It was probably because she didn't jump into bed with him at his first suggestion.

That had to be it.

She was too young to consider getting serious with. How much could they possibly have in common with their age difference? As she aptly pointed out, she had things to do with her life, which probably didn't include marriage and babies for a while. Hell, he hadn't even known he was ready for that until three days ago.

That reminded him—would it be creepy to ask to visit Cassie and the baby again so soon?

While the pharmaceutical rep ended up not being the love interest he'd originally intended, she did turn out to be a good friend. Her husband wasn't happy about it until Cooper started being the third wheel on a few occasions, and Luke realized he had nothing to worry about from the fellow Marine.

Cooper could be a philanderer, but he wasn't a home wrecker, and frankly, the baby thing had kinda freaked him out. That is until he met the perfect little angel when she was born. Now he was freaked out because he wanted one.

He pulled into the diner's parking lot and surveyed the cars in the area near the back where he assumed the staff parked. Which car was hers?

He had his money on the older, white Honda Accord with the license plate *KitKat,* in dire need of new tires.

Although he had a mint condition Ford Gran Torino in his garage, his everyday car was a charcoal grey BMW M3. No personalized plates though. He didn't need everyone on base knowing which ride was his.

The familiar jingle of the bell greeted him when he opened the door. His eyes went to his spot at the counter, noting it was occupied and there was a younger girl in the server's area of the square. Where was his kitten? After seeing her license plate, he decided that was going to be her new nickname instead of Kaytits.

Kitten suited her better anyway.

He found her waiting on a couple in a booth by the far wall, so he started toward her. The bright smile she greeted him with made his heart soar. He liked that she was so glad to see him. The feeling was mutual.

She must be busy or at least had been because her hair was falling out of her ponytail, and her cheeks were flushed pink. Sort of like he envisioned she'd look like when she was underneath him in his bed.

26

"Hi! Just have a seat in any of the booths along the wall," she called from where she stood, taking the other patrons' order.

He sat down in the first one he came to and watched her interact with her customers. She was so fucking cute. Her easy smile was contagious, and when she went off to put their order in, they were still grinning at something she'd said.

"Do you want coffee?" she asked when she reappeared and began to wipe down a table a few yards from his.

"I think I'll have a Coke today," he loudly replied so she could hear him.

"I'm on it," she said with a wink and walked away, returning a minute later with a large soda she sat down in front of him, along with a menu and a straw.

"How are you?" he asked as he tapped the straw on the peeling, fake-wood linoleum top to try to push the white wrapper away.

"I'm good. You got here just in time, things have finally died down."

"So does that mean you'll be able to pay extra attention to me?"

Her little smirk was adorable when she teased, "Maaaybe. You are my best tipper after all."

"I appreciate good service," he bantered back.

Her face turned somber, yet expressive. "No, seriously. You've been incredibly generous, and I really appreciate it, but I hope you don't think..." her voice tapered off.

"That I'm trying to buy a date? No, Katie, I don't have to pay women to spend time with me. You're going to go out with me because you can't resist my charm." He leaned back with a smirk.

"You are charming," she muttered, almost begrudgingly.

That caused him to grin broader.

"Do you need a few minutes to decide?" she asked, changing the subject.

"What's good today?"

A look passed over her features that seemed to indicate she had something flirtatious to say in response, but it was quickly masked. He'd help her out.

"Besides you, I mean."

That prompted the eye roll he knew it would, followed by a small smile she tried to hide.

"My favorite is the patty melt," she offered.

"Sounds perfect," he said, handing her back the menu.

"Fries and a chocolate shake?" she asked as she wrote on her notepad.

"You know me well."

That prompted her to pause her pen and look up over her pad at him. "Hardly," she sniffed, then turned on her heel toward the kitchen.

"Oh, Kitten, you will. You will," he murmured, his cock springing to life as he watched her sashay to the back of the restaurant.

*

Kate

He came back.

She'd thought about him on the drive here, wondering if he'd really show up again today.

Okay, she'd thought about him more than just on her drive—like when she'd spent extra time on her hair and makeup getting ready for work. Fortunately, her life kept her busy enough, she didn't have time to dwell on him. Except when she was alone in bed that is.

She'd dreamt of Cooper holding her all night long, but instead of waking up from the sexy dream feeling happy and hopeful, it depressed her. It could never happen in real life.

Her life wasn't easy. Still, she wouldn't change it for the world. Not even for a chance to sleep in Adonis' arms all night long. However, just because she couldn't spend the night asleep in his arms didn't necessarily preclude her from spending a couple of hours awake in them.

Kate found herself loitering at his booth. It was a good thing he was such a good tipper because the service her other tables received when he was in the restaurant was definitely lacking.

"So what time do you get off?" he asked with a flirtatious smile.

"Three."

He glanced at his watch that read two twenty-five. "I really did come at the right time. Do you need to go home and change after work?"

"Change for what?"

"For our date."

"We're going on a date? I didn't know that," she teased.

"Well, at least I'm hoping we are, Kitten."

Her left eyebrow raised. "Kitten?"

"Yeah, kitten. It suits you. Kittens can be soft and adorable or playful and feisty. Then there's your sex kitten... Something tells me you have the potential to be all three."

"At the same time?" she smirked.

Cooper cocked his head, thinking about her question. "Maybe. I think I'd like to experience that, actually."

She shook her head with a slight smile. This cocky man knew how to unsettle her, no doubt about it.

"So, you didn't answer me. Should I pick you up at your house?"

A feeling of panic rose in her chest at the thought of him coming to her upstairs apartment. That's the only reason she could come up with for what she said next.

"No, I'll meet you."

His triumphant smile made her want to smack his sexy face.

Or kiss it.

Maybe smack it, then kiss it.

She glowered at his arrogant ass. "I need to check on my other tables."

"I'll be here when you get back, Kitten," he chuckled.

"My name's Kate," she groused as she walked away.

"Katie Kitten," Cooper called after her.

The man was completely insufferable, yet she found she couldn't stop smiling.

Did she really just agree to meet him after work? She wished Carol were here, she'd help her figure out what to do. Although Kate had a pretty good idea what the older waitress would tell her. *Go have fun.*

She had no doubt any time spent with Cooper Johnson would be fun, both in and out of bed. And therein lied the possible problem.

As she absent-mindedly gathered his plate from the kitchen, Kate couldn't believe she'd already decided she was going to sleep with him, barring anything weird happening that would suddenly make her change her mind. Seeing him sitting in the booth in the white graphic t-shirt that showcased his muscular arms and chest and showed off his tan skin, she couldn't envision what that would even be.

Setting his lunch in front of him, she asked if he needed anything else at the moment. His sly smile made her tingly, but she tried to sound unaffected when she scolded, "Like ketchup, mustard, or more soda."

Cooper sat there smugly. "I'm all set for now."

"I'll check back soon."

She had turned to leave him when he grabbed her wrist.

"Hurry back, Kitten," he whispered with a wink.

Damn him and his chiseled jaw and kissable lips.

31

Chapter Six

Cooper

His little kitten was meeting him after her shift. *Fuck yeah.*

Should he meet her at the bar near his house or just give her his address with the pretense they'd leave from there?

The funny thing was he really thought he'd enjoy hanging out at his neighborhood tavern with her, having a few beers and shooting pool, almost as much as he'd like to fuck her. He guessed he'd do both. They had all night, and neither of them had to work tomorrow. There was no reason to rush things.

Just then, he heard Cassie's voice in his head saying *ten dates.*

No, the ten-date rule wasn't intended for Katie. But for some reason, the thought of not seeing her again after tonight bothered him.

He was sure after he'd slept with her, he'd feel differently, it was just the conquest. Once he'd had her in his bed, he'd be able to send her on her merry way, with a smile, of course, and she'd be out of his system.

When she reappeared at his booth to present him with his check, he handed her his phone.

"Plug your number in," he ordered. "And I'll text you my address."

Cooper was surprised when she did so without argument and immediately sent her his address. He heard her phone buzz in her apron pocket, indicating not only had she given him her real number, but she'd gotten his information.

"So, in like, an hour?" he asked hopefully.

Katie pursed her lips. "Oh, no. I can't get there until after nine. I have to go home, and... take care of things before I can leave."

He scowled, she was cheating him out of at least five hours with her.

She scowled back in return, and before he could protest, let him know the time was non-negotiable. "I understand if you'd rather not get together tonight. Maybe another time."

He made a conscious effort to keep his tone light. "No, I still want to see you tonight. I'm just disappointed I have to wait is all."

"Thanks for understanding," was all she offered. No explanation for what was so important she couldn't make it until much later.

"What do you like to drink?"

Her smirk had a hint of suspicion to it, and she tilted her head. "Why?"

"I want to make sure I have it so we can have a cocktail before going out. Believe it or not, my mother did raise me to be a gentleman and a good host."

Her smirk turned into a genuine smile. "Beer will be fine."

"That's it? Nothing stronger? Vodka? Tequila? Scotch? Whiskey? Gin?"

"I got sick on gin the night of my twenty-first birthday and haven't been able to drink it since. I don't really care for whiskey or scotch, and I'm afraid every time I've drunk vodka, I've done things I've regretted. And you know the country song, 'Tequila Makes Her Clothes Fall Off' by Joe Nichols? Yeah, it could have been written about me."

"Tequila it is," he said with a chuckle.

"*Beer will be fine*," she reiterated sternly. "Soda would probably be an even smarter choice."

He ignored her soda comment. "We can grab a late dinner unless you can't wait that long to eat."

"I'll just eat at home," she offered.

"How about we compromise, and you eat a light meal at home so you can still have something with me? I'm going to be hungry again at nine o'clock tonight."

"That sounds like a plan."

She walked him toward the front, stopping just short of the cash register to take his ticket, then telling him, "It's on me today."

He shook his head. "You don't have to do that."

"Well, I want to," she challenged with her hands on her hips.

He slipped two twenties in her apron pocket without her knowing as he brushed a kiss against her forehead.

"Thank you. I'll see you later."

His little waitress was blushing. *Blushing*. From a simple kiss to her forehead.

That got him wondering how much experience she had.

When she looked up at him with her big brown eyes, his dick moved.

Tonight was either going to be a lot of fun or a total bust.

****

Kate

He smelled so good when he got in her personal space to kiss her forehead, like soap and some expensive aftershave. Meanwhile, she was sure she smelled like greasy burgers and French fries. That shit was embedded in her clothes, and the only way it was coming out would be to burn them.

Seriously.

Ah, the joys of working in a restaurant. The money was okay. She probably could be making more at an office job, but Frank always worked around her school schedule and never had a problem if she was needed at home. Flexibility was important, not to mention the people she worked with cared about her and were always doing little things to help her out. Between the restaurant staff, Mrs. Neal, and her few close friends, she had an amazing support system.

She tried as often as she could to show her appreciation in ways she could afford—baking cookies, birthday cakes, little cards just because, things like that, but she still knew the scales were tipped in her favor.

She loved her tribe—big and small.

Cooper walked toward the door and turned around with a smile, pausing before he pushed it open with his rear-end.

"See you tonight? Are you sure you don't just want me to pick you up?"

The idea made her neck sweat.

"No. I'll be okay."

"Text me when you leave your house, okay? And call me if you get lost."

"I'll do that," she promised, and he opened the door, the bells jingling as he did.

"See you later, Kitten," he said with a wink that seemed to insinuate a few dirty thoughts.

Was she ready for this?

She watched him stride to a grey car that probably cost more than four years of college tuition. There was no denying he was sexy as hell, and the thought of seeing him naked made her bite her bottom lip.

One night of fun. That's what he offered, nothing to get her off-track from her goals of a better life, and she was going to take him up on it. She deserved one night. Hopefully, it would be as incredible as she imagined it was going to be and would be enough to satisfy her until she had more to offer than a night.

Just one thing worried her. What if it was better than she imagined, and instead of satisfying her for the time being, it simply whet her appetite?

Kate shook her head.

No.

Nothing was going to keep her from getting her degree and providing her son a better life.

Nothing.

Chapter Seven

Cooper

He was actually nervous about his date with the little, busty waitress tonight.

Him. Captain Cooper Johnson. Nervous about a date.

The last time that happened, he was in high school with acne and still wearing braces.

Having five hours to kill before she got there wasn't helping things. He kept a spotless house, so he didn't have any cleaning to do to prepare for her arrival. He didn't, however, keep a stocked refrigerator or pantry and decided to go to the trendy, neighborhood grocery store to buy the beer she said she liked and premade hors d'oeuvres to have before they went out. While he was shopping, he opted to pick up dinner ingredients, too, just in case they ended up staying in.

He guessed since her favorite selection at the diner was a patty melt, she'd like the top sirloin steak he bought, along with the potatoes, onions, baby-cut carrots, green beans, and squash he'd mix with spices and put in tinfoil on the grill. Cooper wasn't much of a chef, but he could grill like a motherfucker.

Even if they went out for dinner and he ended up eating it for dinner tomorrow, the vegetable preparation and steak marinade helped him pass the time.

At eight forty-five, he heard his phone ding, indicating he had a text, and his cock got instantly hard when he saw it was from his kitten.

Katie: Hi! I'm on my way. My GPS says fifteen minutes.

Cooper immediately replied. **Can't wait—hurry! Just kidding, drive carefully. See you soon.**

Should he light candles?

He decided that might come off as cheesy. It would be like having Barry White already coming through the speakers when she walked in the door. He did, however, dim the lights—just a little and turned the Jason Aldean Pandora station on low for background music.

A four-minute shower, teeth brushed, quick dab of cologne, change of clothes, and he was ready with two minutes to spare. He saw her headlights turn into the driveway of his stucco and mission tile roof tract house and was out the door and waiting for her in the driveway.

Yeah, he was coming off as eager, and he didn't give a shit. He was excited to see her.

Katie quickly got out of her little white Honda before he had a chance to meet her at her door, slipping her purse over her shoulder as she closed the car door. Cooper had to consciously keep his mouth from hanging open—she was a fucking knockout.

Her thick brown hair was loosely curled and cascading over her shoulders to the middle of her back, and he immediately caught the scent of her shampoo when she stood in front of him. She had on more makeup than he'd seen her wear at the diner, and her tight, dark jeans with blingy back pockets made him have to subtly adjust himself. Or maybe it was her cleavage in the black tank top she dressed up with a silver, half-moon collar necklace, hoop earrings, and strappy black high heels.

He stood in front of his garage, openly admiring his date, and let out a low whistle.

"Damn, Kitten. You look gorgeous."

She looked down at the professionally stained tan concrete with a small smile. "Thank you."

Cooper reached for her hand. "Come on in," and started walking her to the front door.

Katie glanced at his landscaping and outdoor lighting as they made their way up the walk. "Wow, your place is gorgeous," she murmured.

He worked his ass off on his lawn and the fact she not only noticed but appreciated it made him like her that much more.

"Thanks," he said, opening the front door and ushering her inside, where she promptly took off her shoes.

"You don't have to do that," he told her.

"It's a rule in my home, so I try to respect it in other people's too," she explained. He now felt compelled to take off his black Chuck Taylor's as well.

She surveyed his home. It was the four bedrooms, three baths ranch model the builder offered, and the saleswoman had convinced him the difference in price between the three and four bedrooms was small compared to what it would be when it came time to sell. Trying to see the place through her eyes, he supposed it was tastefully furnished, nothing that screamed a bachelor lived there, other than maybe the big television and bar in the great room.

"Do you live here alone?" The tone she used suggested her question was out of curiosity and not suspicion.

"Just me."

Katie nodded her head and looked around again. "It's really beautiful. You're very neat."

"You get that drilled into you at basic, and it never goes away," he replied with a chuckle.

"So, you're in the service?" she asked, tilting her head.

"Marines, almost thirteen years now."

She nodded her head again. "I wouldn't have guessed that."

"No?"

"No, you strike me as someone who travels around selling surfboards all day."

Although he was unsure if he should be insulted, he threw his head back and laughed. There was some appeal to that idea.

"Would you like the tour?" he asked, gesturing to the rest of the house.

"I'd love it."

Cooper walked her through the open floor plan, and she giggled when they got to the bedrooms.

"You have an empty room?"

He shrugged. "I haven't gotten around to buying any furniture for it yet."

"And how long have you lived here?"

"About four years," he said with a grin and closed the door.

"Well, your office and guest room are very nicely decorated, anyway."

Cooper paused in the hall to take in her easy smile. She was smokin' hot, and he was having a hard time keeping his hands to himself, but the realization of how genuine she was hit him square in the gut. Suddenly, he understood the appeal of the ten-date rule. He wanted more than one night with her, and he hadn't even fucked her yet.

Too bad all she was looking for was one night.

That left him with no choice. He'd have to rock her world tonight so she'd be begging for a chance at a second date.

*

Kate

She was way at out of her league with this guy. She knew it the second she turned into his upscale community in the beat-up Honda Civic she'd gotten as a high school graduation present from her parents, back when they were still proud of her.

Kate had nothing he could possibly be interested in, other than sex, and she planned on giving that to him tonight in spades. She had four years to make up for.

Four years is too long to go without sex even if you're a busy, single mom. She'd been telling herself that ever since Cooper had propositioned her in the diner, and she seriously began to consider his offer. It was the only justification she could think of for why she'd been so willing to be so easy.

Not that she hadn't been propositioned before. There were a few good-looking guys in her classes who'd asked her out. She'd made the mistake of telling the first guy who wanted to have dinner with her that she had to find a sitter for her son and promptly never heard from him again. That was when she decided having a young kid and trying to date didn't mix. It turned out she didn't miss it... that is, until the day Adonis walked into the diner.

He had definitely done something to her hormones because from the day he first asked for her phone number, she hadn't stopped thinking about him. Not to mention, fantasizing about him. Even as out of her element as she felt here, she'd wanted nothing more than to wrap her arms around him since the second she rushed to get out of her Honda so he wouldn't notice Sam's car seat in the back. She'd actually considered taking it out before she left her apartment but ruled against it. It was way too much of a pain in the ass to reinstall.

So, now she was on a date with a hot, older, sexy man who was way out of her league, and the sole purpose of her being there was to have sex for the first time since she got pregnant with her son. Katie knew it was slutty, but at the moment, she didn't care. She'd worry about regret tomorrow. It was all about tonight.

Cooper escorted her to the other side of the house to continue the tour, pausing in the kitchen when Katie mentioned, "Something smells good."

"Egg rolls and lasagna bites. I thought we could eat something before going out."

He shook his head, grumbling *shit* under his breath before asking, "Can I get you something to drink? I bought you beer, I just got distracted looking at you and forgot to offer you one."

That made the corners of her mouth turn up. "I don't want to carry a drink through your house and risk spilling."

"My floors are moppable," he teased.

"How much more is there to see?" she asked, looking at the short hall they hadn't been down.

"Just the master suite." His voice was huskier than it had been a second ago.

His stare was deliberate and intense, and she shifted on her feet, wringing her hands in front of her. Why was she feeling self-conscious now? Isn't this why she came here?

"A beer sounds great."

He knew he'd unnerved her, and one side of his sexy mouth lifted into a lopsided smile.

"I'll be right back. Do you want a glass?"

His mama did raise him right.

"No, thanks."

He returned seconds later with two Leinenkugel's Summer Shandys.

Clinking his beer neck against hers before taking a sip, Cooper swallowed his drink and inspected the label closer. "I'd never tried this before. It's good."

"I don't drink it very often, but I love it. The taste just reminds me of summer, which I guess is appropriate since you can only buy it March through August."

"I guess that would make sense then," he said with a laugh, then took her hand to lead her down the hall.

Her breathing picked up, not knowing what to expect next. Once they reached his bedroom, was he going to try to seduce her already?

She glanced at him in his medium blue Levis that hugged his ass beautifully and the Army-green vintage t-shirt of the punk band, The Clash, which showcased his arms and chest nicely and decided it wouldn't be the worst thing that could happen.

His bedroom matched the rest of his house. Masculine décor, neat and orderly with modern furniture that looked like he'd bought it at Crate and Barrel.

He remained a perfect gentleman even when pointing out the hot tub on the small, private patio area outside the sliding glass door in his room. It would have been the perfect opportunity for him to insinuate getting naked in later, but instead, just explained how it was great for helping him recuperate after a hard workout.

He didn't even allude to the hard workout being sex. Was he no longer interested in her?

She crossed her arms over her chest, pushing her boobs up higher, and saw his eyes darken while he subtly adjusted himself. Okay, he was still interested, so why wasn't he making any attempt to at least kiss her? They were alone in his bedroom, for goodness sake, what was he waiting for? An invitation?

One thing she'd discovered in her twenty-five years on earth, if you want something done, you have to do it yourself.

They were standing in his ridiculously huge walk-in closet when she made her move and pressed on his chest so he'd sit down on the built-in bench. He seemed surprised at her boldness and even more surprised when she straddled him and wrapped her arms around his neck to stare into his eyes.

"Were you planning on kissing me tonight?"

He slowly brought his arms around her back and gently caressed his hands up and down her spine. God, she liked how that felt.

With a soft chuckle, he responded to her question. "I was planning on kissing you. I was just trying to figure out the right time to do it."

Kate bit her bottom lip, her bravado running out fast. With as much courage as she could muster, she whispered, "Now works," and gently lowered her mouth on his.

His mouth parted slightly, and he let her control the tempo as they nipped and tugged one another's lips. When their tongues started to tangle, he inhaled deeply through his nose and tightened his hold around her as he took command.

Cooper pulled her hips down on his erection, subtly rocking into her as he angled his mouth to deepen the kiss.

She moaned softly, which seemed to excite him more.

"Katie, my little kitten, you have no idea what you do to me," he harshly whispered against her ear while digging his fingers in her hair.

After tugging on her hair to expose her neck to him, he buried his face between her shoulder and chin, sending goosebumps down her body.

She felt herself getting wetter, and she clutched the back of his head as she began grinding against his hard cock. A low growl escaped his throat, and he began to knead her left breast while moving his lips along her jawline before capturing her mouth again with his.

God, she wanted him. It had been so long since a man had touched her like this, and if she had to wait another second to feel his bare skin against hers, she'd die. Having too much to live for, she began to tug at his shirt.

Beep beep beep.

He broke the kiss, panting, "Fuuuck."

Her furrowed brows asked the unspoken question.

"Appetizers are ready," he explained, nudging her off his lap.

Fuuuck was right.

Cooper grabbed her hand again and led her to the kitchen where the rude noise was coming from. She wanted nothing more than to throw the cockblocking snack offenders in the garbage.

46

They didn't even smell good anymore.

Chapter Eight

Cooper

Appetizers had sounded like a good idea at the time. He thought he'd make a good impression by being a well-mannered host. Now, eff that. If he wasn't worried about setting the smoke alarm off, he'd have let the fuckers burn.

Shutting the timer off and taking the lasagna rolls and egg rolls out of the oven, he set the pan on the stove top, tossed the oven mitts on the counter, and wrapped his arms around her waist.

"Sorry to ruin the mood," he murmured.

"You didn't ruin it," she assured him as she wound her hands behind his neck.

Cooper grabbed her hand.

"These need to cool, come with me," he said while pulling her into the living room, unable to keep his eyes off her once they stood in the center of the room.

"Alexa, dim the lights and play something romantic," he commanded with a smirk.

Katie gave a shy grin while the digital assistant responded to his instructions, and he pulled her against him as an old song, 'Just You and I,' by Crystal Gale and Eddie Rabbit flowed from the speakers.

Her head rested on his shoulder as he moved her around the area rug. Listening to the lyrics about a couple sharing love and building dreams together was bittersweet. He wanted the opportunity to explore those possibilities with this woman in his arms, and she wasn't going to let him.

Oh, the karma gods were having a good laugh at his expense tonight.

Still, Cooper felt content as they quietly swayed to the rhythm in the softly lit room. Her hands skimmed up and down his back, and she softly began to kiss his neck, making his cock go hard against her stomach.

At that moment, part of him wanted to proposition her with the ten-date rule but was afraid he'd freak her out. His best chance at getting her to see him again would be to sleep with her because he knew if she thought he was interested in getting serious, he'd never stand a chance.

Ah, irony and karma—the dynamic duo.

Still, he was going to take his time with her tonight. It had to be serendipity that Sam Hunt came on just then, singing about going slow and being unhurried with his lover in 'Body Like a Back Road.'

Her hand stroking his hard length over his jeans indicated she didn't share this mindset. Cooper drew in a deep breath when she cupped, then gently squeezed his balls, purring in his ear, "You are so sexy."

The Marine skimmed his hands over her curves, settling on her hips to pull her closer. "So are you."

He leaned down and caught her lips with his, kissing her slowly while fighting the urge to rip her clothes off and eat her pussy right there on the blue and green striped Persian rug. He really did want to take his time with her, but the way she was returning his kiss, she was making it pretty damn difficult.

49

"Katie," he panted as he leaned his forehead against hers, gently applying the brakes. "We need to stop, or I'm going to fuck you right here on the floor."

"Would that be so bad?" she asked while attempting to unbutton his jeans.

Cooper wasn't surprised to learn she was amenable to the idea of floor sex, confirming that, for her, tonight was solely about lust.

But he wanted more.

Grabbing her hands to stop her from undoing his Levi's, he brought her inner, left wrist to his lips while holding her right hand tight to her side.

"Slow down, baby girl. There's no need to rush," he murmured against the skin just below her palm, then pulled her hand down against her other side, entwining his fingers in hers.

The hurt in her eyes when she looked up at him was unmistakable. Did she think he was rejecting her? That couldn't be further from the truth.

He lowered his lips onto hers again, kissing her thoroughly until she was moaning softly.

"I'm going to take my time and savor you, Kitten," he explained as he released her fingers to run his hands up her sides and gently squeeze her tits over her tank top, then dropped his mouth on hers to continue exploring.

Her hands slid under his t-shirt, inching her way up his back until her forearms were on his bare skin pulling him closer.

Cooper broke the kiss when she had his shirt poised to pull over his head. He let her slip it off him, then buried his face in the crook of her neck. Katie tilted her head to the side, nestling her fingers in his hair.

His dick was rock hard and straining to be released from the confines of his jeans. Her subtle grinding against his thigh wasn't helping matters.

He moved from her neck to her breastbone, pushing her right tit upward as he moved to bite her nipple over the fabric of her tank. Even through the cotton, he could feel it was hard as a pebble. He moved his other hand to pinch and twist her left nipple while continuing to tend to the right with his mouth.

The Marine pulled away to push the straps of both her tank and bra down her arms until the tops of her bare breasts were exposed to him.

He had been right. Her tits were fucking magnificent, and he stared in awe so long, she shuffled uncomfortably in front of him.

"You are so beautiful, Kitten," he harshly whispered as he slowly traced her exposed flesh with his index finger. "So. Fucking. Beautiful."

She let out a shuddering breath, and he yanked her clothing down to fully display her boobs to him, groaning when he caught sight of her.

Her skin was soft and supple with a hint of honeysuckle as he gently started to suck the flesh of her curves. Her sharp intake of breath, followed by the goose pimples covering her body head to toe let him know he was doing something right.

Which was good since his mission tonight was to make her see stars so she'd come back again without a second thought.

She arched against him, and Cooper brought his hands under her ass and lifted her up. She automatically wrapped her legs around his waist, and he started toward the master suite, maneuvering as best as he could through the house while she kissed his neck and pressed her center heat subtly against his cock.

In his bedroom, he pulled the comforter back before gently depositing her on his king size bed. Her brown hair was splayed across the pillow, and her makeup was impressively still intact, save for her lipstick. Her sumptuous tits were still hanging out of her black tank top, beckoning to him. He reached for the hem of her shirt, and she laid her hands flat against the bottom, blocking him from pulling it off.

"Can we dim the lights?" she timidly asked.

Having used the dimmer switch earlier, the overhead lights were already low, so her question caught him off guard. He loved her body and couldn't understand what she was self-conscious about. But he wanted her comfortable, so he switched on the lamp on his dresser and turned off the main light.

Stalking back toward the bed, he noticed her tank top lying on the floor next to the bed and the sheet tucked under her armpits.

"I think you forgot something," he mused.

She produced her jeans from under the covers.

"You mean these?" she smirked.

He felt somewhat deprived of the opportunity to take those off her. He had been looking forward to sensuously torturing her while undressing, her. It's okay, he was nothing if not adaptable.

"What about your socks?"

"I didn't wear any, remember?" she giggled.

"How about your panties?"

He slid under the sheet and rolled next to her, getting his answer when his hand rested on her satin and lace hip.

"Um, aren't you forgetting something?" she asked coyly, tugging on his belt loop.

"Nope, I want to concentrate on you first, Kitten."

"But I—" she paused, her voice growing raspier as she continued, "I want to feel your skin, not your jeans."

Fuuuuck.

Who was he to deny a lady her request?

"Do you want to take them off or shall I?" he asked with a small smirk as he laid flat. He was curious how bold she really was. He had a feeling just asking him to take his pants off was a stretch for her.

When she slid her naked tits onto his bare chest and reached down to undo his fly, he felt his cock aching for release from his jeans. She undid the top button but paused before pulling his zipper down.

"I know this is probably not when we should be having this conversation," she murmured, biting the corner of her lip, "but I haven't—"

Cooper sat up on his elbows, cutting her off. "Kitten, you're not a—"

"What?" then realized what he was referring to. "Oh, no. God, no. You don't have to worry, this isn't my first time. I was going to say I haven't *done this in a while*. But we need to discuss safe sex before we go any further."

She was fucking adorable.

"No discussion necessary, baby girl, I always play safe. Always."

She was obviously feeling awkward now and laughed uncomfortably. "Appetizers anyone?"

He grabbed her and pulled her underneath him, smiling as he looked down at her pretty face.

"Actually, I would like an appetizer," he growled, stroking her slit beneath her panties.

She gasped and subtly spread her legs wider as she bowed into his touch.

He could feel the fabric becoming wetter while he continued rubbing her over her satin thong.

When she began to fumble with his zipper, he slid down her body and nestled between her thighs while pushing the denim down his legs. His mouth rested on her soaked center, and he breathed hotly into the patch of satin covering the object of his desire.

He could taste her through the material and couldn't wait any longer. Sliding her panties to her ankles, he pulled her lips apart and with a flat tongue, licked her folds up and down. He smiled when he noticed her fat clit peeking out at him and began to suck it. Her pussy was gushing when he slid his middle finger inside her and began to finger fuck her as he devoured her clit. She was panting and bucking against his face, and he pinned her in place using his forearm across her hips.

The sound of her arousal filled the room as he slid a second finger into her tight, little hole. Judging by how hard her pussy gripped his fingers, he believed her that it had been a long time since she was last fucked. He was going to make her cum so many times tonight, she was going to lose count.

Her fervent cries of "Ohmygod, yes, yes, yes!" followed by her body convulsing made his cock leak precum.

There's one.

He slowed the rhythm of his ministrations and gave her glistening pussy one last, long lick, smiling when it caused her to jump and try to close her legs.

He moved up her clammy body, kissing her sweetly when she whimpered, "Wow."

"That was sexy as hell," he said in a low voice, brushing her hair across her forehead.

She took a deep breath and nodded slightly in agreement, glancing up at him shyly.

"Can I, um..." she didn't finish her thought, instead reached between his legs to convey what she was thinking.

With a smirk, he rolled onto his back, indicating she could, indeed, play with his cock.

Katie was timid as she began kissing down his core until she was settled between his legs. He couldn't figure her out. Sometimes she was fierce and bold, others, shy and timid. He suspected she wanted to appear aggressive but didn't have much experience being so, at least sexually.

It would be his pleasure to provide her with the opportunity to practice.

Chapter Nine

Kate

The naked Marine lying next to her just gave her the first orgasm she'd ever had with a man. And it was freakin' amazing. Better than any she'd had with her battery operated 'friend,' Buzz Lightyear, that's for sure. Especially because the real-life version wanted to cuddle her after blowing her mind.

Kate had other plans though. Since tonight was a night of firsts, she wanted to return the favor and make Cooper come with her mouth.

She'd given blowjobs before but never to completion. Partly because she wasn't confident in her abilities, but mainly because she'd never been interested in tasting a man's seed. Especially since she'd never been with someone who was very concerned about her orgasm. Cooper's sole focus on her was such a turn-on, and she was suddenly feeling sexier, bolder, and friskier than she ever had.

Kissing down his six-pack to the sexy 'V' above his hip bones that was like a big directional sign to paradise, she was suddenly intimidated again, his perfect body a reminder just how over her head she was with this man. Then her face reached his cock jutting out.

Holy shit.

She'd felt his length in her hand but actually seeing it was a completely different experience.

How the hell is that going to fit in my mouth?

She was nothing if not a trooper, so she'd give it the old college try. Never mind that she hadn't finished college yet.

She circled the tip of his dick with her tongue, tasting a bead of his precum. Cooper drew a sharp breath when she took him as deep in her mouth as she could, the bulbous head pulsed reflexively in her throat. She slurped off his cock and began stroking his slippery shaft as she bobbed her head up and down, her hand and mouth meeting in the middle of his length.

"Katie, fuck," he snarled, gripping her hair and slowing her pace.

Alarmed at his reaction, she immediately stopped what she was doing.

"Did I hurt you?"

"God, no, woman. It feels incredible. *Too* incredible."

She giggled as she resumed stroking him.

"How can it feel too good?" she asked, just before slipping his cock back in her mouth.

He fisted her hair to control the tempo and growled, "You know damn well how."

Running her tongue up and down his shaft, Kate dipped her head between his legs and circled her tongue over his balls. His low groan continued feeding her ego and helping her confidence. She'd never sucked a man's balls, but again, tonight was a night of firsts.

His scent was masculine but clean, like he'd just showered, which she appreciated. Surprisingly, she liked it and was getting more turned on, especially because he seemed to be enjoying what she was doing.

Cooper steered her lips back to his shaft and guided her up and down his cock by her hair, grunting as he began to thrust deeper into her mouth.

She could taste the saltiness of his precum.

Suddenly, he stopped. At first, she thought it was because he was coming, then quickly realized it was to prevent it from actually happening.

He drew her face to his and began to kiss her.

"You're pretty damn good at that," he whispered between kisses.

How should she respond? *Thank you?*

She opted for, "I like doing it," then wondered if that made her sound slutty, so she quickly added, "to you."

"Well, that makes two of us," he chuckled, then reached into his nightstand drawer, pulling out a small square package. "But I need to be inside your tight pussy, Kitten."

He slipped the condom on and slid between her legs, lining his cock up with her opening but not pressing forward. She raised her hips up, trying to maneuver him inside her, but he drew back with a smile, resting on his forearms as he shrouded her upper body with his.

With his face inches above hers, he stared into her eyes before capturing her lips between his, plunging his cock into her waiting entrance. She reflexively bowed against his body while they moaned in unison as he filled her pussy. The Marine let her get used to his size before he methodically began to move in and out, murmuring in her ear as he did.

"Fuck, Katie, you feel so good."

All she could do was whimper in response, "So do you."

"So tight and wet," he groaned.

As much as she hated her Caesarean scars, at that moment, she was grateful that was how she'd delivered Sam. Even though it meant she'd never wear a bikini or have sex with the lights on again, Cooper said her pussy was tight. Tonight, it seemed like a fair tradeoff although the next time she was at the beach in her one-piece bathing suit, she'd probably have a change of heart.

Her clit was still buzzing from the orgasm he'd given her with his tongue and fingers, so when he leaned back on his heels and began to rub his cock on her magic button, she thrashed her head as her pussy responded.

"Do you like that, baby girl?" he growled, vibrating his hard shaft back and forth over her nub.

Her breath was becoming faster and shallower, and she panted out, "Oh, fuck, yes."

Cooper slammed his cock back inside her dripping pussy and began to use his middle and index fingers to polish her clit in unison with his hip thrusts.

She felt another climax starting to creep up from her toes and felt her entire body tense up.

"Come all over my cock, Kitten," he demanded through gritted teeth. "Let me feel you, baby."

Her body flashed hot, then cool, and she raised off the mattress as she came, crying out in ecstasy while Cooper continued pounding her pussy. He gripped her hips with both hands and began to make short, erratic thrusts, moaning,

"Oh, fuck, Katie, I'm coming. Fuuuuck...." Followed by slamming into her hard and holding her, grunting his release.

It was the most erotic sound she'd ever heard and triggered another orgasm.

How was that even possible?

She felt her cunt milking his cock as she rode the euphoric wave.

Ohmygod. She finally understood what all the fuss about sex was.

He collapsed on top of her, wrapping his arms around her upper body while he caught his breath.

"Holy fuck, Katie," he panted in her neck.

Holy fuck was an understatement.

"Wow, Cooper Johnson," she whispered as she ran her fingers through his hair. "That was amazing."

Cooper slowly rolled off her onto his back, his breathing gradually evening out before he got up to dispatch his condom. He came back with a hand towel and tended to her, then lay back down beside her, pulling her tight against him in a spooning position.

His warm, hard naked body next to hers, coupled with the multiple orgasms he'd just given her, and the fact she'd been going since six a.m. when Sam woke her up, lulled her to close her eyes and wiggle further into his arms.

It was only supposed to be for a few minutes.

Chapter Ten

Cooper

He lifted up from the bed to glance at the clock—3:24 a.m.—then nuzzled the neck of the sexy brunette in his arms.

God, she smells like heaven.

He ran his hand over her naked hip and pulled her tighter into his body. She fucking *felt* like heaven too. Katie moaned and turned over, burrowing into his chest with a sigh and a smile. A guy could get used to this.

"God, you're beautiful," he murmured against the top of her head.

Cooper felt her body tense, then she sat up like a shot.

"Ohmygod, what time is it?" Her hand was frantically wiping the sleep from her eye as she surveyed the room for a clock.

"It's okay, Kitten. It's just after three, go back to sleep."

"Oh no!" she cried, scrambling from the bed. "Oh no, oh no, oh no!" she continued as she rushed around the room in a frenzy, retrieving her clothes, then running into his bathroom with the pile she'd collected.

What the hell was that all about?

She was back into the bedroom less than four minutes later, her hair smoothed into place, and the smeared makeup under her eyes gone. He had managed to put on his boxers and watched her scuttle about as he sat on the edge of his bed, still half-awake and thoroughly confused. Women didn't leave his bed in the middle of the night. If anything, he had to kick them out in the morning.

"My phone, do you know where my phone is?" she asked as she scurried around his bedroom searching for the device.

He grabbed her by the wrist and pulled her in between his legs, trying to calm her down.

"Katie, what's going on? Come back to bed—we'll find it in the morning."

"I can't, Cooper. I have to go," she said, gently trying to tug away from his grasp.

He wrapped his arms around her, laying his head on her chest. He could hear her heart beating a mile a minute.

"Are you okay?"

"I just have to go. I didn't mean to fall asleep."

"I'm glad you did," he tried reassuring her. Did she think he didn't want her there? That didn't make any sense, he was all but begging her to stay. Something else had to be going on.

Holy shit, did she still live with her parents?

He decided not to ask. No sense in embarrassing her at this hour. But he was going to find out what the hell was going on, eventually.

Grabbing her hand, he guided her to the main part of the house to help her find her phone. He spotted it on the kitchen counter next to the cold, uneaten appetizers.

"Here it is." He handed it to her and gestured to the food. "I'm sorry I didn't feed you."

"I hate that we let it go to waste. I'm so sorry."

"Maybe you could come back tomorrow, and we could reheat it? Or better yet, I can grill some steaks and veggies."

Her smile was polite when she looked up at him. "You don't have to do this. We both know what tonight was. I mean, it was, hands down, the best sex of my life, so thank you very much, but really... It's okay. We don't have to pretend it's something it's not for the sake of making it less awkward now."

"But what if I want to see you again?" His tone reeked of desperation.

She shook her head with the same polite smile. Actually, maybe it was a little sadder now due to his patheticness.

"Cooper. One night, remember? That's all this was supposed to be."

"But what if I want more?"

"I have to go," she whispered and started walking toward the door.

He stood in the doorway, watching her put her high heels on, then grasped her around the waist and pulled her against his bare chest.

"Can I call you?"

Katie pursed her lips as if poised to tell him no, then reluctantly murmured, "Okay."

He smiled and leaned down to kiss her softly on the mouth, then pressed his forehead against hers with his eyes closed. All he could think was he wished she would stay.

"Don't feel like you have to call because of what happened tonight. I came here with my eyes wide open."

"Katie," he said softly, "I *want* to call you. I *want* to see you again."

Tears filled her eyes when she answered in a hushed tone, "I don't think that's a good idea, Cooper."

He was determined not to lose this battle.

"It's late. Let's talk about this tomorrow. Can I take you to lunch or dinner? Both?"

"I can't tomorrow."

"Maybe I could bring some takeout over?"

The idea visibly upset her. What the hell was going on in her life? Was she married?

No, that couldn't be it. She didn't wear a wedding ring, plus, she hadn't had sex in a long time, not to mention her coworker was pushing her to go out with him.

Cooper was pretty sure she lived with her parents. It was a logical assumption since she was still in college. *God, she's just a baby.* What the hell was he doing, trying to date her?

Then she smiled and kissed his cheek, murmuring, "I had a lot of fun tonight. Thank you," and it all made sense why he wanted to date her.

"I'll call you tomorrow," he promised as she opened the security door.

"Um, why don't you text? It'd be easier for me to chat that way."

He almost said, "So your parents don't overhear?" but decided to let her have her secret.

For now.

He was going to have to meet them eventually though.

"Text me when you get home. I mean it. I won't be able to fall back asleep until I know you're safe and sound in bed."

"I will," she assured him and started toward her car, seeming startled he was following her out. "What are you doing? You're in your underwear!"

"Making sure you get in your car safely," he snarled, offended she thought he'd just shut the door and let her go to her car alone.

She smiled, "Such a gentleman. You don't have to walk me to my car so the whole neighborhood sees you in your skivvies. Just wait here and watch me."

Although he doubted any of his neighbors were up at this hour, it was kind of chilly out. Katie gave him a peck on the lips and scurried to her car, not leaving him any room to argue. Once inside, she started the engine, waved, blew him a kiss, then backed out of his drive, only turning on her headlights once the Honda was on the street.

He closed the door and walked into the kitchen to clean up and argue with himself.

She was way too young for him.

The sex was amazing.

He wanted to settle down soon—it couldn't be with her. She was only interested in something that wouldn't distract her from reaching her goals.

God, he liked how he felt when he was around her.

She lived with her parents and obviously had a curfew.

Just her smile made him happy.

And those fucking tits.

Boom. Mic drop.

Argument over.

Chapter Eleven

Kate

She couldn't believe she was coming home at four o'clock in the morning. Mrs. Neal had been more than happy to have Sam stay with her tonight so Kate could go on her date and had even suggested just having him spend the night, but the younger woman insisted she'd be home at a reasonable time.

Now, she had a dilemma.

Kate had a key to Mrs. Neal's so she could pick up Sammy when she worked the late shift at the diner, but the latest she'd ever been was half past midnight. Did she risk disturbing her neighbor at this hour to collect her son?

She didn't want to wake up her generous landlord, but she also wasn't sure how she felt about Sam not waking up in his bed in the morning.

The decision was made for her as she crept up the walk after parking the Honda in the detached garage. She'd just finished sending Cooper a text she'd made it home and looked up to find Mrs. Neal waiting at her front door in her bathrobe, looking down from the wraparound porch with a smile.

"Did you have a nice time?" she asked before taking a sip from the mug in her hands.

Kate took the porch steps two at a time. "I did, but I am so sorry to be this late. We fell asleep watching a movie. I can't apologize enough for bothering you at this time of night."

"Nonsense, I was awake, so you are not bothering me in the least," the French woman chastised. "You should have just stayed at your friend's. Sam is perfectly fine here, and he loves my breakfast. Go to your apartment and get some sleep. And don't you dare come down those stairs until after nine."

Tears threatened to spill from Kate's tired eyes as she hugged her landlord. The young mother really had no idea what she would do without this beautiful soul. The day she answered Mrs. Neal's ad to rent her upstairs apartment was one of the luckiest of her life.

"Thank you," she whispered, kissing her cheek. "Are you sure you don't want me to take him now? He tends to be an early riser."

"Minette," Mrs. Neal addressed her using her favorite pet name for Kate, "I will be awake until my early afternoon nap. Sam and I will be fine until you come down later."

It dawned on Kate that both Mrs. Neal and Cooper's pet name for her was kitten, just in different languages.

"Cooper calls me kitten, too," she mused with a smile.

"Cooper? Is that who you went out with tonight?"

Kate nodded.

"I can't wait to meet this brilliant young man," the older woman said with a twinkle in her eye.

Kate was too tired to explain that was never going to happen. She couldn't very well tell her sophisticated landlord tonight had been nothing but a one-night stand. It had been hard enough to admit it to her slutty self.

"Maybe someday," she mused, then turned toward the outside stairs leading to her apartment, pausing to ask, "Are you sure you don't want me to take Sam?"

Kate conceded it was a half-hearted attempt at best. She was tired, and the idea of getting up with her son in less than two hours wasn't exactly appealing.

Mrs. Neal waved her off. "Positive. Goodnight sweet girl. See you after nine," then promptly closed and locked the door.

Kate was going to have to bake Mrs. Neal's favorite cookies tomorrow to show her appreciation, but right now, her pillow was calling her name.

When she was snuggled into bed in her oversized pink t-shirt that had *Bed Hair, Don't Care* in big white letters on the front, hugging her body pillow, she sighed. If only the pillow was a certain sexy Marine.

"I dub thee, Sir Cooper Johnson," she mimicked in a royal voice as she squeezed the down alternative cushion. "Dilly dilly."

"Goodnight Sir Johnson," she murmured as she drifted off into a slumber filled with sexy dreams.

****

Cooper

The clock read 5:55 a.m. Another byproduct of basic that had been drilled into him. No matter what time he went to bed or when his alarm was set for, he woke up every day at five minutes before six.

Kate hadn't responded yet to the text he'd sent her after she let him know she'd arrived home safely.

I had a great time tonight. I'd love to do it again soon.

He assumed she was sleeping in like normal people do on the weekends.

His jogging shoes were tied, and he was out the door to pound the pavement of the trails maintained for the residents of his neighborhood. It was one of the many amenities his hefty, monthly HOA fee covered. Maybe he'd take advantage of the community pool later.

He wondered if Katie would like to join him, which led him to think about what she'd look like in a bikini, which led him to think about how she looked last night when she was naked underneath him. That caused his dick to get hard, so he had to stop at one of the exercise stations along the jogging trail and think about baseball statistics to get his erection to go away.

He started back down the path, and his thoughts once again turned to Katie as his shoes made a rhythmic noise on the concrete.

Did she jog? Maybe they could go together sometime, like one morning after she'd spent the night.

What was she studying in school? He pictured her as a librarian or a nurse. He had no idea why other than the fantasy of what she'd look like in either profession.

Did she have siblings? He could see her as the doting older sister or the baby of the family.

There was so much he wanted to know about this girl.

Her hopes and dreams... not to mention her fantasies.

What big things did she want to accomplish that she didn't have time to date? Did she ever want to settle down—

maybe have a family someday? What kind of man did she see herself ending up with? Had she ever had a serious boyfriend? What turned her on?

He wondered what her parents would think of him. Parents always freaking loved him and the idea of their daughter dating him.

Of course, the last set of parents he'd met was over thirteen years ago when he was still in college. His little kitten's parents might not be thrilled with the idea of their Katie dating an older man. He'd just have to prove he was worthy. He could do that.

He turned the corner and headed back to his house. As the sweat dripped from his body, he couldn't help but wonder, *am I worthy of her?*

Cooper began to analyze his merit.

Educated—check.

Solid career—check.

Good family—check.

Honorable—check.

Dependable—check.

Track record when it came to women—fuuuuck.

In his defense, he'd never met anyone like Katie...

Jesus, I don't even know her last name.

Cooper shook his head. How could he be so infatuated with this girl? Everything was telling him they were incompatible, and he should just chalk it up to being the last hurrah he'd told himself it was going to be.

But the thought of not seeing her again made his chest physically hurt. The fact he was feeling like this after only one official date told him he needed to pursue her or he'd regret it for the rest of his life.

No regrets. Maybe that'd be his next tattoo because he was about to start courting his sweet Katie Kitten.

Let the chips fall where they may.

Chapter Twelve

Kate

"Mommy!" Sam shrieked as he came running from the kitchen when he heard her walk through Mrs. Neal's door at eight thirty in the morning.

"Did you forget how to tell time, Minette?" the beautiful French woman asked, wiping her hands on a towel when she appeared in the doorway. "It's not nine o'clock yet," she scolded.

"I know, but I slept as late as I could," Kate said, standing with her son in her arms. She kissed the little boy's sandy brown hair and asked, "Were you good for Mrs. Neal?"

Sam nodded solemnly.

Kate tilted her head. "Are you sure?"

"I had an accident," he whispered.

"Oh no. What happened?"

"I didn't make it to the potty in time."

"Did Mrs. Neal help you change your clothes?"

Again, he nodded soberly. "She said that doesn't mean I'm a bad boy though."

"Of course it doesn't, baby. Why would you think it did?"

"Miss Terri says I'm a bad boy when I have accidents at school."

She suddenly felt sick to her stomach.

Just another way Kate was failing her son—placing him in Promises Preschool, a shitty pre-K school because that's all she could afford. He was on a waiting list for the preschool the college offered at a subsidized rate for students, but unfortunately, she didn't know when, or if, he was going to be admitted.

"Miss Terri made a mistake saying that, sweetie. Everybody has accidents, it doesn't mean you're bad."

She made a mental note to talk to the school's assistant director, Terri Amonson on Tuesday. Kate doubted it would do much good, although the gray-haired woman would smile and pretend she was on her side.

She was sure the older woman would tell her. "I completely agree with you, but I'm just doing what I'm told,"

I'm just doing what I'm told. That seemed to be the lady's mantra. Kate wondered if Terri was capable of owning a decision she made.

She really needed to find a new daycare.

Mrs. Neal seemed to be having the same thoughts because she glanced at Sam before looking at Kate and saying sternly, "We need to talk about him coming here more."

The young mother shook her head. "We impose on you too much as it is, Mrs. Neal. I'll figure something out."

"Minette, for the millionth time, call me Noelle. And having that sweet child here is no imposition at all." She gestured toward the kitchen, "Come on, mon petit fils needs to finish his breakfast. Have you eaten?"

Mon petit fils. *My grandson.*

Mrs. Neal feeling that way about her child was bittersweet since her own mother barely acknowledged him. Amelia Katherine Connelly thought her first grandchild was the consequence of her normally rule-abiding, conscientious daughter finally rebelling at twenty, resulting in her entire future being flushed down the toilet. The woman was at mass four times a week, saying a rosary when she learned Eric Kingston didn't want anything to do with being a father and had quickly distanced himself from Kate—eventually, refusing her calls and blocking her number.

Her parents wanted her to give the baby up for adoption, citing she had nothing to offer a child without a husband or a career. When she decided to keep him, they refused to help her financially or with childcare so she could stay in college. Without a support system, Kate was forced to drop out of school at the end of her sophomore year and get a job. Meanwhile, Eric graduated with a degree in business and started the grooming process in his father's business. Last she'd heard, he was engaged to a perky, blonde, Pi Beta Phi alum who was perfect for his and his family's image.

Fuck him.

His refusal to even admit Sam was his made Kate all the more determined to provide her son with everything he deserved. Although she hated her son not having a father in his life or on his birth certificate, Kate truly believed it was Eric's loss.

She was positive of it every time she watched her little angel sleeping. Or when he belly laughed or whispered in her ear, "I love you, Mommy," after presenting her with a beautiful rock he found while outside playing.

Eric could have a dozen babies with Pi Beta Phi Barbie— they'd never be as perfect as Sam Jason Connelly.

Although she had a paper she needed to write today, Kate decided she'd stay up late tonight and work on it. Today was going to be about making memories with her son.

****

She was cleaning up the kitchen after Sam went down for his afternoon nap. They'd been to the park, then came home and baked cookies and had made a bit of a mess. She needed to get the kitchen cleaned so she could dirty it again preparing their meals for the week. And there was that paper hanging over her head she should be working on.

Her phone buzzed on the kitchen table, and she flipped it over, seeing a text from a number not in her digital address book.

Still thinking about last night. When can I see you again?

She had purposefully not entered Cooper into her contacts list, believing last night was a one-and-done kinda thing.

This conversation was going to be too complicated to have over text, and since Sam was sleeping, she dialed the number. He answered on the second ring.

"Well, hello there. What a nice surprise."

That made her smile.

"Hi," she said, suddenly feeling shy for calling. The silence that followed was awkward.

She murmured, "So, um..." at the same time he stammered, "Well, I..."

With a giggle, she prompted, "Go ahead."

"I was wondering what you're doing for dinner tonight. Do you want to come over? I can grill some steaks, we could maybe sit in the hot tub, pick up where we left off last night..."

Kate closed her eyes with a smile at the delicious thought, then squeezed them tight, wincing when reality hit her.

"I can't. I have a paper I need to work on, and things I need to get done to prepare for the week."

"What's your paper about?"

"Emerging market volatility for the upcoming quarter."

"Oh." He sounded surprised at her response. "What are you majoring in?"

"Finance," she said with a sigh.

Chuckling, he replied, "Doesn't sound like you're excited about that."

"Well, it's not pre-med."

"Is that what you want to do?"

Shit. She knew where this conversation was going to go.

"A long time ago, I thought it was, but things change. A career in finance will allow me to be financially secure sooner, and I won't have to go to school forever, then work insane hours for five years in a residency program."

"So, if money were no object, what would you do?"

That was easy. "I'd teach."

The idea of being able to make a difference in so many kids' lives was enticing, not to mention being on her own kid's schedule, but the abysmal salary made it impossible to even consider as a single mother.

"So why aren't you doing that?"

What's with all the questions, dude?

"Maybe someday, I will. After I'm more established, I'll go back and get my Master's and possibly teach college." This was getting too personal. "What about you?"

"I'm in the Marines until they make me retire," he responded quickly as if he'd thought about it often.

"So, you must like what you do?"

"Most days, I love it. There are days I wonder why the hell I joined, but those are few and far between."

"So, did you enlist right out of high school?"

"No, I got my degree then enlisted. I went straight from basic training to Officer Candidate School."

She had no idea what any of that meant but assumed it was impressive, so she replied, "Oh, very cool."

There was another lull in the conversation until he asked, "So, when can I see you again?"

Ah, the reason she'd called him to begin with.

"Cooper, between work and school, my life is really hectic. I don't know when that could even be a possibility."

"Kitten, you have to eat, right? Can't I at least take you out for dinner some night this week?"

"I work every night."

"Then we'll have a late dinner."

She loved and hated that he seemed to have all the solutions and wasn't taking no for an answer.

"I'll have to see if..." She almost slipped and said, *if I can get a sitter* but caught herself in time. "What my exam schedule this week is, so I'll know when and what I need to study for."

She could tell he was grinning when he told her, "I can help you when you do. We could have a study session that included a rewards system, hehe. I majored in business, so I'm not completely clueless."

A study session with him rewarding her could be quite motivating, and no, clueless was not a word she would ever use to describe Cooper Johnson. Sexy, smart, and relentless were better descriptors of the man.

"How about I look at my syllabi and see what my schedule this week looks like, then I'll text you tonight?"

"That sounds good."

"Okay, then..."

"Hey, Katie? Thanks for calling, baby. Just hearing your voice made my day."

Well, shit. So much for letting him down easy.

"It was nice talking to you. I'll text you later," she replied and quickly hung up before he started to make her swoon.

Goddammit. She didn't have time for swooning. She had things to do.

But would one more night in bed with him really be that big of a deal?

Chapter Thirteen

Cooper

She texted him her availability that week, and he was smiling the rest of the night.

Katie K: I can have dinner tomorrow.

He may or may not have done a fist pump in the air after reading her message. Since he didn't know her last name, he'd entered her in his list of contacts as *Katie K*. *K* for Kitten.

Cooper: What time should I pick you up?

Katie K: I'll just come to you. Will 6:30 work?

He'd had a feeling that would be her answer.

Cooper: 6:30 is perfect. Are you okay with steaks at my place?

Katie K: Steaks sound great. What should I bring?

Cooper: Just your sexy self, Kitten. I've got the rest covered.

Katie K: LOL See you tomorrow.

He couldn't wait.

The next day at work kept him hopping, which he was grateful for. He'd gone in early so he would be sure to leave by five, giving him plenty of time to stop by the store, get home, changed, and chop fresh veggies for the tinfoil bake with the steaks on the grill.

He bought a premade salad at the deli department of the market, along with a half-gallon of Cookies and Cream Blue Bell ice cream. He didn't know what she'd like for dessert, so he decided to go with his favorite.

It was a beautiful spring night, so he set the patio table for them to eat outside and made sure there was some firewood in case they wanted to sit by the fire pit later. He'd prefer keeping her warm in his bed, but he wanted to prove he was interested in getting to know her, so he was going to try to take it slow tonight.

Try being the operative word.

When he answered his front door and saw her standing there in a red checkered sundress, red heels, and red lipstick, he realized his resolve might not be that strong. The vision of her red lips sliding down his cock flashed in his mind, and he moved to grab her hand to escort her inside in an attempt to keep his khaki shorts from tenting in the crotch.

"You look amazing," he uttered as he leaned down to kiss her cheek.

It was then he noticed she had a pie in her hand and a backpack slung over her right shoulder.

"It's my books," she answered sheepishly when he asked hopefully if she was planning on spending the night. "I have finals this week, so I thought I'd take you up on helping me study."

That might be the perfect way to spend the evening with their clothes on so he could get to know her better. And it was *her* idea.

Things were looking promising with Miss Katie Kitten.

Which reminded him...

"I have something important to ask you," he said solemnly as he took the pie and backpack from her and guided her toward the kitchen.

"Oh? What is it?" she asked nervously, taking a seat in the chair at the table he pulled out for her.

Cooper set the dessert on the counter on his way to the refrigerator, pulling out a Summer Shandy left over from Saturday night and holding it up in a silent question if she wanted it. She nodded, and he asked, "Do you want a glass?" while opening the bottle for her, then grabbed another bottle for himself. Katie shook her head, and he handed her the bottle, sitting down at the table with a serious expression.

"What's your important question?"

He leaned closer, draping his arm on the back of her chair kitty-corner from where he sat. "What's your last name?"

Instead of grinning like he expected her to, she furrowed her brows.

"Why do you want to know?"

Was she serious?

"Because I like you and want to get to know you better. Because we've slept together and that's usually something someone knows about the person they've had sex with."

She remained silent, and he was feeling offended.

"Jesus, I'm not going to stalk you if that's what you're worried about. I don't need to coerce women to date me, Katie. It's not like..."

"Connelly," she whispered, swiftly shutting down his affronted rant.

Now he felt like a dick for getting his ire up. Cooper cupped her face in both hands and stared into her eyes with a smile.

"It's nice to meet you, Katie Connelly," he murmured, then lowered his mouth to hers.

She didn't immediately return the kiss, it took some coaxing on his part for her to respond, but when she did, he was instantly hard. He'd never met anyone he enjoyed kissing like he did her.

Every time, she tasted like cinnamon, and their lips responded perfectly to each other's attention—like they'd been kissing each other for years instead of days.

"I fucking adore you, Kitten," he confessed when they broke the kiss.

"You're not so bad yourself, Mr. Johnson."

It wasn't a declaration of adoration, but he'd take it.

It was a start in the right direction, at least.

*

Kate

I shouldn't have come tonight.

She had tried convincing herself seeing him *just one more time* wouldn't hurt anything, but the second he opened the door and looked at her with such affection, she knew she was in trouble. There was no way she wasn't going to want to keep seeing him.

Hell, she didn't even mind him calling her Katie or kitten. It was actually endearing.

Dammit.

She should have just told him about Sam upfront, then she wouldn't be in this predicament. He would have either never pursued her in the first place, or he'd have been content with the one-night thing they'd originally agreed on.

Now, things felt disingenuous. She was keeping her son a secret like she was ashamed of him, and that bothered her. Kate wasn't ashamed of Sam, but to bring him up now made her wonder if Cooper would think she was trying to pull a fast one.

Like Eric had accused her of doing when she told him she was pregnant.

That decided it. Tonight was the last time she could see the Marine. So she better make it memorable.

"Let me get the grill started, then I can help you study," he said after kissing her within an inch of her sanity.

She didn't want to eat. Or study. She wanted to be naked with him in his comfy, king-size bed. But seeing as she was feeling a little slutty knowing they'd had sex and he didn't even know her last name, she decided a little decorum was in order.

"What can I do?" she asked, following him into the kitchen.

"Just stand there and let me look at you," he grinned as he began pulling platters from the refrigerator.

Kate wasn't subtle with her eye roll.

His grin turned into a laugh. "Seriously, everything is ready, all I need to do is fire up the grill and let it cook."

She didn't like feeling useless, which he must have sensed because he handed her a large bowl of salad while setting three bottles of dressing on the counter. "Here, take these out to the patio table."

He may have forgotten what she did for a living because he seemed impressed when she managed to carry the salad bowl and all three bottles in one trip.

"Anything else?" she asked from the doorway to the backyard.

"Just the drinks. Do you want anything other than beer?"

"Maybe some ice water," she answered while picking up their beer bottles from the table. "I'll get it. Do you want any?"

"Yeah, actually, that sounds good."

She brought out the drinks and set them on the metal and beveled glass table as he placed a large tinfoil bundle on the upper rack of the grill, closing the lid without adding their New York strips.

"The steak won't take long, but the vegetables take a while to cook," he explained. "So we've got some time to study. Do you have a study guide or something I can quiz you with?"

Kate tried to hide her sigh. She was hoping he'd suggest other ways of passing the time while they waited for the tinfoil's contents to barbeque.

God, I'm such a slut.

The idea was actually kind of funny since normally she was the farthest thing from slutty. She'd only been with three other guys before Cooper. One was her first serious boyfriend who she lost her virginity to on prom night their senior year. They dated steadily all summer until they went off to different colleges in the fall. One was a drunken one-night stand—not her proudest moment. And the last one was Sam's dad who she dated for three months before finally sleeping with him right before he left for Europe on spring break. She wanted to make sure he didn't forget about her while he was gone.

God, she had been so naïve.

They continued seeing each other when he returned, right up until finals when she found out she was pregnant, and he dropped her like a hot potato. Needless to say, she pretty much bombed all her exams, subsequently dropping her GPA, which caused her to lose all her scholarships. Not that it mattered. She decided to withdraw after the semester, anyway.

Right before Sam turned one, Mrs. Neal encouraged her to think about going back to school. She started out taking one class that spring semester, then increased it to two in the fall. Between work and trying to be a good mom, eight credit hours seemed to be the most she could manage a semester, which meant earning her degree was going to be a marathon, but she knew she'd get there in the end.

Kate never went after Eric for child support, having decided it was better not to have to worry about him wanting custody one day. Sure, it meant she struggled more than she would have to if he helped her financially, but this way, he had no claim to her son.

Fuck him.

Cooper's voice brought her back to the present.

"Hey, where'd you go just now? Judging by your scowl, I'm betting it wasn't your happy place."

"Oh, I was just thinking about how impossible one of my professors is to please."

"Which class?"

"Macro and International Economics."

"What are your other classes?"

"Corporate Finance," she answered.

He nodded. "Sounds interesting. What else?"

"That's it."

"You go part-time?"

This would be the perfect opportunity to tell him about Sam, but since she wasn't going to see him after tonight, she didn't see the point.

"Yeah. It's going to take longer, but I won't have any student loans when I graduate," she offered in explanation.

"Your parents aren't helping you?"

She scoffed involuntarily. "Hardly."

Cooper seemed to be contemplating what she said as if he were puzzled by her admission and opened his mouth like he was poised to ask follow-up questions.

A change of topic was needed-*now*, and she shoved the study guide for her Corporate Finance final at him.

"Fire away!"

Kate could see the internal debate he was having with himself, but he finally decided on quizzing her. They were about three quarters through the review materials when he stood up.

"I think we can start the steaks."

"Good. I need a break."

"You're really prepared for this exam. I have no doubt you're going to ace it," he said, kissing the tip of her nose before tending to the grill.

His observation made her feel proud of herself. Something she hadn't felt in a long time. He always managed to make her feel worthy around him even when she was just waiting tables.

It was a nice feeling, one she could get used to.

If only that was a possibility.

Chapter Fourteen

Cooper

His kitten was fucking brilliant. No wonder she had better things to do than spend time with a jarhead like him.

Yeah, he'd graduated with a degree in business, but there was no *cum laude* attached to it—magna or summa. The only cum associated with his degree was the sexual kind. Which may explain his lack of academic honors.

Still, there was something about the way she made him feel that had him believing he could be a positive part of her life. He knew he was her biggest fan.

When she was laughing out loud as they ate, completely at ease and herself, he knew he needed to be with her. He didn't care about their age difference or that they were at different stages in their lives—he'd wait until she was ready to settle down. Or he'd convinced her to.

Probably the latter because not only was he impatient, he usually got what he wanted. And he wanted Katie Connelly. More importantly, he didn't want anyone else. Not even as a backup plan. That was how he knew she was special.

He needed to remember to cancel his date with Allison on Saturday. He'd asked her a couple of weeks ago to the spring ball that was happening this weekend.

Fuck, that was probably going to cost him at least a few hundred dollars when he uninvited her with such short notice. It was a dick move, and he knew it, but he wouldn't leave her holding the bag for all the things he was sure she'd already bought.

Allison was actually someone he had considered in the running to settle down with after he'd had his fling with Katie. The idea made him chuckle now.

No one but his kitten would do. He could only imagine how perfect their kids were going to be.

"What are you doing this Saturday," he asked, once their dinner plates had been cleared, and they were situated on the outdoor loveseat in front of the fire pit.

"Um, I have a thing that I have to go to," she replied cryptically.

"Can you cancel it? I'd love for you to be my date at the Spring Ball on the base."

She visibly paled. *Did she not dance?*

"No, I can't. I made these plans a while ago. People are counting on me."

He didn't try to disguise his disappointment and was heartened when she asked, "How many people usually go to those things?"

"To the balls?"

She nodded her head.

"I dunno. Maybe five or six hundred."

"Wow, that many. Must be hard to mingle."

"I usually just find my seat and stay put. If I bring a date, I'll dance with her, of course, but for the most part, the only socializing I do is with the people at my table and those I run into at the bar."

She nodded her head, lost in thought.

"Let me know if you reconsider," he told her. "It's always a good time. I think we'd have fun."

"I really can't. I'm sorry."

Cooper started to caress her inner thigh—he couldn't help himself. Her dress had ridden up her legs when she crossed them while sitting next to him, and her creamy, toned flesh was just too damn tempting.

"Are you ready for dessert?" she purred in his ear as she leaned over and brushed her tits against his shoulder.

He wasted no time and slid his arms around her middle, pulling her onto his lap before capturing her lips with his.

She was not timid when she returned his kiss. Sliding her arms around his neck, she tugged him closer while winding her fingers in his hair.

"I think you are the sexiest man I've ever met," she whispered as she nuzzled her nose against his face.

"I *know* you're the sexiest woman I've ever met," he countered.

He wanted to tell her it was so much more than sex though. She had captivated him. He wanted to know everything about her. Starting with what the hell she was doing on Saturday she couldn't be his date to the dance.

"Are you sure you can't come with me on Saturday? If I don't have a date, there won't even be any point in going. Do you know how bad it'll look if I don't go?" He was sort of teasing, but he wasn't above using a little old-fashioned guilt.

What she said next kind of knocked the wind out of sails and had him backpedaling.

"Cooper, I shouldn't even be here tonight. We agreed we were only going on one date, remember? But I thought when you asked me to come over tonight it was, well, casual, and there wouldn't be any harm in... seeing you again."

Seeing you again-code for *sleeping with you again*.

She only wanted to fuck him.

Shouldn't that be the ideal situation?

Under any other circumstances, it probably would be. But goddammit, he wanted more with her.

So much more.

He had no idea how to handle this woman without scaring her off, but it was obvious he was going to have to rock her world again in his bed.

Ouch. Twist his arm.

He began tracing the plunging neckline of her checkered dress with his index finger.

"Well, I'm glad I'm able to see you again." Then as if unable to control his damn mouth, he added, "I really like you, Katie. I want to keep seeing you." He began kissing her neck, murmuring against her skin as he moved from one side to the other. "Again. And again. And again."

She tilted her head, giving him easier access to her throat, but whispered in protest, "Cooper, let's just enjoy tonight."

Oh, he was going to make sure they enjoyed tonight.

She was going to enjoy it so much, she was going to be wrecked for any other man.

*

Kate

Cooper lifted her in his arms and began carrying her to his bedroom while she nestled her face against his shoulder.

She loved the scent of him—very clean with just a hint of cologne to tease her pheromones.

Setting her gently on her feet at the side of his bed, he slid the straps of her sundress and bra down her arms and began kissing her bare shoulders. His mouth was reverent on her flesh, causing her skin to erupt in goosebumps. He chuckled softly when he felt them as he caressed her skin.

Yeah, you know how to turn me on.

Her hand slid down to the front of his shorts, and she rubbed his huge hard on over the fabric. Apparently, she knew how to turn him on, too.

She felt the zipper on her dress being slowly lowered, her dress dropping to her feet. She had on white lace panties that matched the bra now haphazardly covering her boobs and her red heels he had insisted she keep on when she walked in his house.

Cooper took a step back to take her in and ran his hand roughshod through his hair.

"Katie," he growled. "Holy fuck..."

At that moment, it was like she was the sexiest woman on the planet. That she'd managed to have that effect on this gorgeous, experienced Marine made her feel powerful and bold.

"Do you like it? I thought about you when I bought the set."

"Hell yes, I like it. I need to take you lingerie shopping so I can buy you everything in the whole damn store."

"I know just how I'd show my appreciation," she purred.

"Kitten, just seeing you wear it would be appreciation enough," he snarled.

She dropped to her knees in front of him and looked up at him innocently as she began to undo the button on his shorts.

"Are you sure I couldn't show my appreciation some other way?"

He took a sharp breath in as she started to lower his zipper.

"On second thought..." he mumbled.

Kate tugged his shorts and boxer briefs down his legs with a knowing smile, and his cock sprang free inches from her face. She cupped his balls, then moved to stroke his shaft slowly up and down, looking up at him.

She was enjoying this game of make-believe. The idea of him buying her an entire store full of lacy lingerie like a baller and her thanking him with her body turned her on.

So much for being a feminist.

But when she ran her tongue up one side of his shaft, circled the tip, then licked down the other side, and he moaned out loud in ecstasy, she'd never felt more empowered. Or turned on. She could smell her own arousal through her lace panties.

Wrapping her lips around his cock's head, she looked up at him as she took him as deep in her throat as she could. Her eyes watered, but she was proud of herself for not gagging.

Cooper threw his head back, groaning, "Fuuuuuck, Kitten."

She began bobbing her head up and down his cock, stroking his base as she did, pressing her thumb on the vein under his crown. She'd read about that in some article—it was supposed to enhance his experience. His increased breathing seemed to indicate there was some truth to it.

He tried to stop her like he had Saturday night, tugging on her arm to get her to stand.

Sex goddess Kate was not happy. She was kind of drunk on the control she was feeling and refused his attempt.

"Katie..." he murmured as he tried to slow her attention to his dick. "Kitten, you have to stop."

"Why?" she quietly demanded before resuming her blowjob.

"Because, baby... you're going to make me come."

She smiled as she increased the tempo.

"And coming is bad?" she asked, playing naïve while jerking faster on his dick wet from her spit. He was having trouble formulating words, and she fucking loved it. Getting him off was turning her on more than anything. She could feel how soaked her panties were.

Cooper pressed on the back of her head, almost instinctively, then consciously seemed to move his hand away and stroke her shoulder, allowing her continued control of the situation.

With one hand she cupped his balls while continuing to stroke and suck his cock. She felt his body start to tense, and he began to gasp.

"Katie..." he cried out in warning. "Fuck, Kitten, I'm going to come."

That caused her to take him deeper into her mouth. She thought that surprised him and turned him on because instantly, he was grunting and thrusting into her mouth, then he let out a long roar as he began to empty himself in her throat.

She swallowed his warm cum without a second thought, something she never imagined she'd ever do. She always envisioned herself as a spitter. Who knew?

Cooper collapsed on the bed, panting, "Oh my God, woman. What the hell did you just do to me?"

With a smirk, Kate crawled up his body.

"I made you come," she whispered seductively in his ear. She really was fucking proud of herself.

When he leapt up and flipped her on her back, growling, "My turn," all she could do was bow her body off the bed in approval.

After all, she knew how to share and take turns.

Chapter Fifteen

Cooper

Mind officially blown.

Cooper was supposed to be the one rocking her world, and instead, she just knocked his upside down.

Granted, he was pretty sure he returned the favor, based on her cries of delight as her body shuddered like he was exorcizing a demon from it. But afterward—when he held her tight in his arms and she sighed with contentment—is what he didn't want to end.

He was gaga over this chick.

Fucking gone.

Like make-room-in-his-closet-for-her-shit kinda gone.

He wanted to fall asleep holding her every night and wake up spooning her every morning. Make her happy any way he could.

Take care of her.

He had just started to drift off to sleep when he felt her kiss his cheek and get out of bed. Instinctively, he knew she was getting up to leave, and he wasn't happy.

"You can't stay?" he asked as he watched her pull her dress on and reach behind to zip it.

"I have to get home," she said with a sad smile.

Cooper felt like maybe he was getting a taste of his own medicine—all the women who'd begged him to stay as he got dressed to get the hell out of their house once he'd had his fun. He always made sure she was satisfied first—he wasn't a dick, but he wasn't a fan of waking up in a foreign bed.

He sat on the edge of the mattress and tugged her wrist until she was situated between his naked thighs. It was déjà vu. They'd just played this scene last Saturday.

"Can't you sleep over?"

She tilted her head as she looked at him and tucked imaginary hair behind his ear. His hair was too short for her to really do it.

"I wish I could."

"Do you think you'll ever spend the night?"

The corners of her lips turned down.

"No, I can't." Tears filled her eyes. "I don't think we should see each other again. I like you too much already."

Oh. Hell. No.

He slid his arms around her waist and pulled her against him. He could feel her soft sobs and knew she wasn't really done with him yet, she just needed some coaxing and assurance.

"Baby," he murmured, "let's just see where this goes. I like you, you like me. The sex is great. Why shouldn't we keep seeing each other?"

She softly answered, "My life is so complicated, Cooper. I don't—I can't—date right now."

He pulled back to take in her tear-streaked face. "I don't want to make your life difficult, Kitten. Let me be your escape from reality."

She smiled wistfully. "I wish it were that easy."

Wiping her cheeks with his thumbs, he told her, "It can be. I promise. Let's just go out, be together, and if you ever feel like I am making your life even more complicated, I will go away. No hard feelings." He could tell he was getting through to her, so he kept talking.

"I just want to spend time with you, Katie. I won't push you for anything more than you're willing to give."

That was a damn lie. He wanted everything from her, and he knew he wouldn't be content with anything less. But he was patient, and he was willing to take things as slowly as she needed to realize they were perfect together.

"I have things I want to accomplish, Cooper."

He rubbed his hands up and down her upper arms. "I know you do, Kitten, and I will never stand in your way. I promise. I will be your biggest cheerleader as you conquer the world."

Hugging her middle, she told him frankly, "I think you will distract me from my goals."

He felt like she was starting to dismiss him and tried not to panic.

"No," he said more urgently than he meant to as he unwrapped her arms from her middle and put them at his sides instead. "I'll be your respite, help you recharge and regroup."

"And you'd be okay with that? What do you get out of it?"

Her question was fucking ridiculous. Cooper held her face between his hands and stared into her eyes.

"What do I get out of it? I get time with you, Katie Connelly," he whispered, then lowered his lips on hers to kiss her slowly.

She wound her arms around his neck as he deepened the kiss, and his cock started to harden against her stomach.

"I have to go," she murmured.

Had he not just promised he wouldn't push her, he would be trying to convince her to stay, but since he was trying to prove he wouldn't complicate her life...

"Okay, Kitten. Let me walk you out."

He found his boxer briefs in his shorts and pulled them on, then walked her to the door where they proceeded to make out for ten more minutes. She finally made it out the door when he called out to her.

"Katie, you forgot your backpack."

"Shit," she muttered and started back toward the house. He jogged to the back patio, gathered her papers and tucked them in the backpack, then met her in the kitchen with the purple JanSport flung over his arm.

They started kissing again, and Cooper had just reached under her ass to lift her onto the counter and fuck her silly when he came to his senses.

"You have to go," he smiled and kissed the tip of her nose.

Katie swallowed hard and nodded. "I have to go."

They reached the front door again, and she whispered, "Just so you know, I don't want to, but I have to."

He kissed her forehead. "Just so you know, I don't want you to, but I understand you have to."

Taking a step back, he asked, "Text me when you get home?"

"I will."

He waited by the door until he saw her drive away.

With a deep breath, he wondered what the hell he was going to do about this woman.

Chapter Sixteen

Kate

Well, so much for not seeing him anymore.

It was going to be okay, it would be on her terms. She could manage to keep him separate from her everyday life. It was like he said, he could be her escape from reality. Kate knew deep down the likelihood of being able to keep Cooper in her own special world was nil, but she wanted it so bad, she was willing to believe her own fib.

Then there was this the ball on Saturday. That had disaster written all over it. Her only hope was there would be so many people, they wouldn't run into each other. Or better yet, he wouldn't attend because he didn't have a date. Still, the gnawing feeling in her stomach got worse as the week progressed.

It was finals week, and she'd asked for evening shifts only so she could study, but knew that meant her budget was going to be tight. She hadn't counted on Cooper showing up every night just in time for her to wait on him before her shift ended. He continued to tip her generously.

Probably too generously. If she had more money in her checking account, she'd be prouder about refusing so much. Or maybe be offended, wondering what his ulterior motives were. But she was broke and couldn't afford pride, and so far, it appeared his only purpose for being there was dinner, followed by walking her to her car once her shift was over and kissing her soundly goodnight

Kate had a feeling he might do something like that and covered Sam's car seat with a blanket emblazoned with *San Diego State University* before she left for work on Tuesday.

He didn't push her to go out until Friday when he knew she'd taken her last exam. Instead of walking her to the Honda, he steered her toward his BMW. Her perplexed look when he opened the passenger door was met with his knowing smirk.

"We're going to celebrate you finishing the semester."

She protested, even as she slid onto the gray, butter-soft leather seat.

"Cooper, I'm in my waitress uniform, and I don't have a change of clothes. I haven't even looked at my hair or makeup since this morning before I left the house, and I'm tired... I really don't feel like going out."

He closed her door and came around to the driver's side. Once inside, he pushed a button, so the overhead light came on and reached in the back seat before presenting her with a dozen red roses wrapped in green florist tissue paper.

"Congratulations on another semester under your belt, Kitten," he said, kissing her cheek.

The gesture made her teary-eyed. She'd never gotten flowers from a man she was dating before. Burying her nose in the petals, she inhaled deeply.

"They're beautiful, thank you. I can't believe you bought me flowers."

"Katie, I told you, I'm your biggest cheerleader."

The idea made her a little giddy. Still, she didn't feel like going out and told him so.

"We're just going back to my place. I've got champagne on ice, the hot tub heater on, and you're going to sit back and relax. You deserve it."

"I have to be back here to get my car by midnight," she warned.

"That gives us three hours, Kitten. Plenty of time for me to spoil you."

On the drive, she noted his car was as meticulous as his house. While he'd never given her the impression he obsessed about keeping his things pristine, she couldn't help but notice how neat and orderly everything about him was. His home, his yard, his clothes, and now his car. She wondered how long he'd last around Sam's sticky fingers before pulling his hair out or reaching for a bucket and a sponge.

She had been trying to keep her love life compartmentalized and away from her real life, and the realization the two could never mix made her not only sad but feel like a phony. She was pretending to be someone she wasn't, and this gorgeous man next to her deserved to know she wasn't the woman he thought.

They pulled into his garage, and he turned to her with his perfect smile.

"What?" she asked.

He shook his head. "Nothing. I'm just glad you're here."

God, she felt like an asshole. It must have shown on her face because he furrowed his brow.

"What's wrong?"

"Nothing," she replied quickly. "I think the week just finally caught up with me is all."

"Come on," Cooper nodded toward the door leading to the house. "Let's get you inside so you can relax." He came around and opened her door, taking the roses from her and helping her out of the car.

"Do you have a vase? I should probably put those in some water."

"I'll take care of that, you just go get out of your clothes and into the hot tub. I'll be in shortly with your champagne."

"But, I..."

"I mean it, Katherine Connelly," he said, trying to sound stern. It only served to make her giggle.

"My name's not Katherine although it's a normal assumption. I'm just Kate Allison Connelly."

His face fell when she mentioned her real name, and she heard him mutter, "Oh, shit."

"What's wrong?"

He smiled in a way she'd never seen before and knew instantly it was fake. She didn't like it.

"Nothing's wrong," he assured her.

Kate knew that was bullshit, but she didn't have any right to demand he tell her what was bothering him. Especially since she was harboring her own den of secrets.

Don't ask, don't tell.

Had that way of doing things ever worked?

It had to, at least tonight.

Instead of dwelling on all the things she was doing wrong, she did as he instructed and was naked in the hot tub on the private patio off his bedroom without another thought. He was right, it was relaxing.

He came out ten minutes later with a navy and white striped towel wrapped around his waist carrying an ice bucket with a green bottle, along with two champagne flutes tucked bottoms down between his fingers. He'd dimmed the lights in his bedroom so the glow in the small enclosed area had lessened, but she still got an eyeful of the beautiful man as he walked toward her in the bubbling, hot water.

He was freaking perfect. Why he was interested in her, she had no idea.

Yes, the sex was ah-mazing, but she had a hard time believing she was anything special, and he certainly wouldn't have a problem getting any woman he desired to go home with him. Ones who were far sexier and more sophisticated than she was that was for sure.

Then he smiled at her, making her feel like the most beautiful woman in the world. She still couldn't come up with an answer why he wanted her, but at that moment, she didn't care. She was content just knowing he did.

*

Cooper

Every minute he spent with Katie made him happy. They didn't even need to be naked, although that definitely had its merits, and he would never complain when they were. But just being with her, talking to her about his day and listening about hers lifted his spirits. He had to run an extra mile in the mornings to make up for eating late night diner food just so he could see her this week.

Worth every step.

He'd bought her a bracelet as a graduation present, but Cassie told him it was too early to give her the aquamarine and gold gift.

"You're going to scare this girl away by giving her something like that so soon," his friend warned when he dropped in to visit her and the new baby. He was still enamored with the tiny person but was discovering Luke's almost-four-year-old son was a freaking riot. The little man's perspectives on life were hilarious.

Without looking up from playing with his toy trucks, he suggested, "Give her a flower. Girls like flowers. And don't forget to brush your teeth. Girls hate stinky breath."

"Flowers and fresh breath—got it."

"He's not wrong," Cassie smiled as she discreetly nursed Sophia Claire.

"So, no on the bracelet, yes to flowers, and positively yes to brushing my teeth," Cooper recapped.

"And you should kiss her a lot. Madrastra likes it when Papa kisses her," the little love expert advised as he smashed two Tonka trucks together.

Cooper looked over at the new mother with a smirk. She simply shrugged and repeated, "He's not wrong."

So, he opted for the roses instead, heeding young Lucas' advice. He'd also brushed his teeth before getting in the hot tub with Katie because he planned on kissing her—a lot.

After popping the cork on the bottle of champagne, he handed her a full glass and clinked his against it.

"To you, Kitten. I'm really proud of you."

That drew a small smile from her as she rested the back of her head against the side of the tub. She looked exhausted, and he wanted nothing more than to tuck her into his bed and hold her all night as she slept in his arms, but she had been adamant about returning to the diner by midnight.

When was she finally going to agree to sleep over? He wanted nothing more than to fall asleep with her in his arms and wake her up in the morning with his head between her legs.

He was going to broach the topic with her again soon, but not tonight. Tonight, he wanted her to feel safe and comfortable.

Her eyes were closed, and her glass of champagne was starting to tip, so he took the flute from her and set it on the edge of the tub then slid his arm around her. She rested her head against his shoulder and sighed with a smile.

"You're right, this is exactly what I needed," she affirmed without even opening her eyes.

Cooper leaned in to kiss her just as she brought her hand up to cover a long yawn. Part of his pampering plans tonight included multiple orgasms, but he was rethinking that idea. She needed to be still and unwind without the added sexual element. Her soft snoring confirmed his assessment.

He knew she ran herself ragged and had to be barely making above minimum wage. What he couldn't understand was why. Why did she have to work so much, and why couldn't she go to school full-time?

She never talked about her family—maybe she was supporting her parents or taking care of her elderly grandma. He didn't know, but he wanted to. He wanted to know everything about her.

Cooper kept a careful eye on the time, wanting to prove she could trust him to honor her wishes, and tonight, her wish was to be at her car by midnight. He'd have her there by eleven fifty-nine.

Which meant, he had about another hour to be with her, but he worried her skin was going to start to prune if she didn't get out of the water soon.

Nudging her, he whispered, "Baby girl, why don't you go lie on my bed for a little while."

That seemed to startle her awake because her eyes flew open, and she urgently asked, "What time is it?"

He smoothed her hair. "Shhh, it's not even eleven. I promise, I'll have you back to your car by twelve. Come on, let's get you out of the water and into bed."

"I can't be late, Cooper," she reiterated as sternly as she could in her tired state.

"Trust me, Katie. I will make sure you're on time."

That seemed good enough for her, and she let him lead her out of the tub to dry her off before getting her situated under his covers. He checked on a few things before slipping in beside her to hold her naked body against his.

His dick started to grow, but he wasn't aroused because he wanted to fuck her. He just liked how she felt in his arms.

Like that's where she belonged.

He set an alarm on his phone for forty-five minutes and drifted off to sleep next to her. It was the best forty-five minutes of rest in his life.

Chapter Seventeen

Kate

She woke to someone gently shaking her shoulders.

"Kitten, it's time to wake up."

It was Cooper's voice coaxing her out of her peaceful slumber. She felt so comfy and cozy, her body was fighting her brain to open her eyes.

"Katie, it's eleven-thirty. You need to get up and get dressed if I'm going to get you back to the diner before midnight," he murmured.

She appreciated the Marine was thoughtful enough to give her a few minutes to wake up and get moving. Her son was not nearly as considerate. Every morning he wanted her up and making him breakfast the second he woke up. Or worse was when her mommy brain registered he was up and being far too quiet, making her jump out of bed even faster.

Being able to stretch and slowly roll out of bed at her own pace felt almost decadent.

"Hi," Cooper said softly when he noticed her eyes open.

"Hi," she responded sheepishly. "I'm sorry I wasn't a very good date tonight."

"Baby girl, you were perfect. I'm glad you were able to get some rest. I'm sure you needed it after your busy week."

"You have no idea," she muttered under her breath as she set her feet on the floor.

He handed her a small, grey UCSD t-shirt and a pair of women's shorts, along with her bra and panties.

"Old girlfriend's?"

"Of course not. I'm not a cad. I bought them for my sister, but just never got around to giving them to her."

"Lucky for me," she teased as she headed to his bathroom to change. She noticed her undergarments appeared to be freshly washed.

Exiting the room, she spotted his dress uniform hanging on his closet's door jamb, and a pang of guilt hit her. When she walked back into his room and found her uniform washed and neatly folded, her conscience was screaming at her with a megaphone. She needed to come clean about tomorrow, lest she run into him there. He had been way too good to her, and she didn't want him to think she was a terrible person.

He was already dressed and smiled when he noticed her standing in his room.

"Ready?"

She bit her lower lip as she tried to summon the courage. *It's like ripping a band-aid off, just do it.* Taking a deep breath, she forced herself to look at him.

"I need to tell you something."

That got his full attention, and he sat on the edge of the bed, waiting for her to continue.

Kate stared at the carving of his footboard.

"About tomorrow. Why I can't go with you."

He drew her hand in his. "Okay?"

"I can't go with you to the ball because..." she hesitated, then blurted out, "I'm already going," then glanced up at his face to gauge his reaction.

Cooper opened his mouth in surprise but kept his expression neutral. She pulled her hand from his in order to wring it with the other in front of her.

"It's not a date-date. I mean, we're not dating romantically or anything. He needed a date, and I said I would go. It was all arranged before I even met you. I'm sorry I didn't tell you."

He nodded his head slowly, a lopsided smile forming on his face as he stroked her biceps.

"Baby girl, it's okay. I have something I need to confess, too. I asked someone a couple of weeks ago, but then I met you and was planning on canceling because I didn't want to go with anyone but you, but, um, I actually forgot to call her. I was still going to bail on her tomorrow morning even though it's a total dick move, but maybe since you're going with someone else..."

"Cooper, you can't cancel on such short notice,' she admonished.

He shrugged. "I didn't feel right going with someone else."

Which only served to make her feel like a bigger asshole than she already did.

"I'm sorry I didn't tell you sooner, I just didn't know how," she offered as an explanation. A lame one if she did say so herself.

He chuckled. "Well, I'm glad you did before I ran into you tomorrow with...?"

"Trevor Neal."

He nodded "Do you think he'll mind if I ask you to dance?"

She countered, "Do you think your date will mind if you ask me to dance?"

He wrapped his arms around her middle and pulled her in closer to him.

"I don't give a damn if anyone minds, I'm dancing with you."

She couldn't help but giggle.

Her admission made her feel one hundred pounds lighter, and she wished she would have told him sooner. Maybe if she had, she would have actually slept this week. As it was, between worrying about exams and running into him tomorrow night at the ball, her sleep had been fraught with nightmares, resulting in her waking up still exhausted.

After the little bit of champagne she'd drank and the warm, soothing water of the hot tub, it finally all caught up with her tonight.

Now, she just had the fact she hadn't told him about her son looming over her head. It was to the point now she couldn't tell him, she'd waited too long.

Good thing he was just her escape from the real world. Nothing more.

Chapter Eighteen

Cooper

He saw Katie immediately when she and Sergeant Neal walked through the front doors and down the ballroom's steps into the receiving line.

She was fucking mesmerizing.

Her tits were begging to be sucked as the tops peeked out from the purple satin dress that hugged her hourglass shape, then flared at the bottom, almost like she was a mermaid. Her brown hair was pinned up with soft ringlets framing her face, and he could tell she was wearing makeup, her dark lipstick, in particular, catching his attention.

Her date slid his hand around her waist as they walked through the line, and Cooper wanted to kill the man with his bare hands as he watched from his vantage point near the entrance where he waited for his date to arrive. He'd sent an Uber for her, citing he needed to be there early and help set up for the awards they were giving out later, so he couldn't get away to pick her up. It was bullshit, but Allison didn't need to know that. He did, however, warn her she would be making a roundtrip via the car service.

Still observing the sergeant paw at his kitten, his fists were clenched tight at his side when Allison approached him in her nude colored dress adorned with sequins splashed in a starburst across her middle.

Allison was a beautiful woman, no doubt, and she'd been okay in bed. She had potential, which was why he had considered her in the running to get serious and have babies with. Then he met a little firecracker waitress who knocked him on his ass, and suddenly, every other woman seemed dull and boring.

He at least tried to fake he was happy to see the blonde, kissing her cheek and smiling at her appreciatively.

"You look lovely. Your dress is stunning."

She traced her finger along his uniform seductively.

"Maybe you can take it off me later?"

He captured her hand and gave a sympathetic smile. "I can't, I'm sorry. I just started seeing someone."

Her eyes flashed as she withdrew her fingers from his grip.

"So why did you invite me?"

"I wasn't dating her when I asked you."

Realizing she was now his second choice, she scoffed indignantly, "I see."

"I hope you understand."

She glared at him, and coldly said, "I'm going to find our seats," then turned on her heel without another word. He guessed they were skipping the receiving line.

I should have just fucking canceled.

Right then, he noticed the sergeant alone at the bar, Katie nowhere to be found.

He'd like to say he was acting on impulse, but after asking around about Trevor Neal today, since the only thing he knew about the man was Cooper had to outrank him, otherwise, he'd know exactly who he was, Cooper had formulated a few ideas before arriving tonight.

The captain approached Trevor with a smile and a handshake, trying to put the lower ranking man at ease.

"Sergeant Neal. Glad to see you could make it tonight. I've heard good things about your unit."

"Thank you, sir."

"And I see you brought a date tonight..."

"Kate Connelly. She's a college student—finance," the younger man offered helpfully. Cooper noticed he didn't mention the waitress part.

"How long have you known her?" he asked as nonchalantly as he could.

Trevor Neal pulled at his collar uncomfortably like he'd just been caught with his hand in the cookie jar.

"Sergeant?" Cooper barked a little harsher than he'd intended.

"Well, um not long, sir. She rents an apartment from my favorite aunt who asked me to take her out and show her a nice time. I guess she's a single mom and doesn't get out much."

It took every ounce of his willpower not to gasp, instead, spitting out a cough as he said, "I see."

He hadn't seen that one coming and felt a little shell-shocked. Cooper Johnson didn't get blindsided easily, but this just floored him.

Single mother? Katie has a kid?

Suddenly, everything fell into place—her refusal to let him drive her home, not spending the night, leaving in a panic after their first night together, not wanting to go on a real date. It wasn't because of something Cooper had done or because she had a curfew, she had a child to protect and worry about. That made him suddenly want to care for her even more than he already did. Her and her kid.

The subordinate continued with a shrug. "She's obviously beautiful, and she's actually really sweet, but if I'm honest, Captain, she's not really my type."

*Fucking right she's not your type. She's **my** type. Mine.*

He no longer wanted to destroy the sergeant's career or kill him with his bare hands. Fortunately, Cooper had perfected his poker face long ago, so his expression remained unchanged when he suggested, "You're putting in for staff sergeant, aren't you? Why don't you join me at my table? I'd like to hear more about the training methods you've been employing."

"Sir?" the sergeant asked with a head tilt. "Isn't the table seating already assigned?"

"Yeah, but I've got room for two more at mine. There shouldn't be a problem." Well, he'd have room once he bounced two of the butterbars that is. "Table thirty-six," he stated like the matter was decided—which it was—then walked away to discourage any further conversation. Not that the younger man would continue the discourse if he knew what was good for him.

Cooper made sure the two seats to the right of him were unoccupied so Sergeant Neal and Miss Katie Connelly would have no other choice but sit there. Allison sat to his left with her face in her phone, oblivious to his seat maneuvering.

He watched Katie and Trevor make their way across the ballroom from their old table. She was adorable as she fidgeted with the straps on her gown as they walked. He could tell she felt out of place by her darting eyes and nervous smile when Trevor stopped and chatted with people. Cooper wondered if the dumbass even bothered to introduce her.

Her look of panic wasn't what he was expecting when the pair finally arrived at table thirty-six, and she realized they were sitting at his table. He stood and pulled the chair next to him out, ensuring Katie was situated right beside him. Her look of panic morphed into a fake smile, and she took her seat.

Cassie's sister, Brenna Roberts was newly married to a high-ranking commander and had silently observed him banish the second lieutenants to different tables and rearrange the seating, so the chairs next to him were vacant. She seemed to be watching with interest as Cooper scooted his chair closer to the brunette once the new arrivals were seated. Mrs. Roberts smiled at Katie, trying to put her at ease.

"I'm sorry, I didn't catch your name. I'm Brenna Roberts," the flawless blonde said as she stretched out her hand.

"Kate," the younger woman said shaking her hand, then cast a nervous glance at Cooper before finishing. "Connelly."

"What do you do, Kate?"

Trevor quickly interjected, "She's a finance student."

Katie glanced down at her lap, not saying anything further. That fucking pissed Cooper off.

"Finance," Brenna marveled. "That must keep you busy."

"Yes," was all the beautiful waitress offered in return, then seemingly tried to shift the spotlight. "What do you do, Brenna?"

The older woman smiled broadly, putting her hand on her husband's forearm as she replied proudly, "I'm Ron Thompson's wife," like that was a job. Cooper supposed being a lieutenant general's wife could probably be a full-time job, but he knew better. So did her husband, who shot her a look, so she hastily added, "And I'm a screenwriter."

He tried to keep from snorting. *A screenwriter* was putting it mildly. Cooper knew she was an Oscar-winner who made more money than God with her movies. Her humility only added to her beauty.

"Oh, wow," Katie said, sitting up in her seat. "I bet that's a lot of fun. Do you go on the red carpet and everything?"

Brenna smiled warmly. "I used to, but that got old, really fast. I'm lucky to be in San Diego, away from the glitz and glamor, but close enough to make a meeting in L.A. when I need to."

The younger girl nodded in understanding.

Brenna gestured between Cooper and Katie. "So how do you two know each other?"

He wasn't sure how to play this, but when Katie quickly glanced between him and Brenna and started to stutter a reply of, "Oh, we don't..." he interjected.

"I met her when I was visiting your sister and the baby at the hospital. Katie's my favorite waitress at Frank's diner." He wanted to throw in, "And I'm going to fucking marry her and have babies with her," but thought it would be bad form since she was another man's date tonight.

She looked at him as if startled he was revealing that.

Yeah, I'm saying it. Fuck Trevor Neal for trying to make you feel embarrassed about it.

The sergeant seemed surprised Cooper knew his date's 'secret,' and looked even more stunned when Cooper threw his arm around her silky, bare shoulder and rubbed her opposite bicep, winking at her with a smile.

"She's the best by far."

"That's so adorable," Allison's patronizing voice shrilled from over his left shoulder. She'd apparently put her phone down to join the conversation. "Is this the little waitress you told me all about? She's not at all how you described."

What a bitch.

He'd not talked about Katie specifically with anyone but Cassie and well, Lucas.

"I'm Cooper's date, Allison," the blonde purred as she clutched his bicep with one hand and stretched the other in front of him to shake his kitten's hand.

He turned toward Allison and scowled, keeping his arm around Katie's shoulder while he did.

"Why would I have told you about Katie? And when would I have? You and I have barely spoken since I called you three weeks ago when I needed a date for tonight."

The bitch backpedaled, "Oh, I must be thinking of someone else."

"Must be," he replied brusquely.

Brenna would have made the perfect diplomat because she immediately tried to ease the situation by engaging his date in conversation.

"I'm detecting a southern accent, Allison. Where are you from originally?"

That got the blonde talking about her favorite subject—herself, and she retracted her claws as she droned on about Alabama.

The first course arrived, and he reluctantly withdrew his hand from Katie's shoulder. The feel of her skin was immediately missed, so he brushed her outer thigh with his thumb under the table. Her shifting away from his touch upset and confused him. He glanced over at her and found she appeared really interested in her salad.

After half of the greens on her plate were gone, she excused herself to use the ladies' room. He waited about twenty seconds before standing and announcing he was going to the bar, asking if anyone needed anything. Luckily, no one did because he wouldn't have gotten it for them, anyway.

He stood outside the women's restroom, feeling like a goddamn stalker, which if you wanted to get technical about it, he probably was. Especially when he practically pounced on her once she exited the door, grabbing her by the elbow and pulling her to a secluded corner of the hallway.

"You look fucking beautiful, Kitten," he growled.

She scowled. "You've had your fun. Point taken."

"What the hell is that supposed to mean?"

"Please. Why did you insist on sitting us at your table? We both knew we were here with other people, Cooper, you didn't have to throw your beautiful date in my face. And *the General's favorite little waitress* bit was the *pièce de résistance*—just in case there was anyone left at our table who might actually think I belong here.

That pissed him off, and he pulled her further into the corner, boxing her in with his body and hovering over her.

"First of all, I fucking want to be with you tonight, Kitten, not Allison, that's why I insisted you sit at my table. Second, I'm only a captain, not a general, but thank you for the promotion. Third, you are my favorite waitress, no contest, what's wrong with saying that? And lastly, if you feel like you don't belong, that's not on me. I've been nothing but welcoming to you."

Her eyes brimmed with tears, and she looked away as she brushed her cheeks with her fingertips. "You're right," she whispered. "You've done nothing wrong. I'm the one who—"

He cut her off by leaning down and catching her mouth with his for a gentle kiss. A kiss she returned immediately, he noted.

Keeping his face close to hers when he broke away, he softly caressed her jaw and stared at her beautiful face, uttering, "I'm so glad you're here."

"Really?" she breathed.

"Really. Now what are we going to do about your date?" he said matter-of-factly.

"What about yours?" she teased.

"Oh, Allison already knew she was getting put in a cab at the end of the night."

"So, you did tell her about me."

"Not in the way she implied. I just explained I had other plans after this ended."

"Pretty sure of yourself."

"Well, at least I *hoped* to have other plans..."

A small smile escaped her lips like she had a secret.

He cocked his head and asked suspiciously, "What?"

"I was hoping that too." She put her hand on his shoulder and confessed in his ear, "Because I don't have to be home until late morning."

A jealous growl escaped his throat.

"Why? Were you planning on staying out all night with Trevor?"

Her eyes got big like she was surprised at the idea, then offended, she pushed him away with both hands.

"No asshole, I was hoping to meet up with you afterward."

Drawing her back into him, he smiled like he knew that and was just teasing her. That way, he could save a little face and smooth her ruffled feathers at the same time.

"I'm glad we didn't have to wait until afterward to meet up."

He felt her relax against him, and she leaned against his shoulder as if in agreement, murmuring, "I feel bad. I don't think this was what Trevor was expecting tonight. We should probably get back."

Sergeant Neal and Allison were now seated next to each other, lost in conversation, barely noticing Cooper and Katie's return just in time for the main course to be served.

Once they were seated in their new chairs, the captain leaned over and whispered in Katie's ear, "Something tells me they'll be okay with me asking you to dance later."

She smiled. "I think you're right."

Cooper wanted to ask her how she was able to arrange to be gone all night but decided he was going to wait and let her tell him about her child on her own terms. If he were honest, he was really waiting to see if she trusted him enough to divulge it to him at all.

He wasn't sure what he was going to do if she hadn't told him by morning.

Chapter Nineteen

Kate

Marines in their dress blue uniforms? Hot. Cooper Johnson in his dress blues? Panty melting, ovary exploding, make her weak in the knees, oh hell yes, *scorching hot.*

Kate was glad her date and Cooper's date appeared to be hitting it off. Trevor even seemed surprised when Cooper interrupted them to ask him permission to dance with Kate.

That's when the sergeant stood and pulled him aside to talk with him privately. Kate concluded their discussion must have had something to do with Trevor asking to take Allison home or asking Cooper to take Kate home because when they were dancing, the sexy blonde man asked, "Did you bring an overnight bag?"

She nodded her head, and he asked as he spun her around the dance floor, "Is it in Trevor's car?"

"Yeah."

Cooper chuckled. "That must have been a nice surprise for him when you walked out the door with it slung over your shoulder."

"Actually, he was the one who suggested it, saying I might want a change of clothes if we went to an after-party on the beach or something."

He snarled at the thought. "I thought you were going to try to meet up with me after?"

Tracing the hair above his neckline in an attempt to soothe his jealousy, she whispered with a grin, "I was. But Trevor didn't need to know that."

That caused him to break out in his trademark smile, and he muttered a sheepish, "Oh," then squeezed her tight.

She liked how she felt in his arms—safe. Protected. Adored. Kate noticed the muscles underneath his uniform as her hand rested on his shoulders while they moved around the dance floor, and she had to keep herself from sighing out loud. Tonight was like a fairytale, but she knew eventually she was going to turn into a pumpkin.

As their bodies swayed to the music, she decided she was going to let herself enjoy being Cinderella for a night. She'd fret about losing her glass slipper later. Right now, the Marine holding her in his arms was staring at her almost reverently, and she felt beautiful.

Cooper twirled her through the French doors leading to the near-empty balcony and pulled her into a dark corner where he pressed her back against the building and began to kiss her passionately. Kate had felt the desire between them slowly building all night and was rejoicing his decision to take her outside for a clandestine rendezvous.

His mouth was firmly planted on hers while his hands urgently caressed and stroked her bare skin. She pressed her hips against his, aching to feel him inside her. He hiked her dress up past her thighs and slid her panties to the side, plunging a finger inside her dripping pussy as he did.

Kate quietly groaned against his lips, and he began to finger fuck her, slowly sinking his middle digit in and out of her until the wet noise coming from between her legs echoed loudly in the otherwise silent night air.

The naughtiness of them slipping away to commit such lewd acts while dressed up and dignified, coupled with the thrill they could get caught, turned her on even more, and she was quickly on the verge of coming.

"Katie," he panted in her ear. "I want to fuck you, right here, right now."

Gee, who was she to argue with that?

She reached down and unzipped his pants, pulling his cock out and stroking his warm, hard length. She smeared his precum with her thumb, rubbing it in circles along his velvety crown, then firmly jerked his shaft.

Spinning her around so her tits were mashed against the cold, rough bricks of the building, Cooper snapped the wisps of fabric that were here her panties, kneeled down, and spread her ass cheeks while he dove his tongue into her crack, then her pussy, grabbing handfuls of her fleshy bum as he devoured her. Kate rested her head in her arms holding her upright against the building and quietly groaned as his tongue darted in and out of her holes. Arching her ass against his mouth, she urged his tongue to go further in her pussy while her arousal dripped down her thighs.

Cooper stood, and she sensed the front of his uniform pants being lowered, then heard the sound of a crinkling wrapper. He brought his hands around to hold her tits for leverage while his cock slowly eased inside her. Both of them quietly moaning in unison as he filled her.

They moved in small, rhythmic thrusts, his low grunting in her ear erotic as fuck. She was making little whimpering noises when suddenly, they heard a group of voices walk onto the patio and grow louder as they came closer to their dark corner. Cooper covered her mouth with one hand as he continued to thrust his dick deep inside her and brought his other hand down to fondle her clit. She felt him smile against the back of her neck as if devilishly delighted with his attempt to make her cum while she had to keep quiet.

He gripped her middle tight when she began to make uncoordinated thrusts, his hand still over her mouth to muffle her cries of ecstasy while she climaxed. The Marine continued penetrating her quietly until, thankfully, the intruders went back inside, and he could fuck her at a feverish pace. His balls slapped her ass until he held her hips still while making one long thrust as he emptied himself inside her with a discreet grunt.

"Fuck, Katie..." he growled in her ear. "You are so goddamn sexy."

The funny thing was, she *felt* sexy.

And only just a tiny bit slutty.

She had to admit, being a slutty Cinderella was kind of fun and exciting. It was so outside of her normal, everyday life. Then he spun her around and looked into her eyes before kissing her thoroughly, and she felt like a princess.

She knew turning into a pumpkin was inevitable, but just for tonight, she was going to let Captain Cooper Johnson be her Prince Charming.

Chapter Twenty

Cooper

He'd just fucked Katie on the balcony at the Marine Corps' spring ball. In his uniform. With his command staff inside. And it was wicked hot.

He tied his condom tight and wrapped it in a cocktail napkin, throwing it in a large garbage can before they headed toward the ballroom doors; her torn panties, however, were safely in his pocket. Cooper paused to appraise her appearance before they made their way back inside. Aside from her lipstick being kissed away, she looked no worse for wear. He was glad. He would have hated to have her embarrassed. With a smile, he kissed her below her ear.

"Shall we?" he asked, ushering her in.

When they reached their table, Katie picked up her clutch and excused herself to the restroom. He watched her hips sashay across the ballroom before looking up and seeing Brenna Thompson smiling knowingly at him. Just what she knew was the question, and he moved to sit next to her and find out.

"I like her," she gestured in the direction Katie had left.

Cooper nodded as he continued watching her walk across the room. "Me too."

"But?" she asked.

He turned his full attention to Cassie's older sister and shook his head. "No buts. I want to be with her. Period."

The corner of Brenna's mouth lifted in approval.

"Can you hear that?" she asked seriously.

He furrowed his brow. There was nothing unusual about the sounds coming from the dance. *What the hell was she talking about?*

"I think I hear hearts breaking all over San Diego tonight," Brenna said with a smirk.

He scoffed. "Pfft. San Diego? Try the world, sweetheart."

She burst out laughing and leaned over to kiss his cheek. "Just don't break her heart, Cooper."

"It's not her heart you should be worried about, Bren," he replied somberly.

The stunning blonde's lips parted slightly in surprise at his admission. He was equally taken aback at the realization the power the little waitress had over him. He'd never allowed a woman to make him feel vulnerable before. Not that he'd *allowed* Katie to. She just had, without him even realizing it.

The fact she had a child made her refusal to let him in her life more credible than when he thought he just had to win her parents over in order to keep her out past her curfew. Being a mother and protecting her kid were pretty legitimate reasons to reject him. Or at least keep him at a distance, which was the furthest thing he wanted.

Cooper wanted, no he needed, to get closer to her. Make her fall in love with him because he was falling in love with her.

Holy shit.

He was falling in love with Katie Connelly, the single mother/sexy waitress/brilliant college student.

Their eyes met across the room as she walked back toward their table, and she smiled brightly at him, her lipstick freshly reapplied.

Yeah, there was no falling about it. He'd already fallen.

"Katie's date asked if I'd give her this," Brenna said, holding up the purple backpack he recognized from the other night.

"Oh, did he leave already?"

Brenna smirked. "Yeah, with your date while you were on the patio with his."

His smile was unapologetic. That was the most erotic thing he'd ever done, and it was well worth the discipline risk.

Cooper gestured to the knapsack. "Thanks for keeping it safe."

"Anytime," she replied just as Katie sat down next to him.

"Oh, my backpack. Did Trevor leave it with you?"

Brenna nodded and handed it to Katie. "I promised I'd make sure you got it."

"Thank you for doing that."

Lieutenant General Thompson appeared at his wife's side and reached for her hand.

"Excuse us, but it's time to take my beautiful bride home."

"Anything you say, husband," Brenna gushed, beaming at her spouse before turning to Cooper and Katie. "Goodnight. It was lovely to meet you, Kate. I hope to see you again soon."

Ron said goodnight to the table then whispered in Brenna's ear, "Come on, darlin'," as he protectively escorted her out the door.

Cooper watched them leave and realized he wanted what they had. Only with some rugrats. And he wanted it with the beautiful woman sitting next to him. Now, he just needed her to want it, too.

*

Kate

Right after Brenna and Ron left, Cooper leaned over and whispered in her ear, "Are you ready to go home?"

The clock hadn't struck midnight, and Cinderella was leaving the ball.

Happily.

"Yes," she said with a contented smile. She couldn't help the warm feeling in her stomach when he asked if she was ready to go *home*. Like they were a real couple, and they shared a home.

Fuck it. This was her fairytale tonight, and she was going to relish it. Actually, she was going to roll around naked in it all night long.

He placed his hand possessively on the small of her back as he guided her toward the exit. They made frequent stops along the way to say goodnight to people who called out to him. He introduced her each and every time as if he was honored to be with her. She'd never felt so wanted before and not just sexually. Cooper truly seemed to like her company

133

while she was dressed as well. She knew the feeling. She really liked him with his clothes on—especially in that sexy uniform.

God, he was hot.

But he was also kind and caring—at least toward her. And so generous. He was definitely an alpha male—that was obvious tonight by the way others spoke to him with such respect. She had to admit, it was a huge turn-on.

She had to remind herself—it was all a fairytale.

The noble Marine wasn't really *her* Prince Charming, and Kate was a far cry from a princess. She was a single mother, barely scraping by, getting her degree eight credits at a time, and only with the help of the generous people she'd had the good fortune of having in her life.

Which reminded her, she hoped Mrs. Neal wouldn't be too upset if she learned Kate left with a Marine other than her nephew. Although she wondered how much Trevor would tell his favorite aunt since he also left with someone else. Another thing to add to her list of things to worry about tomorrow.

Tonight, she was Cinderella, and the clock hadn't struck midnight, and she still had both glass slippers on. Except this happy ending was going to have an entirely different meaning than the storybooks.

Wink, wink.

Chapter Twenty-One

Cooper

He couldn't stop smiling the entire drive back to his place. Katie was coming home with him tonight, and he was going to wake up with her in his arms.

Greatest night of his life. Hands down.

And the best part was it was far from over. The Marine captain was having a hard time believing she was actually going home with him, and she seemed as happy about it as he was. It was almost too good to be true.

He kept stealing glances at her as he steered the BMW through the light traffic on the streets that Saturday night, half expecting her to have changed her mind. But she didn't, just looked over at him and smiled back as he laced his fingers through hers.

"You look really beautiful tonight," he murmured and brought her fingertips to his lips.

She seemed shy at his compliment and whispered, "Thank you," while tucking some stray hairs behind her ear and looking down. They'd driven another block when she spoke again.

"Can I tell you something?"

He took a quick breath in, expecting this to be when she told him about her child.

"Of course. Anything."

"I've never met a man who is sexier than you are in that uniform."

Not quite the secret admission he was expecting. Still, it made him smile.

"I'm glad you like it," he chuckled.

Her hand was suddenly squeezing his inner thigh then began to move up toward his cock.

"Oh, I think it's safe to say I more than just like it," she flirted.

He felt himself getting hard at her touch, which didn't take much, considering he was at half-mast every time he looked at her tonight in that sexy as fuck dress.

Cooper slightly tilted his hips forward, encouraging her to touch him higher. She briefly squeezed his sac then ran her hand over the crease of his thigh, smirking with satisfaction at the obvious bulge in his uniform.

"Baby girl..." he growled.

Kate sensually palmed his cock over his pants, pressing her tits against his arm as she leaned over to whisper in his ear, "Yes?"

"I'm going to pull this car over and fuck you in the back seat if you don't stop," he warned.

She seemed to perceive his threat as a challenge, and tugged his zipper down, slipping her tiny hand through the fly and fishing around through the flap on his boxer briefs until she had direct contact with his shaft.

Her hand felt so fucking good wrapped around his dick. She began to tug up and down as her tits threatened to spill out the top of her dress from the awkward position she was in stretched over the console.

He groaned at both the sensation and the sight of mounds of creamy flesh. Fuck, he wanted her. Not only in his bed, but in his life.

Cooper imagined what that would look like. Getting up in the morning, sitting at the breakfast table with her kid—did she have a son or daughter?—before he headed to work, and she got ready for her day at school. They'd meet at home after their day was done, maybe he'd stop by daycare and pick the little rugrat up, and the two of them would have dinner ready for her when she got home. They'd all three eat as a family, and Katie and Cooper would clean up while little Susie or Johnny watched cartoons. He'd steal kisses and play grabass as they loaded the dishwasher and tidied the kitchen as a team before putting the kiddo to bed, reading a bedtime story until he or she nodded off. Then he'd take his little kitten to bed and make love to her until she fell asleep in his arms. Only to wake up and do it all over again until he got her pregnant, so they'd have two babies to take care of. And eventually three, maybe even four.

He wanted all of that—with her.

His little daydream, coupled with her stroking had him so fucking hard, he was contemplating making good on his threat and pulling the car over and fucking her on the leather interior in the back.

But it was probably not in his best interest to get caught with his uniform around his ankles, driving his cock into her sweet little cunt with her evening gown bunched around her hips in some vacant parking lot. He could hold on until they got to his house.

Or so he thought until she unbuckled his belt and undid his button, freeing his cock in its entirety while she lowered her mouth down on him with a devilish grin.

"You slutty little kitten," he gasped as she engulfed his cock in her throat.

Katie slurped off his cock, slowly stroking the shaft.

"Do you want me to stop?" she feigned innocently.

"Don't you fucking dare," he snarled through gritted teeth and fisted her hair in his hand, ruining her styled updo. Cooper didn't want her to stop, but he was going to control the tempo. He wasn't blowing his load in the car, there were still lots of things he planned on doing to his little kitten tonight.

First on his list—fuck those sumptuous tits of hers.

As determined as he was not to come, Katie seemed equally determined to make him.

Not happening, sweetheart.

Did Quintana's batting average go up after last night's game? The Padres' season was looking promising, too bad they traded Dalbec.

When that didn't work, he tugged her off his cock by her hair.

"Fuck, Katie." His tone was almost scolding.

He was chastising his girl for being too good at giving head. What the fuck was wrong with him? But he wanted to go all night with her and coming twice before they even got back to his place might hamper that. So, as much as he'd like nothing better than to erupt in her mouth, he tucked himself back into his pants.

Her grin was seductively wicked when she rubbed him briefly, then sat back in her seat.

"Why did you stop?" she pouted.

She knew damn well why.

Cooper veered the car into an empty parking lot in a strip mall, threw it into park, and grabbed her face, dragging her lips to his.

Kneading her hair, he kissed her hard. Katie wrapped her hands around his neck and pulled him even closer, holding the back of his head when his mouth began moving against her throat.

"God, Katie," he groaned frantically against her skin in between kisses and love bites. "You drive me insane."

He reached across her body to press the button to lean her seat back, then tugged her dress up around her waist and pushed her legs wide apart. He could see her pink pussy glistening with juices in the dim fluorescent lighting coming through the windshield of the abandoned parking lot.

His fingers began to move up and down her slit, exploring her folds, spreading her lips apart with his index finger and thumb while he continued rubbing her puffy pussy. She was so slick and soft, and when he plunged two fingers inside her, she arched her back and gasped.

He watched her face—her eyes closed, head thrown back—as she made little whimpering sounds while his digits moved in and out of her, his thumb strumming her clit.

Cooper leaned over and replaced his thumb with his tongue, flicking her hooded knot. Quick lashes at first, then using flat strokes, he began to lick her like an ice cream cone. She spread her legs wider, and he began to suck her fat, little nub while finger fucking her faster.

She was drenched and curving against his hand as his index and middle fingers moved in and out of her tight hole while his tongue continued its assault on her button. He could hear her getting wetter and felt her clit getting stiffer, and she was starting to gasp in between her mewls of passion.

His kitten was so fucking sexy, he was ready to come in his pants just watching her get off.

"That's it baby girl," he growled into her wet center. "You're going to come on my face, aren't you?"

She moaned in agreement as he doubled his efforts. His tongue and fingers bringing her closer and closer to climax. Katie started to tense. Cooper pinned her in place so he could finish fucking her to completion. She tasted so fucking good. He moaned into her folds as she bucked her sweet hips against his face while she went over the edge.

He didn't let her finish before he was tongue fucking her hole, lapping up every drop of her delicious nectar. She tried pushing him away, but he grabbed her hands and held them down until he finished licking her clean. At first, she fought him, but he felt her slowly relax as she moaned and began to grind her hips against his mouth.

He smiled when he felt her stomach start to clench. Yeah, he was going to make her come three times, and they hadn't even made it to his house.

Her tight little pussy began to quiver as he tongued her to another orgasm. Her gasps became cries when her body started to convulse, her head thrashing back and forth in ecstasy. His underwear was wet from all the precum that had leaked out of his cock.

She was so fucking hot.

Cooper sat up and adjusted himself in his pants, hit the defrost button on the center console to try to defog his windshield, murmuring, "Buckle up," before slipping the car in drive.

Katie lay sprawled against her seat, her sweet little cunt still on full display for him as she recovered and mindlessly put her seatbelt on with her seat leaning back.

Her dress had slipped below her tits so one nipple was playing peekaboo. It was all he could to keep from pulling over again just to suck on it.

Finally, she whispered, her eyes still closed, "Oh my God. I didn't think something like that was possible."

"Something like what was possible?" He had a good idea what she was referring to but wanted her to have to say it out loud.

"Coming two times in a row like that. I thought it was a myth. Another first for me with you."

"Another? What else has been a first with me?"

Her eyes flew open when she realized she'd revealed too much. He couldn't help but smile while trying to keep his chest from puffing out.

Fuck yeah. There's plenty more 'firsts' where that came from, baby girl.

He didn't say anything more, just chuckled and stroked her thigh before tugging her dress down, letting the subject drop. He'd let her mull her admission over while he remained silent—for now. There was a lot they still needed to talk about.

Cooper realized Katie wasn't going to tell him a damn thing until she felt safe doing so, and that became his mission of the night. Well, another mission. Titty fucking her was still pretty high on his list of the night's priorities.

They pulled into his community, and he noticed her looking at his neighbors' houses as they drove through the streets leading to his place.

"It's so beautiful in here," she mused as she trailed her finger over the walnut on the door panel.

"It's a great place for families with kids," he replied, trying to not-so-subtly bring kids into the conversation.

She turned to him with a thoughtful look.

"Is that why you bought it?"

He decided his best course of action with her would always be honesty and shook his head.

"No. I bought it for the resale potential, but I've been rethinking that. I think I would like to raise my family in this neighborhood. It's got great schools and is a really tight-knit community where the kids seem to feel safe playing outside. I think it'd be a great place for our kids to grow up."

He expected her to flinch at *our* kids. She didn't—just smiled with amusement.

"*Our* kids?"

"However many you want," he replied unapologetically with a grin.

Her expression turned serious.

"I explained to you, Cooper, I have things I need to do."

Cooper shrugged. "Who says you can't do them and have kids at the same time? It doesn't have to be either-or, Katie. People have both careers and families all the time."

"I just can't get sidetracked. You acted like you understood. Please don't try to make what's going on between us more than it is."

He wanted to scream, *"But I want more!"* but felt like his best course of action at the moment was to back off. Katie Connelly was going to have to call the shots. Or at least think she was.

With a grim smile, he said, "I know, I'm sorry. You're right. For the record, I wouldn't mind more, but I know you have things to accomplish first."

He could see her eyes well with tears as he pressed the garage door opener.

Shaking her head, she whispered, "I have to, Cooper. I hope you understand."

The funny thing is, he *did* understand.

He understood she was a single mom who was fighting to provide her kid with a better life, and she struggled and worked her ass off for every damn thing she had.

Was it so terrible he wanted to carry some of her burden? He got the impression she would think so, as if relying on him would somehow make her weak and vulnerable.

That got him thinking. What kind of asshole must her baby daddy be to leave her scraping to get by? Was he the reason she was so unwilling to let her guard down now?

His work cut was out for him, but he was willing to put in the effort to prove to her he was worthy. When she smiled weakly at him, he wanted to pull her into his lap and fix every single problem she had.

This feeling of possessiveness and the desire to take care of her was definitely a new experience for him. The way his cock moved, watching her hips sway when she sauntered into his house? Not so much.

Chapter Twenty-Two

Kate

She was naked, shoving her tits together while Cooper straddled her tummy and slid his fat cock between her oiled-up globes, another first for her as he whispered words of adoration.

"Katie... You are so fucking beautiful..." he groaned. "I love your tits, Kitten. I love your sexy body. I love your hair, your face... I fucking love—" He abruptly stopped his words, but not his thrusts between her boobs.

It was sexier than she imagined being titty fucked would be. The visual was hot as hell, and she was feeling pretty impressed with how her glistening boobs looked wrapped around Cooper's thick cock.

It didn't hurt that the man whose legs were draped around her middle was a magnificent specimen of the male species—the V that formed at his hipbones, the ripples in his stomach, his broad chest, handsome face... She was still having trouble wrapping her head around why he was interested in seeing her, especially after meeting his date tonight—a gorgeous Southern belle who was an accomplished advertising executive.

What the hell did Kate have to offer Cooper that someone like Allison didn't?

Established in her career? Nope.

Beautiful and sophisticated? Nope.

Experienced—sexually and in life in general? Ha.

Barely making ends meet? Yep.

145

A little curvier than she'd like to be? Definitely.

Three and a half-year-old son? Check.

Yet, regardless, every time they were together, it was so easy. Everything between them—their conversation, laughter, chemistry, sex—nothing felt forced or awkward, other than when she was attempting to keep her home life separate from him.

They were having such a great time together, why ruin it by mixing the two? But it was exactly the reason things could never be serious between them.

"Katie," he growled, "I want to be inside you when I come, baby."

"Ohhhh," the thought made her moan out loud.

He slid a condom on and lined his cock up to her entrance, sinking deep inside as he hovered over her in a plank position. His forearms were at her sides when suddenly, he moved to embrace her, murmuring her name reverently into her neck as he moved in and out of her.

"Katie... Baby... You feel so good."

She cooed her agreement, and his breathing started to pick up as did his pace.

"Fuck, Kitten... I'm gonna come," he grunted, then squeezed her tight, holding her still as he thrust inside her hard and deep. The noise from his throat was guttural while he burst inside her.

Cooper left his face buried in her neck while catching his breath, not pulling out and kept her held in a tight embrace.

"God, Katie..." he growled against her skin once his breathing evened out, "you are so fucking amazing," then slid off her and made his way to the bathroom. He was back in a matter of seconds with his arms around her middle, pulling her back into him in a spooning position. He kissed her shoulders and her ears as he attempted pillow talk.

"I'm so glad you came home with me tonight."

"Me too," she whispered in agreement.

"I don't think I'm going to want to let you go in the morning."

Part of her wanted to admonish him for talking like that, but part of her was still letting herself live the fairy tale tonight and loved it.

She didn't say anything, but rolled over and burrowed into his chest. He had just a smattering of blonde hair on his breastbone and smelled like the clean, spicy cologne he used. She inhaled his scent deeply and sighed.

"Tonight was like a fairytale," she confided.

"I agree," he said, kissing her temple.

"I don't want tomorrow and reality to come."

"This could be our reality, Kitten if you let it."

Tears threatened to spill from her eyes and onto his bare chest.

"No, it couldn't. I—"

"Have things to do, I know," he interrupted.

She traced circles on his skin, her cheek flat against his body.

"It's more than that, Cooper. My life is really complicated. But at the same time, compared to yours, it's

147

probably simple. I don't have a mortgage or a car payment or a career."

He tilted her chin, so she was looking at him.

"No, you just have work, school, and bills you're trying to pay while keeping your head above water. Not to mention being a... student with things going on at home."

His phrasing seemed odd, and for a second, she panicked that he knew about Sam, but then realized there was no way he could know about her son, she was just being paranoid. If he knew about Sam, she certainly wouldn't be in his bed tonight.

"We're just at different stages in life. We would never work in the long run."

"I don't believe that for a second, Katie, but I'm not going to waste our precious time together tonight trying to convince you otherwise. I'm just going to enjoy being with you here, all night long."

That brought a smile to her lips as she closed her eyes and nuzzled against his side. His arm remained around her, and the last thought she had before drifting off into a peaceful slumber was how well her body fit against his.

****

Cooper

He watched her sleeping next to him for a long time before nodding off too.

Smitten would be the understatement of the year regarding how he felt about her. He was fucking gone over her.

What if it's just because she doesn't want me? The thrill of the chase and all that?

Maybe she was right to keep him at a distance, away from her kid.

But he wanted a baby with her, and he wanted to meet hers and see if there was any way Cooper could be part of her child's life as well. And that had nothing to do with the thrill of the chase. That had to do with adoring this down-to-earth, beautiful woman in his bed. He'd never met anyone quite like her.

He loved being able to touch her all night long, and his subconscious knew the entire time she lay next to him. Part of him was calmed by her presence while another part of his brain was on alert she was going to leave before he woke up.

Luckily she didn't drive here.

When he remembered that little tidbit, he was able to relax and sleep more soundly, only to be jolted awake when he reached for her, and she was missing. His feet were on the floor when he called out, "Katie?"

What fucking time was it?

He heard water running in his bathroom, then the bathroom door open, and the light switch off. It had to be early, it was still dark out.

She was clad in one of his t-shirts with the bottom of her bare ass peeking out from the hem when he caught a glimpse of her in the moonlight walking from the bathroom.

"Hey," she whispered as she crawled up the bed and hugged him from behind as he sat on the edge of the bed. "I'm sorry if I woke you. I tried to be quiet, then I stubbed my toe on your stupid ottoman."

"Are you okay?" he asked as he rubbed his eyes.

"I'm pretty sure nothing's broken, so I'll survive."

Cooper laid down, pulling her next to him.

"I didn't know where you were," he murmured. "I was worried you'd left."

He felt her smile against his chest before she kissed his skin tenderly.

"I promise I will never do that."

Stroking her hair, he felt his eyes grow heavy. "Good because if you do, I'll come find you."

He realized that might have come off a little stalker-ish, but he was just trying to convey he wasn't letting her get away without fighting for her. Her giggle assured him that was how she took it.

"Go back to sleep, silly."

It struck him how much she sounded like a mother just then, and he smiled when he snarled against her hair, "Yes, Mom."

Cooper was too tired to be sure if her body really stiffened when he said that or if he imagined it. He'd try to figure out a way to talk to her about things tomorrow. For now, she was in his arms, and that was enough. At least to let him sleep easy, anyway.

"Goodnight, Cooper," she uttered softly. "Sweet dreams."

"Goodnight, baby girl. I'll see you in the morning."

He again felt her smile against his chest. "Yes, you will. I promise."

He tightened his arms around her as a contented sigh escaped him.

Best night ever.

Chapter Twenty-Three

Kate

She was awake with Cooper's arm around her waist, looking at the sun starting to peek through the high window near the ceiling.

It was tomorrow, and she was a pumpkin again.

She was feeling guilty about not feeling guilty for spending the night with the Marine captain—she knew Sam was being spoiled rotten by Mrs. Neal.

It had been an amazing night—one she'd remember forever—but it was time to get back to reality and her life.

Maybe she'd hear soon from the investment company about the summer internship she'd applied for. Kate knew if she didn't get a response from them this week, the chances of her actually getting something were nil. Most of her classmates already had their internships lined up, but Kate had waited to apply for anything, hoping she'd hear from the daycare on campus so she'd feel better about leaving Sam. No such luck yet, so she'd decided to forego it this summer.

But Dan Correll, her Corporate Finance professor pulled her aside and suggested she apply for this internship, explaining it was only fifteen hours a week and they would work around her schedule at the diner.

"This would be a great company for you to eventually end up with," Professor Correll explained. "They have great benefits and an outstanding daycare for their employees. I really think you'd be an ideal fit for their team. Interning for them would be the perfect way to get your foot in the door."

Dr. Correll had known about Sam since Kate had to explain why she missed a week of school when her son got the flu. From then on, he seemed to have been extra helpful—not in a he felt sorry for her way, more like he'd been in her shoes once and was paying it forward. Kate would have to remember to do the same someday.

She looked at the beautiful man lying next to her and smiled wistfully. If only things could be different—if she'd met him later once Sam was older or even earlier before she made the mistake of getting involved with Eric. But that would mean she wouldn't have Sam, and Kate wouldn't trade that little boy for anything.

Slipping out of bed, she padded to the kitchen to see what Cooper had in his refrigerator to make them for breakfast. She thought it was funny she was awake this early without her little human alarm clock to get her up.

Maybe it was because she slept so soundly in the sexy Marine's arms without having to have her guard up and mom ears on.

The pancake batter had just been poured into the frying pan when she felt arms go around her waist and her host's chin on her shoulder.

"Good morning, beautiful," he murmured. "You're up early. I was hoping to wake you up with my head between your legs."

Kate giggled. "I can go back to bed and pretend to be asleep after breakfast if you want."

"I think that is an excellent idea." He smiled against her hair. "What can I do to help?"

153

"Put the butter and syrup on the table. I couldn't find where you kept your syrup, the butter is already on the counter. You have a few eggs in the fridge, do you want me to make you some?"

"Yes, please."

"Scrambled? Fried?" she asked.

"Over medium."

The feeling of domesticity was in the air. She knew he could feel it when he stood at the refrigerator and held up a container of orange juice.

"Juice or coffee? Or both?"

"Just juice, thanks."

Watching him walk around his kitchen in only his boxer briefs and messy hair felt so intimate. Especially when he would caress her naked ass as he passed by or when he kissed her neck while she flipped pancakes.

"I like having you here when I wake up," he murmured in her ear.

She briefly leaned against his bare chest with a smile.

"It is nice," she conceded, then began to transfer pancakes from the griddle to the plate. "Your eggs should be ready in just another minute."

She was attempting to keep moving and avoid what she knew was coming from him—talk about their relationship that couldn't happen. He took the plate she was taking to the table, and set it on the counter, pulling her into him.

"Katie..." he said softly.

She refused to look at him but could feel his eyes on her face as she stared at the pewter knobs on his dark walnut cabinets.

"It's just Kate," she murmured defiantly.

She sensed his smirk even though she didn't look up.

"Kate," he placated, "I want to keep seeing you—and waking up with you."

The eggs needed to be flipped, so she pulled away to tend to them.

"It's not that easy. How many times do I have to explain?"

"But that's just it, baby girl. You haven't explained anything. Not the *why* anyway, other than *you have things to do*. We all have things to do. Why can't we do them together?"

She slid the eggs onto a plate and set the frying pan down on the stove harshly.

"I have a son, Cooper. A three-year-old little boy." There, she'd said it. Now, she could go back to the way her life was before she met him. The thought made her sad, but at the same time, it was a relief to not keep up this pretense any longer. She turned slowly, expecting him to be staring at her stunned and figuring a way to get her out of his house as soon as possible. Instead, he was grinning.

"What's his name? When do I get to meet him?" he asked as he slid into his chair at the breakfast table.

She was surprised at his lack of surprise, and it took her a second to answer his question.

"His name is Sam. Sam Jason Connelly."

"Connelly... does that mean dad's not in the picture?"

"His choice, his loss." She tried to keep her tone even, but the words sounded bitter even to her own ears.

Cooper looked at her thoughtfully. "Yeah, I can imagine it is his loss." He took a bite of food before repeating, "So, when do I get to meet him?"

Kate shook her head. "I don't know if that's a very good idea. I don't want to confuse him."

He gestured to the empty chair across the table and waited until she sat down.

"He must know what it means to have friends, right? Can't you just introduce me as your friend until you're comfortable letting him know more?"

She eyed his handsome face. He seemed genuinely excited about the idea of meeting her son.

"You're not freaked out?"

His eyebrows drew together in a scowl, and he forked two pancakes onto her plate.

"Not in the least. Did you think I would be? Is that why you never mentioned him before?"

"I guess." She shrugged and started buttering the hotcakes. "You just don't strike me as the type who dates a lot of single mothers."

He handed her the syrup.

"You're right, I don't. But I've never dated anyone quite like you either, Katie. I get you and your son are a package deal, so if I want to be with you, that includes him, and I have no problem with that."

She was skeptical but tried to give him the benefit of the doubt. He'd never done anything to suggest he'd be anything but honest with her.

Still, Kate couldn't help the nagging feeling Captain Cooper Johnson was too good to be true. Which was a problem, considering she'd finally admitted to herself she wanted to date the gorgeous Marine.

She'd have to go the extra mile and not lose focus on her goals, not to mention, concentrate on keeping her heart safe and not letting her son get too attached. She could do that.

He smiled at her across the table, and her insides felt warm with happiness.

She'd at least try, anyway.

*

Cooper

She'd confided in him about her son. That made him so fucking happy. She'd trusted him enough to share her secret with him, and that was huge in his book.

"So, can I meet him today?" Cooper asked before taking a sip of his coffee, carefully watching her reaction over his mug.

Katie bit her bottom lip as she cut her pancakes into bite-size pieces, and after what felt like an eternity, nodded in approval. "When you take me home later."

It was like he was in seventh grade all over again when he won a contest to meet his basketball idol, Michael Jordan— only better.

Meeting her son was going to have a much more profound effect on his life, and Cooper was excited—maybe a little nervous. From the way she was gnawing on her lip, Katie was too.

"It'll be okay, Kitten. Kids love me."

Granted, his only point of reference was Cassie and Luke's son, Lucas, but he counted, plus, he was about the same age as Sam, so that boded well for Cooper.

"I'm sure he will. That's what I'm worried about."

He swallowed a snarl. *What the hell was that supposed to mean?*

"That would be a bad thing?"

She slouched back in her chair and sighed.

"No, of course not. It's just… I don't want him thinking…" She took another deep breath and dropped her shoulders in defeat. "He's been asking about dads since he started going to daycare. I worry he'll get the wrong idea about who you are if you're around him too much."

"You worry too much, Kitten." He leaned across the table and kissed her cheek. "Let's get through today, then we'll concentrate on next time." She didn't look convinced, and he cupped her face, caressing her jaw with his thumb.

"Trust me, baby girl, it's going to be fine."

She nodded reluctantly, and Cooper kissed her. Chaste at first, but as she relaxed and her mouth yielded to his, he became more demanding. Their tongues tangled, and soon, her arms were wrapped around his neck while he tugged her onto his lap to straddle him.

Her hips began to move in small circles on his steel rod jutting up through the fabric of his gray boxer briefs, and he angled his mouth to deepen the kiss. His hands on her bare ass only served to make his cock harder, and her wet pussy grinding on him was driving him insane.

He moved from her mouth down her neck, lifting his t-shirt she was wearing over her head. Her tits were glorious, and he paused to take her in before lowering his mouth to a nipple and suckling. Katie arched back, her hands behind her on his thighs, exposing herself fully to him.

She was starting to grind harder against him, and she tugged on his waistband, springing his erection from the boxer briefs. Her hand tried maneuvering his cock inside her, but he came to his senses just in time.

"Baby, I don't have a condom on."

"I don't care," she panted. "I'm on the pill, and I'm clean."

So was he. He'd just gotten tested at his last physical—not that he was worried. He was adamant about condom usage and hadn't gone bareback with a woman since his steady girlfriend in college.

But when Katie slipped his unwrapped cock into her warm, inviting pussy, he never wanted to wear a rubber again.

She rolled her hips over him like a sexy cowgirl riding a bull, her head thrown back. He looked up at her in awe as he began to knead her breasts, dipping his head to suck and bite her perky, pink nipples.

She let out a long groan and arched back.

Grabbing her butt, Cooper stood and deposited her on the counter so he could fuck her standing up. With her ankles at his shoulders, he moved deeply in and out of her pussy as slowly as he could manage. She felt so fucking good, he wanted to last as long as he could.

He had serious doubts about his endurance when Katie held herself under her thighs and spread her legs wide. He started to strum her clit as he fucked her harder, her tits bouncing with every push not helping him in the stamina department. Fortunately, he felt her getting wetter and starting to tense up.

He pulled his cock out and started to rub her button with it, and she bowed against him as he began to stroke her faster with his dick.

Goddamn, that's hot.

Cooper slammed back inside her and took over polishing her clit with his fingers again.

"Yes! Oh fuck, Cooper! Yes! Right there. Don't stop, fuck, don't stop!" she pleaded.

She began to convulse around his shaft, milking his orgasm from him until he was flooding her womb with spurt after spurt of cum. He grunted as he slammed his release deep inside her. It was the best orgasm of his life.

Bareback is the shit.

He leaned down and kissed her mouth, murmuring against her lips when they pulled apart, "Fuuuuuck, Katie. You are incredible."

That elicited a giggle.

"You're not so bad yourself."

Without pulling out, he reached over and grabbed a dishtowel from a drawer, wiping her inner thighs before slipping his cock out of her and cleaning her pussy as his cum drained out of her.

For the record, creampies are sexy as fuck.

"Do we have time to go back to bed before we have to get ready?" he asked.

She glanced at the clock on the microwave and nodded.

"Oh yeah, at least a couple of hours."

He lifted her off the counter, and she wrapped her legs around his middle while he carried her to his bedroom.

He laid her down on the bed, and she moved over so he could slip in next to her. Embracing her naked body, he closed his eyes and inhaled her scent thinking, *a Sunday morning nap with my sexy, future little baby mama is just what the doctor ordered.*

He couldn't wait to wake up and meet Sam.

Chapter Twenty-Four

Kate

"Should we stop so I can get him a present?" Cooper asked as they drove to her apartment.

"What? No, of course not."

He glanced at her as he steered the BMW along the streets. "Are you sure?"

"Babe, I'm positive. He doesn't need anything, and he will like you just fine without having to bribe him."

"You called me babe," he grinned. "You've never called me that before, I like it."

She shook her head and grinned back in spite of herself.

"Should we take him to the beach? Maybe get some ice cream?" he questioned eagerly.

Kate put her hand on this thigh.

"Cooper, baby, relax. Let's just pick him up from Mrs. Neal and see how he's feeling."

He raised an eyebrow. "Mrs. Neal... any relation to your date?"

"She's his aunt and my landlady. Trevor needed a date, and she suggested he ask me. I don't know if she was trying to play matchmaker or if he really felt like he needed to go with someone. I guess he told Noelle it would help with his chances for a promotion."

Cooper nodded thoughtfully. "He's right. Commanders look for things like that to show he's serious and settled down."

With a grin, she teased, "Is that why you want to date me? Are you up for a promotion, too?"

His arrogant smug was all alpha-male.

"Sweetheart, I'm fucking good at what I do. My work speaks for itself, I don't need to be in a relationship to prove I've got my head on right."

She had an overwhelming desire to jump him right there in the car as he drove down the road. Apparently arrogant pricks were her jam. Who knew? Maybe what was different about Cooper's arrogance was he seemed to have the goods to back it up.

They pulled up to the light blue Victorian home where she lived, and she tried to see it through his eyes. It was well-maintained, quaint, with white lattice work and a beautiful, white wrap-around porch on the first level with stairs running up the side leading to her second-story apartment that occupied about two-thirds of the upper level.

He put the car in park and pushed the power button, turning the car off, then turned to face her with a shaky smile on his face.

She squeezed his hand. "He's going to love you." Kate found it adorable he was nervous about her three-year-old son not liking him.

The truth was, Sam was going to love him, and that frightened her. She and Cooper were not long-term material, and she worried if introducing Cooper to her son was the wrong thing to do.

"Remember, you're my *friend*," she said sternly.

He leaned over the console and kissed her slowly, holding the back of her head in his palm. He knew just how to kiss her to turn her to mush every time. She kept her eyes closed for a few seconds after he pulled away and opened them to find him smirking at her.

"Just friends. Got it."

Arrogant prick.

He carried her overnight bag up the walk to Mrs. Neal's porch, and as they approached the French woman's screen door, Sam came barreling out of it.

"Mommy!" he squealed and hugged her leg tight. "You're back!"

She kneeled down and embraced the wiggly boy and knew the instant he noticed Cooper because he went still.

"Mommy, who's that?" he whispered.

Kate stood and turned to Cooper. "Sammy, this is my friend, Cooper."

Cooper stepped forward with a smile.

"Hi, Sam."

Sammy eyed him thoughtfully but didn't say anything, so Kate tried again.

"Cooper was also at the dance I went to last night."

That made her son's eyes grow big.

"Did you wear a uniform, too?"

Cooper chuckled and dropped to his knee, so he was eye to eye with the little boy.

"I did. I'm a Marine too. Didn't your mommy look beautiful last night?"

Sam nodded in agreement as he inspected the captain.

"Are you a daddy?" he asked-almost suspiciously.

Kate fought back a choking cough and started to answer, but Cooper beat her to it.

"Not yet, but I hope to be someday soon."

The gorgeous blonde man glanced up at her as he said it. His look leaving no doubt the meaning behind his words. He shook her little guy's hand before he stood up.

"It's nice to meet you, Sam."

She may have swooned a little at the sight of the sexy blonde shaking her son's hand, and Sam so business-like in his responding handshake.

"Nice to meet you, too, Coopah."

Kate's hand came to her chest. Maybe she was doing something right and wasn't failing too badly at this motherhood thing.

Then her child farted loudly and erupted in a fit of giggles, which were apparently contagious because she looked up and saw Cooper shaking with silent laughter.

"Sam Jason Connelly!"

"'Scuse me," his little voice said, still snickering.

"Child," she sighed while shaking her head and ruffling his hair, then turned her attention to Cooper. "I swear I'm raising him better than that."

*

Cooper

This kid is fucking awesome.

Once he farted and began laughing hysterically, it was like looking at Cooper's four-year-old self. Okay, and his twelve-year-old self, but that was beside the point.

The mother mortification was a bonus, and he couldn't help laughing at Katie's reaction—only he tried to do it quietly so as not to piss her off.

"I swear I'm raising him better than that," she lamented, and he caught himself from wrapping his hand around her waist and kissing her hair in reassurance. Instead, he shrugged and jammed his hands in his front pockets as he rocked on his heels.

"He's a boy. Farts are funny."

She rolled her eyes.

"I do not understand that, at all."

"Moms aren't supposed to," he chuckled.

"Yeah, Mommy, you're not s'posed to. Only boys do," came Sam's little voice, then Cooper felt his fingers being gripped.

He looked down at the light-brown-haired boy beaming up at him like he'd hung the moon. With a glance at Katie, he noticed a scowl on her face at what she was witnessing.

Shit.

Abort! Abort!

Except he didn't know how to without being a dick, so he continued holding the little guy's hand.

"Coopah, do you want to see my firetrucks?"

Katie's folded her arms at her chest, her lips still turned down.

"Why don't we ask your mom if that's okay."

Just that acknowledgment seemed to soothe her ruffled feathers a little, and she smiled slightly at her son.

"We need to go inside and get your things, and thank Mrs. Neal for letting you stay over last night, buddy."

"Aw, can't you do that, Mommy? I want to show Coopah my trucks."

"No." She shook her head. "You need to help clean up any mess you made and make sure you say thank you to Mrs. Neal before you can show Cooper your toys."

He took a deep sigh and conceded, "Okay," before he headed inside.

Katie went to follow suit, but Cooper pulled her to the side of the screen door, sliding his hand to her hip. Looking down at her face, he searched her eyes with his.

"He's a great kid, Katie. You're a terrific mom."

That seemed to embarrass her because she looked away as she shrugged and said, "Well, I try anyway."

He gripped her hip to emphasize his words, "You are," then leaned down to catch her lips with his.

"Minette?" a woman's voice with a French accent called from the door, followed by a slight gasp, and "Oh..."

Katie jerked away from him, but he kept his hand firmly on her hip, only reluctantly pulling away when she turned toward the house.

"Mrs. Neal, this is Cooper. He is, um, a captain with the Marines."

The beautiful, older woman opened the screen door with a huge grin.

"So were you at the ball last night as well?"

He nodded, and her grin grew wider as they stepped inside.

"So you had a nice time, Minette?"

His little kitten smiled.

"I did. How was Sam? Did he give you any trouble?"

"Mon petit fils?" Mrs. Neal waved her hand dismissively. "Never. He's perfect."

Her heels clicked on her real-wood floors through a dining room and into a kitchen. She called over her shoulder, "Are you hungry? Can I make you some lunch?"

Kate shook her head and answered loudly, "Thank you, no."

"Sam hasn't had lunch yet, but he had a late breakfast. He actually slept in until seven."

That caused Kate's eyebrows to rise.

"Seven?"

The older woman appeared in the kitchen doorway, wiping her hands on a towel.

"Before you ask, I did not keep him up past his bedtime. He's probably going through a growth spurt."

Cooper remembered those days when he was in his teens. It seemed like he couldn't get enough sleep or food from the age of fourteen until he turned twenty and stopped growing.

"Let's take him to Sullivan's for lunch," Cooper suggested. "You're welcome to come too, Mrs. Neal."

"No, I will be taking my afternoon nap early," the French landlady said with an affectionate grin.

"I'm sorry if he wore you out," Katie said contritely as she started to walk through the house picking up his toys.

"Nonsense," Mrs. Neal said, handing Cooper a bright red rolling suitcase that looked like a car with eyes.

Katie was standing at the wide threshold of a room with her hand on her hip.

"Sam Connelly. That's not picking up your mess."

Cooper approached where she stood watching the boy laying on the circular, woven area rug in the living room, playing with his cars.

Completely unfazed at his mother's scolding, he looked up and said, "Wanna play cars with me, Coopah?"

"I thought you were going to show me your firetrucks, buddy? Do what your mom says, then we can go play with those."

That was all the encouragement the little man needed, and he was on his feet scrambling to put away his cars.

She looked over at him and smiled, mouthing, "Thanks."

He winked at her with a small grin. It was his pleasure. The kid was great for his ego.

After he'd made the final dump of toys into a toy box in the corner of the room, Sam ran and grabbed Cooper's hand.

"Let's go!"

Cooper needed to be a team player with Katie. Their kids were always going to know they were a unit.

"Let's make sure your mom is ready first." He directed his attention to the beautiful brunette. "Mom? Are you ready?"

She smiled in amusement at her son's enthusiasm, and Cooper's attempt at redirecting him.

"Yes. Give Mrs. Neal a hug and tell her thank you."

Sam enthusiastically ran toward Mrs. Neal, who kneeled down and allowed him to bear hug her around the neck and give her cheek a sloppy kiss.

"I love you, Mrs. Neal."

She kissed his cheek and whispered, "Je t'aime aussi."

"Thank you for making me cookies."

She stood, acting embarrassed.

"Shh... That was supposed to be our secret, remember?"

"Oops! I'm sowwy."

"What kind of cookies?" Katie asked.

"Chocolate chip," Sam replied enthusiastically.

"Yum, my favorite," Cooper interjected.

That was all the encouragement Noelle needed because she left the room and returned with two freezer-size Ziploc bags of cookies—one for Sam and one for Cooper.

"Wow, thank you, Mrs. Neal. I can't remember the last time I had homemade cookies."

The older woman eyed Katie. "You haven't made him cookies yet?"

His little kitten blushed and shook her head.

"Minette is famous for her cookies. She bakes them for everyone," Mrs. Neal explained. She then looked him up and down, appraising him and said, "Hmph."

Cooper guarded his Ziploc at that point, fearful she'd take them back—as if the fact Katie hadn't made him cookies was somehow a reflection of a character flaw of his.

"I haven't really had a chance to bake lately, Mrs. Neal. Besides, I didn't know what his favorite was until just now."

"For the record, I'm not a cookie snob. Any homemade kind will always be appreciated."

Store-bought cookies—a wretched result of bachelor life.

"Well, we will definitely make you a batch sometime soon. Sam is an excellent helper."

The little man nodded solemnly.

They walked toward the door, Katie hugged Mrs. Neal and thanked her again, then they were out the screen door and walking up a wooden staircase on the side of the house. Sam was in the lead, using both his hands on the railing with bright white paint, Katie carried his cookies and followed close behind as her son maneuvered the steps.

Following up the rear with the red car suitcase, Katie's overnight duffle, and his own bag of cookies, Cooper could tell even though she was letting Sam climb the stairs on his own, she really wanted to carry him.

They finally reached the landing, and she unlocked her door, pushing it open for her son to go in first. Cooper entered into a bright yellow kitchen. The décor was dated, and her table was probably a thrift shop find, but it was clean and homey. Cheerful.

Sam immediately took his shoes off without being told and put them on the mat near the door. Kate did the same, so Cooper followed suit.

"Where should I put these?" he asked, gesturing to the two bags.

"I'll show you!" Sam exclaimed.

The two adults shared a knowing smile as Cooper walked by her, probably a little closer than a friend would, skimming her hip with his free hand.

Her living room was also modestly decorated but clean. There were pictures adorning her walls of Sam in various stages of his short life. Cooper paused in front of a blown-up candid of the two of them genuinely laughing.

"I fucking love this picture."

Her eyes grew wide.

"Little pitchers."

He knew she was referring to the saying, *little pitchers have big ears* because growing up, his mother frequently said that to his father when his dad swore.

"Oh, shit, sorry."

That drew a dressing-down look from her.

"I mean, sorry. But I love this picture. Where was it taken?"

"Mrs. Neal took it at the park last spring."

He noticed there were none of her family.

"Where does your family live?"

He was surprised when she said, "La Mesa," a suburb of San Diego.

"Do you see them often?"

She glanced down the hall where Sam had disappeared.

"No. They think I made a mistake, not opting for adoption and have chosen to not be very supportive to drive their point home."

Right then, he wanted to hug her, take care of her, spoil her and buy her and her son every fucking thing their heart desired. He didn't want her to worry about another goddamn thing for the rest of her life. Fuck her parents, fuck Sam's dad—she had him now.

Instead, he just looked at her in awe, muttering, "You're pretty fucking amazing."

She ignored the compliment like he knew she would.

"Cooper Johnson, I will wash *your* mouth out with soap when my son starts dropping f-bombs."

"I promise, I'll try harder," he pledged, then leaned over to whisper in her ear, "but I really want to f-bomb you later." With a grin, he dropped a kiss on her nose and headed down the hall to Sam's room, leaving her in the living room, watching him and shaking her head.

Yeah, baby girl, you're right-you've never met anyone like me. Get used to it, cuz' I ain't going nowhere.

Chapter Twenty-Five

Kate

She decided to see how long it would take before Cooper found an excuse to leave. She went into her bedroom and began unpacking her overnight bag.

After she finished, Kate paused at Sam's bedroom door and heard the two of them engaged in a spirited conversation. Actually, her son was educating Cooper on how firetrucks operated. Cooper was great and played along.

Sam: No, Coopah, not like that. Firetrucks have to drive this way, see?

Cooper: Oh, I didn't know that. Okay. Show me one more time.

She smiled and went into the kitchen to make her menu list for the week and figure out what ingredients she'd need from the store. With school out, she could probably get away with not preparing their meals in advance this week like she usually did on Sundays.

Kate was a little surprised Cooper had lasted this long and snuck down the hall to eavesdrop some more. Only this time, silence.

Peeking her head around the corner, she found Cooper stretched out on the play mat, his left hand wrapped around one of Sam's throw pillows tucked under his head, his ankles crossed, and his right hand on her son's back. Sam was sprawled on the Marine's large chest, his little hand still gripping his favorite firetruck. Both of them fast asleep.

She escaped to the tiny bathroom they shared, buried her face in a towel, and began to sob. She'd perfected the silent breakdown over the years—she'd never want Sam to hear her, but sometimes she just needed to bawl. This was one of those moments.

I'm an utter failure.

She had tried to be both mother and father to her baby, but seeing Sam so in awe of Cooper and them sleeping like that, made her realize Sam deserved to have a dad in his life. Had she failed him like her parents said by not giving him up for adoption to a two-parent family? Right now, she hated Eric Kingston more than she ever had for denying her son a father. And as irrational as it was, she was feeling pissed off at Cooper too—he got to come in and be this great guy, then go home at the end of the day, without a second thought about Sam or her.

Because he doesn't owe you anything.

She'd let her rational side have its say soon enough, right now, she was in the middle of a pity party, thank you very much. The truth was, maybe she was also feeling sorry for herself because maybe, just maybe, she wanted Cooper Johnson to have a second thought about her and Sam after he left today. Some of these tears might be because she was mourning the loss of what she could never have with him, and it was so damn unfair.

They seemed to work so well together, and he really seemed to like her kid, but there was no way she was letting her guard down. She couldn't afford to. There was too much riding on her keeping her act together—her future career,

Sam's stability, her heart, and maybe, even her son's heart too.

She allowed herself another minute of hard crying with her face buried in the towel, then pulled her shoulders back, wiped her red eyes, and splashed her face with cold water.

Welcome back, rational Kate. Now, get in your bedroom and put some makeup on.

With a deep breath, she opened the bathroom door and was startled to find Cooper leaning against the opposite wall, his hands in his pockets.

Kate stepped out and looked away nervously, trying to hide her tear marred face.

"Oh, um, I'm sorry, I didn't realize you needed to use the restroom. It's all yours," she said as she tried to make her escape to her bedroom.

He softly grabbed her by the elbow and pulled her around to face him, not having said a word. She kept her eyes on their stocking feet, so with his knuckle, he gently lifted her chin to look at him.

Cooper scanned her red eyes with his. His face was so full of concern, her bottom lip trembled at the idea he cared about her.

"Baby... what's wrong?"

She shook her head slightly and tried to look away.

"Tell me what's wrong," he said, his voice more demanding this time.

How could she explain without sounding like a needy lunatic?

"I don't want us to get too attached to you, Cooper," she whispered. "We just can't."

"And you're afraid you already are," he stated knowingly. She nodded.

"Kate Allison Connelly... I promise I won't break your heart. Just give us a chance."

"I can't, Cooper," she said, choking back a sob.

"Why the hell not?" he snarled.

"Because it wouldn't be fair to Sam. He..."

Cooper cut her off by dropping his mouth on hers and swallowing her words. She tried in vain to resist him and continue her thought, but she'd be the first to admit, it was a half-hearted attempt at best.

A whimper escaped her as she wrapped her arms around his neck and realized she was past the point of not getting too attached. While she was confident she would still be able to recover if he walked out her door tonight, and they never saw him again, she knew if she spent much more time with him, that wouldn't be the case. Especially if he continued to treat her and Sam with such tenderness.

Although, she'd be okay with him being a little rough-handed in the bedroom.

Ohmygod. I'm such a slut.

Something she apparently embraced because she began to grind against his hard dick, right there in her crowded little hallway.

"How long does he usually nap for?" he whispered huskily in her ear as he kneaded her boobs over her blouse.

"Usually about an hour," she panted.

177

"Perfect," he said and scooped her up in his arms to carry her into her bedroom.

I'm far too fat for him to be doing this.

She expected him to stagger as he transported her across the room or at least break into a sweat. He did neither, delicately depositing her on her full-size bed before climbing on top of her to continue his attention to her mouth and tits.

How could she still want him this badly after how much sex they'd already had this weekend? But, God help her, she did.

He started rubbing her slit over her black shorts, and she could feel how wet her pussy was getting, his other hand inching the hem of her top higher.

"Wait, did you lock the door?"

*

Cooper

He chuckled. This was what it was going to be like having sex from now on, making sure the bedroom door is locked and closed. Small price to pay.

"I did, but I'll double check just to be sure."

He knew she wouldn't relax until he reassured her he'd locked the door. It was a good thing he checked because he hadn't, but he didn't tell her that.

"All set," he said as he climbed back onto her small bed.

Cooper was either going to have to buy her a bigger bed so he could sleep over, or a bed for Sam to put in his empty room so they could stay at his place. He'd finally found a use for his fourth bedroom. Maybe they could go furniture shopping this week and get it decorated. A firetruck theme seemed like a good idea.

He lifted her shirt and caught sight of her tits spilling out of her bra, and all other thoughts fell by the wayside. The woman had the best fucking boobs he'd ever seen, kissed, sucked, or fucked—hands down.

Pulling the cups down, he bared them and began suckling her nipple while a hand wandered between her thighs. He gently bit down, then switched to her other breast—being sure to provide both with equal attention. He rubbed the fabric of her shorts between her slit, feeling the heat generating from her pussy until she was urgently bucking against his hand.

"Do you want me to fuck you, baby girl?" he teased.

"Oh, God, yes. Please, Cooper, fuck me. Fuck me hard."

Your wish is my command, Kitten.

Cooper tugged her to the side of the bed, standing her upright to easily dispatch her shorts and panties, then turned her around, undid her bra, and bent her at the waist, so her face and chest lay across her comforter.

He took a step back to whip his shirt over his head, unbuckle his belt, and drop his jeans and underwear, but when he moved forward to slide his cock between her legs, the vulnerability of her spread-eagled position was too much for him, and he dropped to his knees

The Marine pulled her ass apart and dove his tongue between her cheeks, circling around her rosebud before licking down her thighs and darting inside her wet pussy. He shoved his face between her legs like it was his last meal, lapping and sucking from her clit to her entrance, then swiping to her ass and back to her sopping peach.

She let out a muffled moan against the bedspread and began pressing against his face when he slid a finger inside and rapidly flicked her clit with his tongue. Her juices slid down her thighs, and he pressed a second finger in, plunging faster and deeper as she raised on her tiptoes and bucked against his mouth.

Both her fists clenched a handful of the white bedding under her, and she bit down on the material as she screamed, "Ohhhhhhh, fuuuuuuck," then began to convulse around his mouth and fingers. He wrapped his arm around her middle, holding her in place, and continued fingering her until she began to push his forehead away.

He stood, slipped the condom over his cock and plunged into her still quivering cunt with gusto.

Cooper fucked her with hard, deep thrusts, and she arched her back as she stuck her ass higher, allowing him to push deeper inside her walls.

"Fuck, Katie, you feel so goddamn good," he quietly snarled as he continued driving inside her. "This. Is. My. Fucking. Pussy," he growled, accentuating each word with a hard slam between her legs, his thighs slapping her ass for added emphasis.

"Yes, oh yes! Your pussy," she whispered.

He wanted to roar so fucking bad as he emptied himself inside her but was cognizant to not wake up Sam and let out a harsh grumble of, "Fuuuuuck," instead as he held her hips tight against him and erupted deep inside her.

Maneuvering one of her legs, so she was facing him, he leaned down and kissed her passionately as he rode his post-orgasmic high. He felt her arms go around his back, holding him tight against her, and he wrapped his arms around her middle, loving how her tits felt mashed against his chest.

He loved everything about how she felt beneath him. Her body was meant to be nestled next to his, she was meant to be his—period. Including her son only sweetened the deal, and soon, he'd put another baby in her belly.

Chapter Twenty-Six

Cooper

"Jesus Christ, Coop, it's only been like, what? Three weeks? A month?" Cassie rolled her eyes in exasperation as he sat on her patio lounger the following Friday afternoon.

"I don't know, how old is Sofia Claire? I met her the day she was born."

"Fuck, just exactly three weeks. You need to pump your brakes, pal."

He didn't want to pump his brakes, he wanted to floor the gas.

"Okay, Miss Double Standard, how long did it take before you knew you loved Luke?"

"That's different," she said, smirking.

"Why?" he demanded.

Her smirk remained intact. "Because that's *my* situation, and I'm doling my prophetic wisdom out about *your* situation."

"So, basically, you're full of shit."

"Basically," Cassie shrugged. Her eyebrows furrowed together as she continued thinking. "Seriously, I don't think you should come guns blazing at this girl. You're liable to scare her off—especially if she's a single mom and has her son to worry about. I think you're much better off taking a soft sell approach."

"What do you mean, soft sell?"

"I don't know... Help her out by doing little things, not grand gestures. Be subtle when you spoil her, be available to be with her but don't smother her."

"So, would new tires on her car be considered a subtle or grand gesture? Cuz' I took care of that today."

She smiled and shook her head.

"A grand, practical gesture."

"New clothes shopping for her new internship position? Cuz' I'm taking her tonight, she just doesn't know it yet.

"Grand, practical spoiling."

He returned her smile.

"I can live with that. I'm so fucking gone over this girl, I can't even explain it, Cass. I bought a goddamn car seat for the BMW today and a toddler bed so she and Sam can sleep over at my house."

"Holy shit. You are in deep. What's so special about her? What makes her *the one*?"

"I've been trying to figure that out since the first day I met her. I guess the best I can come up with is I like how she makes me feel when I'm with her and can't stop thinking about her when I'm not. The fact her having a kid didn't even faze me, but rather, I think he's an awesome boy who I want to help her raise kind of sealed it. Now, I just want to marry her and knock her up so I can have one of those," he said, gesturing to the sleeping newborn in his friend's arms.

She looked at him thoughtfully.

"I always knew someday the right woman would come along, knock you on your ass, and get you to quit being such a manwhore."

"I haven't even looked at another woman since the morning I met her. No shit. Like, not even interested."

The radiant, new mother shook her head with a smile.

"I'm really happy for you. I hope it works out."

"Me too," he murmured. "Me too."

Just then his phone rang, Katie's picture appearing on his screen, and he looked over at Cassie with a smile.

"It's her."

"Do you want to take it inside?"

"Nah, I'll just talk dirty in code in front of you."

The dark blonde rolled her eyes, and he hit the answer button.

"Hello?"

"Cooper Alan Johnson, did you steal my car and put new tires on it?" her sexy voice demanded.

He quickly glanced over at Cassie and saw her smirking. She obviously heard Katie reprimanding him, but he refused to be apologetic.

"Baby girl, those goddamn bald tires were dangerous and an accident waiting to happen. I wasn't going to let you drive around on them another day, let alone take Sam anywhere on them."

That seemed to knock the wind out of her sails, except now she was sniffling.

"I know. You're right. Thank you. I'll pay you back as soon as..."

"The hell you will," he interrupted and stood from the lounger, walking toward Cassie's house. "Jesus, Katie, would you just let me take care of you and Sam?"

"You know the answer to that, Cooper," she said quietly.

"Fine," he replied, biting back a snarl as he closed the sliding door behind him. "How about you just let me do something nice for you, then?"

"It's too much..."

"Kitten, I'm pretty good with my money—if I couldn't afford it, I wouldn't have done it. Now, tell me you got a sitter for tonight, and I can pick you up at six."

Sniffles again.

"I don't mean to sound ungrateful, I'm sorry. Thank you for doing that for me. I know I've needed new tires for a while, but I haven't been able to afford them. That was really generous of you, I don't know how I'll ever be able to say thank you enough."

"Chocolate chip cookies and a blow job and we're even," he instantly replied. That was a no-brainer.

He could tell she was smiling now.

"Cookies and sex are worth that much to you?" she teased. "You make it seem like you're desperate."

"I'm a simple creature, Katie. Feed me and fuck me, and I'll be happy."

"Oh my God, you're impossible," she sighed.

"But you love me," he said grinning into the receiver.

"That I do," she said wistfully.

Holy shit. Did she just say she loved me?

He almost told her he loved her back, but decided against it, instead, choosing not to acknowledge it at all. Tonight, when he told her for the first time he loved her, he was going to be looking in her eyes.

"So, six o'clock?" he asked.

"I don't know yet. The teenage girl up the street hasn't called me back, Mrs. Neal has him right now, so I wouldn't feel right asking her to take him tonight too, and Carol is working the evening shift."

He glanced out the sliding glass window. Maybe Cassie knew someone.

"Let me call you right back, baby."

Chapter Twenty-Seven

Kate

They were on their way to Cooper's friends' house for cocktails. Cassie was the sister of Brenna Thompson, the screenwriter who had been so nice to her at the Marine Ball. Her husband, Luke, was a former Marine who was now a sergeant with the San Diego SWAT team. The newlyweds had a newborn and a son Sam's age. which was the reason Cooper gave for including him tonight when she couldn't find a sitter.

"If Lucas and Sam get along, Cass said Sammy could stay with them while we go have dinner. And dessert."

He eyed her with a grin as he stood in her bedroom doorway, explaining the plans while she got ready.

"And if they don't get along?"

"I can't imagine they won't, but if for some reason that happens, he'll just come to dinner with us."

He said it with a shrug like *problem solved.*

"Why don't you pack an overnight bag for both of you, so you can sleep at my house tonight," he suggested as he leaned against the doorjamb.

"Cooper, I don't want Sam to have to sleep on the floor or the couch."

"He won't, baby. I bought him a bed and a few things today. We can turn my empty room into his room."

That made her eyes well with tears.

"You... you did that?" she whispered.

He stood up straight and looked at her anxiously.

"Is that okay? I tried to get a bed similar to the one I saw in his room, and I got him firetruck sheets and a comforter. I also bought him a few toys, but I'll let you decide when he can have those. Oh, and I picked up some donuts for the morning, but we can get stop by the store if that's not an acceptable breakfast."

She walked to where he stood and caressed the side of his face.

"I can't believe you did all that for him," she said as she skimmed her fingertips through the hair over his ear.

"I want to be in your lives, Kitten. That means having a place for Sam in my home, too."

"I don't want to confuse him."

"Just like Cassie, Luke, and Lucas are your friends—or at least, they will be after tonight—that's all I have to be to him for now. We're going over to their house, then we'll go over to mine. He's spent the night at Mrs. Neal's before, that's what he'll do at my place. I'm just your friend."

He made it sound so damn easy. But, in her head, she knew her son was going to view Cooper differently than he did everyone else. How could he not? Other than Mrs. Neal, no one had looked out and cared for her and her son like Cooper had. Kids were perceptive, Sam would pick up on that. Plus, he wanted a daddy, and the sexy Marine had slowly been easing into that role every time they saw him this week.

Her heart wanted to believe it was possible if for no other reason than she wanted to keep spending time with him, so guess which won out?

She stroked his jawline with the backs of her fingers and murmured, "Just our friend, huh?"

"Well, in front of Sam, yes. He doesn't need to know what naughty things I do to his mother behind closed doors," he winked as he grabbed her hand and kissed her knuckles. "Finish getting ready, baby girl, they're expecting us in less than an hour. Do you want me to pack Sam's suitcase while I wait?"

"Um, sure. It's in his closet, the red..."

"Car one, I know. PJs, clothes for tomorrow, how many pairs of underwear? Does he have accidents at night?"

"He doesn't usually at home, but sometimes he doesn't make it to the bathroom in time when he's at daycare or Mrs. Neal's. Maybe just pack an extra pair of pajamas, a set of clothes, and three pairs of underwear, and socks. He can show you where everything is in his dresser and closet. Don't forget his toothbrush."

"I'm on it. You can feel free to forget to pack your jammies though, Mommy," he said, kissing her cheek before turning around with a grin.

She knew just the little teddy she was going to remember to pack. She'd bought it a few years ago at a party at Carol's house where they were selling negligees and sexy clothing—sort of like a Tupperware or Pampered Chef get-together, only sluttier. Kate had never worn what she bought before, she'd never had a reason to, but she knew exactly what drawer it was stashed in.

Throw in her black Come Fuck Me heels, CFMs for short, and she was going to have Cooper Johnson at her mercy tonight. And maybe if she was lucky, she'd be at his in return—except she kinda already was.

****

Cooper

Kate looked back at Sam, happily kicking his feet in his new car seat in the back seat of Cooper's BMW as they drove to Cassie and Luke's beach house.

The Marine captain could see her in his peripheral vision, staring at him now and subtly shaking her head while he maneuvered in and out of traffic.

"I can't believe you bought him a car seat too, and a Nuna RAVA to boot. You do realize you spent about two hundred dollars more than you needed to? Not to mention, he's going to outgrow it in about a year and a half, and you'll have to get him a new one that has the booster option." She quickly corrected herself, "I mean, not that you'll have to do that."

He grabbed her hand and squeezed.

"I will be getting the booster option. I didn't know what to get, so I figured the most expensive probably meant the safest."

"I'm sure the saleswoman was more than happy to let you believe that too," she smirked as she quickly withdrew her hand from his grasp as inconspicuously as possible.

"That nice older woman? No way would she have steered me wrong. Although I think I did help her make her sales quota for the day, between the car seat, bed, and toy… er, other stuff I bought," he said with a wink and glanced in his rearview mirror at Sam, humming along as he looked out the window. "He seems comfortable anyway."

"Did you buy him a Tempurpedic toddler mattress too?" she teased.

He raised his eyebrows. "Do they make those? Because if they do, we are definitely getting him one."

"You really are impossible," she muttered with a smile and looked out the passenger window.

"You really do love me though," he mused.

She turned to give him a stern look.

"I love all my friends," she said loudly for Sam's benefit.

Shit.

This act of only being her friend was harder than he'd thought it was going to be. Especially when Katie called him on his every faux pas, and he had several each time they were together. Although he'd thought he was doing pretty damn good, considering he hadn't grabbed her and kissed her in front of her son in spite of practically dying to anytime they were in the same room together.

"But I'm your favorite friend, right?" he teased hopefully.

"You're one of my favorites," was all she would admit to.

"*One* of? Who do you like more than me?" Cooper demanded.

"You're my favorite friend, Coopah," the little man chimed in from the back seat.

He met Sam's eyes in the rearview mirror.

"Thank you, buddy. You and your mom are my favorite friends too."

Then, with a smug look, he looked over at Katie, only to find her chewing her bottom lip in distress. Now was obviously not the time to gloat about being her son's favorite since that was a clear cause of concern for her.

"It's going to be okay, Kitten," he murmured.

Cooper wanted to hold her hand in comfort but figured that would just compound the issue. She looked over at him with a fake smile. He fucking hated it.

"I know."

He wasn't convinced and called her on it.

"Do you?"

She sat quietly for a few seconds, staring at the walnut dashboard, then turned back to him as she mustered a genuine small smile.

"Yes, I do."

"Good," he said and squeezed her hand, anyway, then let go. It was brief, and Sam probably didn't even notice, but she still scowled slightly. She's lucky he didn't kiss her hand.

Actually, no.

He's lucky he didn't do that because he got the feeling she would put the kibosh on that shit and not let him spend time with them anymore. Cooper knew he had to prove himself to her before she'd let Sam see him as a father figure or her romantic interest, and he respected the hell out of her for it.

It still didn't mean it made any easier to behave as just a friend.

Chapter Twenty-Eight

Kate

Cassie was just as charming and beautiful as her sister Brenna had been when Kate met her at the ball, and her husband Luke was the sexy, protective alpha male when it came to his wife and new baby, but he did hand Cooper the newborn when the blonde man asked to hold Sofia Claire.

Kate's ovaries exploded at the sight. Seriously. *Ka-boom.* She felt them bursting inside her womb as she watched the six-foot-two Marine delicately holding the tiny little girl and talking softly, but animatedly to her.

Sofia seemed to be as in love with Cooper as everyone else was because the baby smiled back at him, cooing her approval of the gorgeous man holding her.

"She likes you," Kate said softly when she came to stand next to him and offer the little one her finger to grasp.

"I told you, kids love me," he bragged with a smirk.

As if on cue, Lucas and Sam, who had become instant best friends the second they were introduced, raced into the family room, yelling for Cooper.

"Coopah, he said you were taking him to the zoo," Sam said, pointing at the little boy who was the spitting image of his dad, Luke.

"Can Sam come?" Lucas, the older and wiser of the two asked on his counterpart's behalf. The blonde man laughed at their enthusiasm.

"Sammy is welcome to come, but he has to ask his mom if it's okay."

The two boys turned to Kate with their best pleading faces as they danced up and down.

"Pleeeease?"

"Well, when is Cooper taking Lucas to the zoo?"

"This Thursday when Cassie takes the baby in for her one-month checkup. I'm taking off work at noon and picking up Lucas. I can swing by and get Sam too."

Kate shook her head. "I have my internship all day, and Mrs. Neal is going out of town, so, unfortunately, he'll be at school."

Cooper effortlessly adjusted Sofia, so her face was at his shoulder, and he patted her back to burp her. The man was a freakin' natural.

"I'll pick him up at daycare then, just give me the address and let me know if there's anything special I need to do to be able to get him."

"I'll just need to put you on the list of people approved to pick him up, and you'll probably need to show your ID."

"Easy peasy." He turned to Sam, who was anxiously awaiting the verdict with his partner-in-crime. "You're in for Thursday, little man!"

The two yelled, "Yay!" and took off running.

Cooper looked over at her and smiled.

"I was going to ask you this weekend if he could come too. They beat me to it. Come over when you're done interning, and I'll make you dinner."

"Oh, that sounds nice, but are you sure you're going to be okay going with them alone? I feel bad I can't go to help, but

I don't think it would reflect very well on me if I asked to rearrange my days the first week," she said with a small laugh.

He shot her a look. "Are you kidding me? No, I don't need help. We're going to have a blast."

"Little boys can be a lot of work," she warned.

"Katie, I'm a fucking captain in the United States Marine Corps. I can handle two three-year-old boys at the zoo."

"Remember he said that," Cassie said to Kate. The new mom stood from her chair to retrieve her little girl, addressing Cooper. "The question is, big guy, can you do it without the boys coming home swearing like sailors?"

"Good point," Kate agreed.

"Please, you two forget who you're talking to. I got this."

Kate and Cassie shared a knowing look but didn't say anything more.

"Baby girl, we've got a reservation at seven," he said, looking at his watch.

Kate looked nervously at Cassie.

"Are you sure you don't mind him staying while we go out?"

"Are you kidding?" Cassie scoffed. "He's wearing Lucas out. The two will be out like a light in an hour. Go, have a great time, and don't worry about hurrying back. Sam will be fine here."

"Thank you," Kate said with a smile as they walked toward the front door. "I'll be happy to return the favor sometime."

"Have a good time, you two. Coop, you know where the spare key is hidden, just let yourselves in when you get back. We'll probably be in bed too."

That got her husband's attention, and there was no denying what the look he gave his bride meant. Cassie smiled, rolled her eyes slightly at him, then winked. Kate could tell the beautiful blonde woman really loved the idea.

Couples goals.

Speaking of...

Cooper growled in her ear as he guided her by the small of her back to the passenger door of his BMW, "Have I mentioned tonight how beautiful you look?"

"You have, actually."

"Well, how you look in that goddamn dress, it bears repeating," he said as he opened her door and waited for her to slide in.

"Thanks," she murmured right before he closed the door.

He got in the driver's seat but didn't start the car, instead, leaned over and kissed her softly on the mouth.

"I love you, Katie Connelly," he whispered when he pulled away, his eyes searching hers.

She'd already slipped today and admitted she felt the same way, so why did him saying it cause a feeling of panic?

He must have sensed her anxiety because he reached up and caressed her face gently and rested his forehead against hers.

"I've never felt this way about a woman before. I promise, I'll never hurt you or Sam."

196

She believed he never would intentionally.

"I love you, too," she breathed out like it was a confessional. "But we need to take things slow, especially for Sam. I don't want him to get too attached to you."

He looked like she'd just slapped him instead of told him she loved him back, and he pulled away and put on his seatbelt before starting the car without another word.

They didn't talk about love again for the rest of the night.

****

Cooper

He didn't know what else he could do to prove to her he was going to stick around for both her and Sam and wasn't going to break their hearts.

The only thing he could do was keep trying. He understood she'd had people let her down, so her lack of trust was understandable. Her own parents and Sam's biological father had, for Christ's sake, who could blame her for being gun shy?

"Where are we going?" she asked as he drove through the streets of San Diego.

"I probably should have asked you if you liked Italian first, but I thought we'd try a little family-owned place Cassie and Luke told me about, Figurino's. They're supposed to have the best ravioli in the city."

"Oh, I love Italian, that sounds yummy."

"We'll find out together if it is," he said and squeezed her thigh.

She looked over at him and smiled tentatively. He could tell she knew he was upset she said she didn't want Sam to get too attached to him.

That was bullshit.

But slow and steady wins the race, so that's how he'd proceed. Eventually, she'd realize it was safe for Sam to get attached—and for her as well.

****

Dinner was fun. They talked and laughed, and she got tipsy on the bottle of red wine he ordered. Slightly drunk Katie was quite talkative and rather flirty. Her hands were on the inside of his thigh whenever she was telling a story, whether it had a sexual undertone to it or not. Her sensual caressing and touching made it that way, regardless. He fucking loved it.

"Are you dating other people?" she asked out of nowhere.

He situated his body in the round booth, so he was directly facing her.

"What? No! Of course not. Why would you ask that? Are you?"

"Since I barely have time to date you, it's safe to assume I'm not."

"I don't like to assume anything," he said quietly before taking a sip of wine.

She gulped the rest of her glass.

"Neither do I, that's why I'm asking."

Cooper refilled her glass. "Well, I'm not. Have I given you a reason to think I don't want to be exclusive with you? Because I do, and if I'm honest, I expect the same."

She shrugged. "You just used a condom the last time we were together even though you know I'm on the pill."

He put his hand on her bicep, subtly grazing her nipple back and forth with his thumb and smirked.

"Baby girl, I didn't want to assume anything. We had done it bareback one time when there wasn't a condom readily available, but then we never talked about it again."

"Well, what's there to talk about? Do you have an STD or something?"

He frowned at the mere idea and turned his body back to face the table, moving his hand around her shoulder.

"No. As a matter of fact, I was just tested before I met you at my annual physical and haven't been with anyone else, so I am one hundred percent certain I'm clean."

"Well, they make you do every test on the planet when you're going to have a baby, and since I haven't been with anyone since the night I got pregnant, I am also one hundred percent sure I'm clean."

She hasn't been with anyone since she got pregnant with Sam? Katie had said the first night they had sex, it had been a while, he just had no idea she was talking four years. The fact she had been so open with him sexually was humbling.

"So, what are you saying, Katie? No more condoms for us? Because I'm completely on board with that if you are."

Her hand trailed up his inner thigh and squeezed his bulge over his trousers.

"That's exactly what I'm saying."

"Check, please."

Chapter Twenty-Nine

Kate

She woke up with a tiny headache, compliments of last night's vino. There on the nightstand was a bottle of water and two white ibuprofen pills, waiting for her as if Cooper knew she'd need them this morning. She sat up, took the medicine, then burrowed next to the thoughtful, gorgeous blonde snoring softly next to her.

With her hand around his middle and her head on his chest, she sighed. Sex with Cooper Johnson was mind-blowing.

But dammit, it was so much more than just the physical act with him.

Yes, it was true, all he had to do was smile and wink at her, and she was ready to jump him, but when she watched him with her son, it made her stomach do flips, and it was so sexy how kind and gentle he was with her but had such a commanding presence with everyone else. When he looked at her like she was the only woman on earth who mattered, it made her knees go weak and her thighs get damp. Waking up in his arms was the best feeling in the world.

And all of it scared the shit out of her.

It nearly destroyed her when Eric bailed on her and their unborn child, wanting nothing more to do with her once she told him she was carrying his baby. Yet somehow, she knew it would pale in comparison to how she would feel once Cooper Johnson grew tired of her if she allowed herself to believe in the fairytale he was selling.

It was inevitable once the thrill of the new relationship wore off, he would move on. She was a broke college student with a three-year-old son. He was a United States Marine Captain with a degree, a career, a mortgage, health insurance, and probably a savings account, and all other things grown-up.

She had nothing to offer him outside the bedroom.

But he loves me.

Yeah, but for how long?

They had gone straight to his house after they left the restaurant last night and had the hottest sex of her life. She had been tipsy and uninhibited, Cooper aggressive and a little rough.

And holy hell was it amazing.

They were all over each other the entire car ride to his place, making out at red lights so intensely, cars were honking their horns because he hadn't notice when the light changed green, then fondling and stroking as he drove until, thankfully, they pulled into his garage.

Once inside, she excused herself to his bathroom—under the pretense of 'freshening up'—where she applied fresh lipstick, brushed her hair and teeth, and slipped into her sexy black lace negligee and CFM shoes.

Cooper was sitting on top of the covers in his boxer briefs, his back against the headboard, his fingers entwined behind his head when she sauntered out of the bathroom. His reaction when she made her appearance made her feel like a porn star.

He rose off the bed and stared at her with such lust as she strutted toward him—the red wine she'd had earlier acting as a fantastic confidence booster.

"You," he shook his head and started again, "You are..." and let out a low whistle while running his hands down her sides. "You are a goddess, Kitten. A. Fucking. Goddess."

At that moment, she was—his goddess.

"How attached are you to this?" he growled as he gestured to her teddy.

"Um, not..."

And he ripped it straight down the middle, leaving her naked, save her high heels.

Wow, was her pussy drenched.

Then, he scooped her up and tossed her on the bed.

"I'm going to fuck you, Kitten, and you're going to come on my cock, over and over until I decide you're done."

She might have had a mini-orgasm right then.

Cooper was true to his word. He fucked her hard and fast, then slow and long, then pinned her down when he came deep inside her pussy. He spanked her clit, smacked her ass, pulled her hair, and talked so deliciously dirty... and she came so many times, she lost count after five.

Kate had nestled in his comfy bed in a just-been-fucked coma when he leaned down and kissed her cheek, fully dressed.

"I'll be back, baby. I'm going to go get Sam."

Sam. Her child. *Shit.* She went to sit up, but he pressed on her shoulder.

"Go back to sleep, Kitten. I can get him. We'll be back before you know it."

"Are you sure?" she mumbled even as she snuggled back under the warm covers.

"Positive." He kissed her temple. "I love you, Katie. I'll be right back."

"I love you, too," she murmured, then drifted back to sleep.

She woke up the next day with his arms around her middle, and minus the little headache, she'd never felt more content.

****

Cooper

She's the one.

He'd never been more sure of anything in his life. Driving home from Cassie's with the little man in his back seat, thinking about Katie asleep naked in his bed, waiting for him to get back made him so fucking happy.

He put Sam in his new bed, then stripped down to his boxers briefs and slid back in next to his little, warm, sexy kitten.

Holy fuck had she been hot as hell tonight. Cooper owed her a new black sexy-thing, but it was so fucking worth it. The sex had been dirty, a little rough, and his baby girl came so many times, his ego wasn't the only thing inflated.

He actually came three times himself.

Bareback really was the shit.

****

There was a weight on his chest, like a real weight.

What the fuck was squeezing his face?

Was that someone's hot breath on him?

"Coopah," came a loud whisper. "Are you awake?"

He opened his eyes and smiled. Sammy's little face was staring intently at him as the little guy got situated on his chest.

"Hey, buddy. Good morning."

"Mommy said to see if you're awake."

Cooper glanced over to where the beautiful woman had slept. The covers had been pulled up neatly, and the pillow smoothed like she'd never even been there. He didn't like that idea.

"I'm awake. Did you already have breakfast?"

He nodded. "Mommy said I could have a donut cuz it's a special 'casion."

"Yeah, we'll go to the grocery store, so there's food your mommy approves of the next time you stay over."

The boy's eyes widened at the idea of there being another time.

Katie walked into the room dressed in one of his t-shirts and a pair of panties and saw her son straddling Cooper's chest.

"Oh God, I'm sorry. Did he wake you up?" She looked at Sam. "Sam, I told you to peek in and see if he was awake."

Cooper sat up and flipped the boy in a backward somersault off him and onto the floor, causing the kiddo to giggle hysterically.

"He was just making sure I didn't sleep too late since we have so much to do today."

Katie crossed her arm and looked at him suspiciously. "Like what? I have to work at the diner at four."

"Plenty of time," he placated with a grin as he walked toward his bathroom.

He went in, used the bathroom, brushed his teeth, washed his hands, and splashed water on his face before coming back out. She and Sammy were no longer in his bedroom, so he threw a pair of gym shorts on and walked toward the kitchen.

Sam was watching cartoons in the living room while she was standing at the kitchen sink, washing the plates they had used for their donuts. He should have known better than to get that sugary shit for breakfast. *Next time.*

Cooper sidled up behind her and kissed the back of her neck, rubbing her ass.

"Good morning," he whispered in her ear. "How'd you sleep?"

"Like a baby," she murmured, keeping with her task.

Speaking of babies... God he wanted one with her. But he'd keep that to himself for now.

"Mmm, me too."

She turned in his arms to face him.

"I'm so sorry Sam woke you. I told him he could check to see if you were awake, but I thought he'd see you were still asleep and know better than to disturb you. I guess he was excited to see you."

"I'm glad he woke me up. I'm usually awake every day at five fifty-five on the dot. Someone must have worn me out last night," he teased as he lightly pinched her ass.

"Who would do such a thing? How rude."

"Oh, it wasn't rude. Far from it. As a matter of fact, I hope she does it again tonight."

She spun back around, trying to get out of his grasp.

"I work at the diner until ten. That's too late to take Sam out," she said as she started to wipe down the kitchen table with a dishrag.

He leaned against the island counter, contemplating which donut he wanted.

"Who's watching him tonight?"

"Mrs. Neal."

Picking up a glazed, he took a bite, then suggested, "Why don't you let him stay here with me? We can hang out and do manly things."

She pursed her lips. "Like what?"

"I don't know. Manly stuff. Grill. Pound nails. Shave. Drink beer. Scratch our nuts and watch sports," he grinned.

She shot him a look and folded her arms.

"Okay, okay, no beer drinking," he laughed, completely unfazed by her stern, maternal posture.

"I think he should stay at Mrs. Neal's. He needs to sleep in his own bed tonight."

He wanted to ask her *why* Sam needed to sleep in his own bed when the one he bought was almost exactly like it, but he already knew what her answer would be. It was like she slammed on the brakes anytime she thought Cooper was getting too close.

What the hell did he have to do, already?

"Okay," he said as he popped the remaining donut in his mouth, then washed his hands in the sink.

He'd keep persevering.

Chapter Thirty

Kate

Her first day interning had been incredible. The morning started off great and just got better as the day went on.

It began when she got ready and put on the tan and black dress Cooper had insisted on buying her. It was beautiful, fit perfectly, and made her feel confident, like she was a real professional. The matching pumps were an added bonus.

She had planned on going to Goodwill to get some business clothes, which she'd probably still do, but he drove her to the mall on Saturday before her shift at the diner and refused to leave until she'd picked out three outfits.

She was definitely baking him cookies on her next day off, not to mention there was another blowjob in his near future.

The problem was, he always reciprocated.

Not like that was necessarily an awful problem to have, but it defeated the purpose of her wanting to pay attention to just his needs and spoil him.

She opened her front door, Sam's daycare bag thrown over her left shoulder, and her purse and backpack over the right, an insulated lunch bag and keys in one hand, and Sam's little hand in her other.

She had let go of Sam's hand to lock the door when he said, "Mommy! Look!"

On her doorstep were a dozen red roses and a bottle of her favorite brand of orange juice, still cold. The card simply read, *Knock 'em dead.*

With a big smile, she dropped all the bags she was lugging on the landing by the door and ushered Sam back inside so she could put the flowers in water.

Tomorrow night, she was going to insist on taking care of that sexy blonde man and not let him return the favor. He was so damn thoughtful. She wished she had more free time to be able to do more little things to show him how much she appreciated him.

She needed to make a more conscious effort to do just that, but right now, she was running low on time and rushed back out the door, reloading her arms and shoulders with the bags.

"Who gave you the flowers, Mommy? Coopah?" Sam asked as he climbed down the steps behind her.

Kate waited for him at the bottom of the stairs. Even Sam knew how much the Marine spoiled her.

"Yes. We are going to have to make him cookies tomorrow. He's been such a thoughtful friend to us."

"He's my favorite friend, next to Lucas," Sam said solemnly as she buckled him in his car seat.

"He's my favorite friend too," she confided.

Shaking the bottle of orange juice absent-mindedly, she came around to the driver's side. There was a post-it on the window with his neat block print that said, *Text me if you can do lunch today. I hope you have a great first day.*

She should ignore him. He was coming on way too strong, especially after she'd told him they needed to take things slow, but all she could think was, *How did I get so lucky to have this man in my life?*

After dropping Sam at daycare, Kate sent Cooper a text through voice recognition as she drove to her intern job.

Kate: What a beautiful way to start my day. Thank you for everything. The roses, the juice, the clothes. You're too generous.

His reply was instant.

Captain Gorgeous: You deserve it, Kitten. Have a great day. Let me know about lunch.

Kate: I'm going to be short on time between the internship, picking Sam up from preschool and dropping him off at Mrs. Neal's, then heading to the diner. I'll be eating in my car between stops.

Captain Gorgeous: Dinner tonight then? I'll bring takeout when you get home.

Kate: It's going to be late when I get home.

Captain Gorgeous: Don't care how late. I'll see you tonight.

She should decline, he'd done too much already, but she knew he wouldn't take no for an answer.

Kate: You're too good to me. XOXO

The people at her internship had been welcoming and helpful, making an extra effort to make her feel appreciated. Which she supposed made sense since they weren't paying her, but still, she hadn't expected to immediately be made to feel like part of the team.

Jason Ellers, her mentoring broker, had an impressive resume of wealth management and appeared like he was going to be hands-on with her training, which she appreciated. She was worried she'd have someone who wouldn't have time to teach her anything, and her biggest responsibility this summer would be making coffee.

Jason was attractive, in his late thirties/early forties, dark hair starting to gray at the temples—although it worked for him, witty, and sharp as a tack. She looked forward to learning as much as she could from him before school started again.

Sam's daily progress report from preschool said he'd had a good day, and he seemed in happy spirits on the ride to Mrs. Neal's. Traffic was light on her way to the diner, so Kate made it there with time to spare, and she even managed to eat her lunch in the car without spilling all over herself.

Today was a good day.

Around six-thirty, Cooper appeared at the restaurant with her son. Sam waved excitedly from their booth as she glanced over at them in surprise while taking a couple's order.

"Mommy!" Sam squealed as she approached their booth, then proclaimed proudly when she stood before them, "Coopah and I are having dinner here."

"Don't be mad," was the first thing the blonde Marine said to her. "Mrs. Neal called me. She had to leave early to go to her son's. I guess the doctors moved his surgery up to tomorrow morning."

Mrs. Neal had been planning on going to her son's house later this week to help care for him after his hernia surgery. He was recently divorced, and she worried he wouldn't heed the doctor's orders and try to do too much, too soon, so she decided to go be with him.

"So, why did she call you? Not only that, but how does she even have your phone number?"

"I gave it to her a while ago in case you or she had an emergency. I guess she thought this constituted an emergency."

Of course, he gave her his number. Always watching out for her and the people she loved.

She glanced around the crowded diner.

"I can try to see if I can get someone to cover..."

"Don't be crazy, that's not why I'm here. Sam and I are locked out of your house, so we decided we'd come get your keys and have dinner while we're here. Right, buddy?"

Sam nodded in solidarity. "Right. Can I still get a milkshake?"

She scowled at the man grinning sheepishly at her.

He turned to Sam and with feigned innocence asked, "What did I say about the milkshake?"

"I have to ask Mommy first." Sam looked at her and bounced in his seat, "So can I?"

"You have to promise to eat all of your cheeseburger."

Her little man nodded solemnly, and she turned to Cooper.

"Do you know what you want?"

"Just something light. I'm having dinner with a beautiful woman later and don't want to ruin my appetite."

Adorably, her son was incensed, not realizing it was her that Cooper was talking about.

"I thought Mommy was your favorite friend," he demanded with a scowl.

"Oh, Sammy. She is. I was just teasing her. It's your mommy I'm having dinner with later."

That placated the little boy in the booster chair.

"Oh, Mommy is the beautiful lady?"

Cooper looked at her when he answered.

"She is indeed. There's nobody else I'd have dinner with but her." He then looked at Sam and tickled his sides. "And you, of course."

"Do you want something like a salad or soup?"

"Yeah, a salad would be perfect. Ranch dressing."

"You got it. Anything to drink other than water?"

"Water works. I'm driving," he said with a wink, then asked Sam, "Unless you want to drive?"

Her little boy erupted in a fit of giggles. As she walked toward the kitchen, she heard him say, "You're funny, Coopah."

He was funny, not to mention, pretty damn amazing.

Her fairy godmother either really loved her by bringing him into her life, or really hated her and was setting her up for a serious fall.

Looking over at her son talking animatedly as Cooper smiled at him, she prayed it was the former.

****

Cooper

He could tell Katie wasn't thrilled about him watching Sam until she got off work but was glad she didn't make a big deal about it.

"I'll stop and pick us up something to eat after I get off work," she told him when he and Sammy got ready to leave the diner.

He shook his head, "Nuh uh. I don't want you stopping anywhere that late. I can pick something up on our way home."

"But then it will be cold by the time I get home."

"Can you bring something from here?" he suggested.

"If you don't mind eating diner food twice in one night."

He smirked. "I'd hardly consider my salad diner food."

"Tell me what you want, and I'll bring it home with me."

Home with me.

Three little words he loved the sound of.

He told her his order and tried to give her money to pay for it, which she refused.

"It's the least I can do since you're watching Sam," she chided.

"Thanks, baby," he said as he kissed her cheek. "I can't wait to hear all about your first day."

That brought a huge smile to her face.

"It was better than I could have ever imagined. I'm really excited about it."

He liked seeing her this enthusiastic.

"Okay, Kitten, we'll see you later." He lifted Sam onto his hip. "Tell your mom goodnight, and you'll see her in the morning."

"Night, Mommy. Have a good shift," Sam told her, reaching out to hug her.

Cooper raised his eyebrow and handed Sam to her. "Shift? He used the word *shift*."

She shrugged and ruffled her son's hair. "I talk about my shifts with him. He knows what it means."

Cooper smiled at her and shook his head in awe.

"Isn't your mommy the best mommy in the world?" he asked Sam.

The little boy nodded enthusiastically.

She rolled her eyes and set him on his feet. "That's the chocolate shake talking. Speaking of, make sure you brush your teeth before you go to bed."

"See? Best mommy," Cooper teased.

She narrowed her eyes at him and warned with a slight smile, "I'll see you later, mister."

"I can't wait," he replied and walked out the diner door holding Sam's hand, the overhead bell announcing their departure, spinning her house key ring around his finger as they walked to his car.

He gave Sam a bath, made sure he brushed his teeth after he put on clean pajamas, then read him a story until he fell asleep—all before eight thirty.

Katie kept her house tidy, so there wasn't much for him to do to help her out while he waited, other than the breakfast dishes in her sink.

There were a few candles in her living room, so he lit those, turned off the lights, laid down on the couch, and the next thing he knew, she was sitting on the edge of the couch, brushing his hair with her fingertips.

"Hey, sleepyhead," she murmured when he opened his eyes.

"Hey, beautiful," he said groggily, sitting up on his elbows.

"There's food on the table."

She had changed into yoga pants and a t-shirt, her hair piled high on her head.

He turned on his side, making room for her.

"Lie here with me first. I need to hold you for a few minutes."

She immediately acquiesced and laid down with her back to his front. He brought his arm around her middle, tugging her hips back to his, and felt his cock jump a little.

Cooper took a deep breath and felt himself relax with her in his arms. Just her presence gave him a sense of calm. He wanted to ask her all about her day, but right now, he just needed to be with her, without words, feel her breathing against him, her body molded to his. The only possible way this could be more perfect, aside from being on a bigger couch, would be if his baby was growing in her belly.

Kate must have sensed his mood because she didn't say anything, just played with the hair on his arm while he held her. If he didn't get up soon, he was going to fall back asleep, and his stomach was reminding him he'd only had a salad tonight.

"Are you hungry?"

"Starving," she confessed.

He pulled them into a seated position, put his chin on her shoulder, and wrapped his arms back around her.

"Aw, baby, I'm sorry. Why didn't you say something? We didn't need to lay there."

"Because I wanted you to hold me for a minute like you asked."

"Come on, let's eat, and you can tell me all about your first day."

They ate from the black takeout containers at the kitchen table, and her eyes lit up when she recapped her experience at the investment firm.

"My mentoring broker seems great, and everyone was really helpful and so nice. It wasn't at all what I feared it would be."

"What were you worried about?"

"I don't know. That'd it be cutthroat, and everyone would be rushing about like you see on Wall Street."

"This is San Diego, Kitten," he laughed. "I think the time change alone takes care of that."

"I know. And that's another thing. Because I'm only an intern, I don't have to be in the office when the market opens, but when I'm doing it for real, I'll have to be to work by six and Sam will be in school by then. Hopefully, I can work something out with Mrs. Neal, and she can get him ready and put him on the bus."

Once again, another reminder she wasn't going to make room in their life for him. She hadn't said it to be cruel. He doubted she even realized how much it bothered him, but it served to reinforce he would always be an outsider.

Just be more patient, the little voice in his head kept telling him.

He'd try. What choice did he have?

****

He could tell she was exhausted as they ate dinner, so he told her to get in the shower while he cleaned up the kitchen. Cooper heard her humming a new song and smiled as he wiped down the table.

The Marine had turned down her full-sized bed and was sitting in his boxer briefs when she came in the bedroom, wrapped in a pink, fluffy towel with her freshly washed hair wet against her shoulders. He could tell by the look on her face she wasn't expecting to find him in her bed, but it must have been a pleasant surprise because she grinned when she dropped the towel, wiggled onto the bed and pulled the sheets to her chest as she snuggled into a spooning position with him. Her wet hair was cold against his chest, causing him to jump, and she giggled, "Sorry."

Cooper wrapped his arms around her but made no sexual advances. She needed to sleep, and frankly, he could use some shuteye too. Sam wore him out.

"You have to be gone before Sammy wakes up," she whispered, then began wiggling her bare butt against his groin.

He smacked her ass. "Baby girl," he warned. "You need to get some sleep."

"No, I don't. I'm off tomorrow."

"Well, damn, in that case..." He pulled his boxers briefs off and began rubbing his already hard cock against her backside while reaching between her legs to fondle her clit and manipulate her folds.

"Fuck, Katie, I love how wet you get for me," he harshly whispered in her ear, the smell of her floral shampoo filling his senses.

She hooked her top leg around his thighs, opening herself to him, and he slid his cock inside her warm, inviting pussy while gripping her tits.

He knew he had to keep quiet in order to not wake the sleeping boy in the other room, so he growled his appreciation at how good she felt as he thrust in and out of her. She buried her face in the pillow to muffle her moans when he reached down to polish her hard button.

"You feel so fucking good," he grunted through gritted teeth. "So. Fucking. Good."

Cooper turned her over onto her stomach, pushed her legs together, sliding his dick in and out. The view was incredible. He couldn't help himself, he smacked her ass. Katie squeezed her pussy and turned to glare at him over her shoulder.

"You need to be quiet," she hissed.

He slid his hand underneath her and began massaging her clit again, intent on making her moan out loud.

"Do you like that, Kitten?" he growled in her ear when he felt her little nub grow harder. "Do you like me stroking your clit?" He chuckled when she grabbed a fistful of comforter and bit down on the pillow.

"Come for me, baby girl," he commanded against her hair. "I want to feel you come all over my thick cock."

Cooper's continued attention to her clit paid off as she began to quiver underneath him, her moans muffled by the down-alternative fluff she'd stuffed in her mouth. He sat up on his knees and began pounding his cock inside her before she even finished climaxing. Her pussy began to milk his dick, and it only took ten thrusts before he was emptying himself deep inside her walls.

He collapsed on top of her, enveloping her frame with his, burrowing his face in the crook of her neck.

"Fuck, Katie," he panted against her skin. She was breathing equally hard and laid perfectly still underneath him until he pulled out and flopped onto his back, his hand on his stomach as he caught his breath.

He slipped out of bed and picked up the towel she had dropped and tended to her dripping pussy, then wiped his junk, wadded it in a ball, and threw it in the clothes hamper she kept in the corner of her bedroom.

Laying back beside her with his feet hanging off the end of the bed, he was reminded he needed to buy her a bigger bed but admitted he liked having no other option than to hold her next to him.

"Goodnight, baby girl," he mumbled.

"Did you set your alarm? You have to be gone before Sam wakes up," she reminded him.

"It's set for five-thirty," he confirmed, then drifted off into a peaceful slumber.

The next thing he knew, a little voice was whispering in his ear, "Coopah, do you want to make me breakfast?"

It was still pitch black out. No, he didn't want to make breakfast. He wanted to fucking sleep. There was no way it was even five o'clock.

"Hey, buddy. Why don't you try to go back to sleep for another hour?" he mumbled.

The little man started to try to climb into bed with them, and Cooper realized they were both still buck naked.

"Whoa, hold on. Can you do me a favor and get me a glass of water? I'll meet you in the kitchen and make you some breakfast."

Katie was going to be pissed when she found out Sam caught him in her bed. Hey, it wasn't his fault the kid was up before the crack of dawn.

But it was his fault for not locking the door. *Wait*, she was the last one in the room after her shower, and she was the one who came to bed naked and started rubbing up against his dick. He wasn't taking the blame for this.

Cooper slipped his boxer briefs back on, along with his jeans and went into the kitchen bare-chested and barefoot to find something to feed Sam at this ridiculous hour. Is this what she had to deal with on a daily basis? If so, she was a fucking saint.

"What do you want for breakfast, little man?" he asked scrubbing his jaw.

"Cereal."

"Okay," he opened the pantry doors and scanned the shelves for the cereal boxes. "What kind?"

"Fwuit Loops."

The Marine searched for a box of Fruit Loops and came up empty-handed.

"There're Cheerios, Cinnamon Life, or Special K." Cooper assumed the Special K was probably Katie's.

"Cheerios," came the way-too-cheerful-for-the-hour reply.

Cooper poured the oat circles in a bowl with his eyes half-closed and managed to dispense the milk without spilling it everywhere. He sat with his head in his hand while Sam happily munched away and tried to engage him in conversation.

"Are you going to make Mommy Cheerios, too?"

"No, bud, Mommy can make her own breakfast."

"Are you going to babysit me today?"

"I have to work. I think your mom is home today."

"Can we spend the night at your house tonight?"

God, he wanted to say yes but knew better.

"We'll have to ask your mom, but if she says yes, you bet."

Cooper was slowly starting to wake up just as Sam finished his breakfast. He wasn't sure what to do with him now. "Do you usually watch cartoons after breakfast?"

The way he said, "Uh huh," was suspect, but Cooper turned on the TV and laid down on the couch while Sam danced and sang along with some purple dinosaur. Maybe he really was allowed to watch cartoons because the kid knew every freaking word to the fucking annoying songs.

Katie appeared in the doorway in a white terrycloth robe. She pursed her lips when she saw him lying on the couch but didn't say anything about his presence.

"Good morning, baby. Are you hungry?"

"Coopah made me Cheerios," Sam responded without looking away from the dancing dinosaur.

She came and sat on the edge of the couch.

"You were supposed to be gone when he woke up," she reminded him softly.

"Um, not sure if you realize what time it is, but he essentially woke me up in the middle of the night."

"I knew this was going to happen if you stayed," she quietly reprimanded. "You should have gotten me up and let me deal with him."

It was probably because he was awake before five fifty-five, but that pissed him off. Why the fuck couldn't she just let him do something nice for her and shut the hell up? Sam knowing he spent the night wasn't the end of the world.

He sat up and headed to her bedroom to retrieve his clothes. He needed to leave before he said something he'd regret.

He came out wearing last night's clothes, knelt down and kissed Sam's cheek, and told him, "Have a good day," then begrudgingly kissed her cheek too. "I hope you're able to get a nap later." He started toward the door.

She followed him, retying the belt on her robe once inside the kitchen, inadvertently flashing her boobs in the process. Even the sight of her tits didn't make his anger dissipate, that's how pissed off he was.

"Have a good day," he said dismissively as he turned to open the door.

Either she was oblivious he was mad, didn't care, or was in denial because she cheerfully told him, "You too," then asked, "Do you think we'll see you tonight?"

"I don't know," he bit back a snarl. "I might have to work late. I'll text you later." He left without kissing her goodbye again. He needed to go home and lie down for another hour. It wouldn't be fair to go in and take his shitty mood out on his staff.

Surprisingly, he was able to fall back asleep when he laid down on his bed. Hopefully, he'd be more amenable when he woke up again.

Chapter Thirty-One

Kate

No more letting Cooper sleep over. She knew she should have told him he couldn't stay, but as usual, when it came to anything related to that Marine, her hormones ran the show. But, God, she liked how he made her feel. He was like a drug, and she probably needed an intervention. Or rehab. Could she check into someplace like the Betty Ford Center for sexy, blonde, alpha male Marine addiction? What would that therapy look like?

Well, Ms. Connelly, we recommend you invest in more romance novels and dildos to fight your Cooper cravings.

Hehe, Cooper cravings—that about summed it up.

And why did he have to be so good to her kid, too?

"Oh, you poor girl. Having a gorgeous man dote over you and your boy," Carol chastised on the phone later that day when Kate called during Sam's afternoon nap to whine about her son catching Cooper in her bed.

"I don't want Sam to get the wrong idea."

"Katie, that's a crock of bullshit, and you know it. Get the wrong idea about what? There's a man in his mother's life who cares about him, too?"

"That his mom's a slut and having sex with someone."

"Sweetheart, I'm not advocating having Sam wake up and find a different man in your bed on a regular basis or not locking the door when you're actually doing the deed, but it's not the end of the world for Sam to know you're in a relationship."

"You know Sam's obsession with dads."

"And is Cooper shying away from that role?"

She sighed and tried not to get mad at her friend who was attempting to be sensible when this was obviously no time for that nonsense.

"Cooper and I are not cut out to be long-term. This is just like a summer fling. I should never have even let Sam meet him."

"First of all, Sam has met him, so you can't unring that bell. Secondly, I thought he told you he loved you? And you felt the same?"

"It's just a crush."

"Katie, sweetheart, you know I love you, so I'm saying this with the best intentions. You are trying to convince yourself this is just a crush because you're scared this could be the real deal, and you're trying to protect yourself. I get it. But honey, sometimes, you gotta take a leap of faith."

"I'm not ready," she replied stubbornly.

"Okay," Carol said. "I just think you've got a good man, and I'd hate for you to lose him because you're trying not to get hurt."

Well, this conversation wasn't making her feel any better.

"I have to go make cookies," was Katie's response.

"Oh, save me some!"

"I'll bring you a batch tomorrow. Thanks for talking to me."

"I love you, Katie Kat."

"Love you, too." Then she hung up the phone and laid her head in her arms on the kitchen table.

Cooper Johnson was not going to be in love with her long-term. This was just a hot and heavy fling that was going to burn out, so she needed to proceed with caution. Her priority had to be protecting Sam, and she had things to do with her life.

She needed to keep reminding herself of that.

And definitely no more sleepovers!

****

"Coopah says we can sleep at his house tonight," was not what Katie wanted to hear from Sam as she mixed the cookie dough ingredients with a big wooden spoon.

She set the ivory and green ceramic bowl on the counter with a thud and tried to get her scowl in check before she turned and answered Sam.

"I don't think that's a good idea, baby. I have my internship tomorrow, and you have to go to daycare. But tomorrow is the zoo, remember?"

The little man jumped up and down.

"I get to see my new friend!"

"I'll bet Lucas is excited to see you, too. Did you have fun playing with him the other night at his house?"

Sam pushed the chair to the counter so he could stand and help her put the dough on the baking sheet.

"His daddy is a policeman."

"I know, sweetie. Mr. Luke has a very important job, keeping people safe."

"Like Coopah?"

"Yes, Cooper's job is keeping our country safe. We're so lucky to have brave men and women like him who do that."

"Coopah is brave," he agreed in an awed whisper.

"Some of these cookies will be for him, okay? To show him how thankful we are for not only helping us yesterday when Mrs. Neal had to leave but because he keeps us safe."

"Should we bake Lucas' daddy some, too? He helps keep us safe," Sam asked thoughtfully.

"I think Lucas' mommy probably already does that for him."

The second she said it, she wanted to take it back. She could see her son's wheels turning, comparing her baking cookies for Cooper to Cassie making cookies for her husband, so she tried to backpedal.

"You know how we bake cookies for people who don't usually have someone who does that for them like Mrs. Neal, Miss Carol, and Mr. Frank. I don't think Cooper has someone who makes him cookies, so I'm sure he'll appreciate it."

"He has us now to bake them."

Shit. Not where she was trying to steer this conversation.

"Yes, he has us as his friends."

"He's lucky he has us."

She loved how Sam didn't mean it to be boastful. To him, he was just stating something he genuinely felt. Cooper was lucky to have them making cookies for him because who didn't love cookies?

"We'll make Miss Carol a batch too."

They finished baking cookies, had dinner, cleaned up, and she never heard from Cooper. That was unusual. He always at least responded to her texts to tell her he was busy, and he'd text later. Today had been radio silence.

Kate had an inkling he was upset with her this morning although she didn't understand why. He knew she didn't want Sammy finding him here, and she certainly didn't want him getting up and taking care of her kid for her. If anyone should be upset, it was her.

He finally texted back after Sam had gone to bed, and she was laying her clothes out for tomorrow's internship.

Captain Gorgeous: Just checking to make sure everything is all set for me to pick Sam up tomorrow.

That's it? No, *Hey, baby girl, how was your day?* or his usual teasing and asking if she missed him?

She eyed the outfit laying on the bed. It was one he'd bought her. Maybe she should have been more adamant in not letting him do that. It still had the tags on, she could return it and have the store credit his account. She slipped the skirt, blouse, and shoes back in her closet and pulled one of her older dresses out. It wasn't quite as stylish as what Cooper had purchased for her, but it would do. She made a mental note to get over to Goodwill this weekend.

Kate: I gave the preschool your information yesterday, but I will remind whoever checks him in you are picking him up in the afternoon.

The three dots indicating he was replying showed up, then disappeared without another message from him. She waited forty-five minutes, then sent another text.

Kate: How was your day?

It showed he'd read the message, but there was no reply from him for another half-hour.

Captain Gorgeous: Busy. How about yours?

Kate: It was fine. Was hoping we'd see you tonight.

Captain Gorgeous: Yeah, sorry. I'm out with friends. I'll see you tomorrow when I drop Sam off after the zoo.

He was out with friends? She thought he was working late that's why he couldn't come over?

Kate: Aren't I picking him up from your place?

Captain Cooper: That's okay. I'll just bring him home when I'm done.

She thought he was going to make dinner tomorrow? What was going on?

Kate: Oh, okay. Do you want to have dinner here?

Was that too obvious of a reminder? Oh, well.

Captain Cooper: No, that's okay. I can feed him before I bring him home if you need me to.

If I need him to? Is he fucking for real?

Kate: No, I like having dinner with him. It's my time to catch up with him about his day.

Captain Dickhead: Okay, sounds good.

He didn't leave her with anything to keep the conversation going, so she simply replied, **Hope you have a good night. Don't drink and drive.**

Captain Dickhead: Took an Uber so I won't. Talk to you tomorrow.

Ouch.

She was not a fan of how easily he dismissed her tonight, but maybe it was a good reality check.

****

Cooper

After he left Katie's this morning and laid back down, he had woken up less grumpy with the world but was still pissed at Katie, so when his buddies invited him for a late dinner and drinks when they got off their shift, he decided not to turn them down this time.

"It's about fucking time you showed your ugly face," Craig Baxter snarled with a smile when Cooper sat down in their usual corner booth at O'Malley's. The beefy SWAT captain gestured to the waitress to bring Cooper a round.

"Hey, cut him some slack, he's got a little hottie who's been keeping him busy," chimed in Sloane Davidson, a dark-haired fellow Marine captain and his former roommate.

"How do you know that?" glowered Cooper.

"Dude, you've had tongues wagging since the ball. Everyone wants to know if she's even legal."

"Fuck you. She's twenty-five and has a son."

Ryan Kennedy, a firefighter who was a good friend of Craig and Luke's, choked on his beer. "You're dating a MILF?"

"I'm dating a *single mom*. Call her a MILF again, and I'll punch you in the fucking throat."

All three started chuckling at his expense.

"Uh oh. I think someone's in loooove," Craig cackled.

Cooper took a deep sigh but didn't refute his friend's assessment.

"Trouble in paradise?" Sloane asked, feigning innocence.

"She keeps pushing me away. Doesn't want her son to get too close to me... says he can't get *too attached* to me. Well, fuck that. *I'm* getting too attached."

Ryan winced. "It's hard dating a single mom."

"How the hell would you know? Lauren have some kids we don't know about?" sneered Craig.

"Because, asshole, I was raised by a single mom. My mom was the same way, and, honestly, I'm glad she was. It would have been confusing as fuck meeting men she was dating but not serious about. She wouldn't even let my stepdad meet us until after they'd been dating for like nine months."

"Well, I'm serious about her. I've already met her kid, and I fucking love him. I'm taking him to the zoo tomorrow with Luke's boy."

"I'm just saying," Ryan replied, "I understand why she wants to be careful. Although it doesn't sound like she wants to be that careful if she's letting you take him to the zoo."

Cooper felt the need to defend her.

"I think she's afraid because Sam is going through a phase where he's asking a lot of questions about dads. She's worried he's going to see me as his dad if he thinks we're a couple."

"So you don't want him thinking like that?" Sloane asked.

"Hell, no, I'd love to be his dad. I love her and would marry her tomorrow if she'd let me, and I'd fucking knock her up next week so we can have another one."

Craig took a swill of beer and narrowed his eyes, "So, I'm not understanding the problem."

"The problem is she doesn't trust me to stick around, and she's hell-bent on making her own way without anyone's help. She thinks I'm going to sidetrack her from her goals."

Ryan looked pained when he said, "I don't know, dude. You might be fighting a losing battle. It doesn't sound like she's on the same page as you."

"She's still pretty young," Sloane interjected.

"She's probably not ready to settle down," Craig added. "She might be doing you a favor by not letting you get too close to her and her kid."

"Fuck you guys," he growled just as his phone dinged with a text from her. He glanced down and saw it read, *How was your day?* He was in no mood to answer that at the moment.

Four beers later, he finally replied. Between the alcohol and his friends talking in his ear, he was a lot more aloof with his answers than usual.

"You're doing the right thing." Craig drunkenly slapped his back when he saw Cooper's obvious distress at playing it cool with her.

"You need to keep your options open," chimed in Sloane.

Ryan was exceptionally quiet, the fucker. He's the one who started all this shit in the first place with his, *I'm the expert on all things about single moms,* and *you might be fighting a losing battle* bullshit.

"Don't throw in the towel just yet," his friend murmured when they poured themselves out of the booth to go home. "Give her some time."

"She's had enough time," Sloane countered. "He needs to start thinking about himself now. He's already crazy about the kid, what happens when she dumps him? How fair is that?"

"Plus, he wants a baby," Craig added his two cents worth. "She's not going to want to have another one."

If he were more sober, he would think his friends were being unfair toward Katie, but he was just tipsy enough, it fired him up, and he bought into the rhetoric. He should have shut his phone off, or at least put it on airplane mode so he couldn't send or receive texts. That's what a smart, sober person would have done.

Alas, he was neither smart nor sober.

Once he was situated in the back of the Uber, he fired off a text to her, not even checking the time before he hit *send.*

Cooper: You don't have to worry. I will make sure to keep my distance from Sam.

She didn't answer, which pissed him off, so he sent another text.

Cooper: We can keep being fuck buddies if you want, but I won't ask anything more from you.

235

Katie Connelly: A) It's 1:30 in the damn morning, and I have a full day at my internship tomorrow. B) Does that mean you don't want to take Sam to the zoo tomorrow? and C) Where the hell is all this coming from?

Oh shit. He hadn't even thought she might be asleep.

Cooper: Sorry. I didn't realize it was this late. We'll talk tomorrow. No, of course, I want to still take Sam. I just want you to know I will be sure he doesn't get 'too attached' to me.'

Katie Connelly: I think that ship may have already sailed, my friend. But yes, we'll talk tomorrow. I hope you made it home safely.

Cooper: In the Uber now. I fucking love you. I wish you knew how much and would let me in your life.

Katie Connelly: It's late, Coop. Let's discuss tomorrow.

He bitterly noticed she didn't tell him she loved him back.

Cooper: Goodnight.

Katie Connelly: Goodnight. Followed by a bunch of different colored hearts.

He was so lame, he'd take it. Those damn purple, blue, and green hearts somehow made him feel better.

Chapter Thirty-Two

Cooper

That was the one thing he liked about drinking beer—no hangover. He was up at his usual five fifty-five, no worse for the wear—physically, anyway. Mentally and emotionally were a completely different story.

He meant what he'd said at the bar, he would marry her tomorrow if she'd let him. He loved her and her son. Sam had wormed his way deep into Cooper's heart, right alongside that fiery waitress.

"What the hell do I need to do to convince her to give us a shot?" he asked out loud as he lathered his face with shaving cream. He hadn't come up with any answers by the time he finished getting ready and drove to work in light, early morning traffic.

Luckily, he had a ton of work to do before he could leave that afternoon for his playdate with the boys, so he didn't have any time to dwell on little Miss Katie Connelly and her insistence on holding him at a distance. That wasn't going to stop him from having a fun afternoon with Sam and Lucas, he decided on his drive to the little boy's daycare.

He pulled into the parking lot and surveyed the facility, completely unimpressed. The building had seen better days— the paint was weathered and peeling, the front full of weeds, and the walkway was crumbling.

"I'm sure it's great," he uttered, trying to convince himself as he approached the faded, red door.

Inside, he was hit with a strong smell of pine cleaner. *It just means it's clean,* he tried reassuring himself as he made his way to the front desk.

After showing his identification, the woman working the front desk area verified he was eligible to pick Sam up and pointed him in the direction of the boy's room. En route in a cramped hallway with gray, industrial carpet and dingy cream-colored walls, he approached a doorway where a bright yellow light was coming from, and a woman was angrily scolding someone.

"I can't believe you did this again. Do we need to start putting a diaper on you because this is becoming ridiculous?"

Then he heard a little voice he immediately recognized, barely above a whisper, say, "I don't want to wear a diaper."

"Then stop acting like a baby!" the woman snapped.

"I'm sorry, Miss Terri. I just couldn't make it in time to…"

"So, are you going to make it in time at the zoo today? Do you think your mom's friend would want to go with such a baby who pees his pants?"

Cooper stepped into the doorway, livid. He didn't disguise his disdain for the woman when he snarled, "His mom's friend will help him change his clothes and not worry about it."

"Coopah," Sam gasped. The little dude wasn't happy to see him like Cooper thought he'd be. Instead, he seemed embarrassed to be caught having his clothes changed, which only served to piss the Marine off even more.

"Hey, buddy. Are you ready to go?" he asked, completely ignoring the woman standing in the small bathroom with him. She was average in almost every way, except she seemed to have gone prematurely gray.

"You must be Captain Johnson, I'm Terri Amonson," the woman said, holding out her hand for him to shake.

Cooper looked at her outstretched hand and knelt down to hug Sam without taking it. Still bent on one knee, he brushed the little boy's bangs to the side with his fingertips and quietly asked, "You ready to go to the zoo and have some fun?" and was finally rewarded with the smile he'd been hoping for.

He stood up and addressed the woman who was now subtly scowling at him, obviously put out he didn't shake her hand.

"Does he have anything else besides the bag?" Cooper asked, nodding toward the bag by her feet he recognized as belonging to Sam.

"No, I don't think so," came her curt reply.

"Would you mind double-checking?"

He wasn't going to flat out say Sam wasn't coming back because he didn't have that authority, but if Sam came back, it would be over Cooper's dead body.

"If he's left anything, Kate can just get it tomorrow."

"He's not coming tomorrow."

Terri raised her eyebrows in challenge, and he crossed his arms over his chest in response—he knew he looked intimidating as hell in that stance.

Don't fuck with a Marine, lady, you're not going to win.

239

Meanwhile, Sam was looking up at him in awe.

"We'll just have Sam make sure he didn't leave anything. Where's your room, buddy?"

His tiny companion proudly grasped his hand and took him to a classroom with child-sized tables, chairs, desks, and furniture in faded colors of blue, yellow, and red, but it seemed clean. Sam tugged him to a cubby that appeared to be labeled by the kiddo himself.

"Did you write that?"

Sammy proudly nodded.

"Wow, I can't believe you already know how to write your name."

"I can write lots of stuff!" the little guy beamed.

"You'll have to show me later after we get back from the zoo."

"Mommy says she's going to make me macaroni and cheese when I get home." Like mac and cheese trumped all.

Fuck. They had originally planned to have dinner at his place tonight, but he effed that up all to hell. Now, on top of him being an idiot in that department, she was going to be livid for him essentially quitting Sam's daycare for her. He'd talk to Cassie about where Lucas went when he picked his other little dude up. Maybe he could get it fixed before he even talked to Katie.

"Sam, do you want to introduce who you have with you?" a young woman in her early twenties asked in front of the class.

All eyes were on them, and Cooper swore he'd never seen Sam with a more delighted smile.

With a puffed-out chest, he said, "This is Coopah. He's going to be my dad."

Oh shit.

The Marine quickly masked his surprise and smiled at twenty sets of eyes staring at him. He wasn't going to embarrass Sam and correct him in front of everyone. The little man had been humiliated enough for one day, but they were going to have a talk in the car.

He finally understood some of Katie's concerns, but at the same time, he really would love the job. Sam was obviously on board, so the only one holding up the show was Katie herself.

Cooper said hello and waved to everyone. The teacher studied him momentarily as if assessing his worthiness to be Sam's dad. Only when Cooper gripped Sam's shoulder and smiled down at him asking, "Are you ready to go?" did the woman's mouth curve up in approval.

"Tell your friends goodbye." *Cuz you're not going to be seeing them here again.* God, he hoped Katie didn't fight him too hard about this, but he was adamant Sam was not returning. Not after what he witnessed in the hall.

He got his companion situated in the car seat in the back of the BMW and came around to start the engine.

"Hey, Sam?"

Little brown eyes met his in the rearview mirror.

"I think you're a pretty terrific kid—you're definitely not a bad boy because you had an accident, okay?"

Sam looked down, embarrassed, and whispered, "Okay."

"Let's talk to Lucas' mommy and see where he goes to preschool. Maybe you could go visit his school and see if you like it."

That caused Sam's face to light up, so Cooper knew he was doing the right thing.

"Are you going to be my daddy like I told my class?" the brown-haired boy asked quietly. Maybe he hoped by announcing it to the class, he was going to make it happen and was looking for confirmation from Cooper.

Aw, kid, don't do this to me. He wanted to say, "Fuck yeah, I am," but Katie would have his ass—and not because he swore in front of Sam.

"I'm someone who will always love and worry about you and do what I can to help you when you need it."

"Like a daddy?"

You're killing me, kid!

"I'll be your best friend, for now, okay?"

"When you marry Mommy, will you be my daddy then?"

Cooper knew better than to go there because if it got back to Katie, whichever way he'd answered would piss her off. Plus, he wasn't even sure Sam's mommy was going to want to date him anymore, let alone marry him.

Sam looked up at him with his big brown eyes, expecting an answer.

Shit.

"I guess if your mommy ever gets married, that man will be lucky to get to be your daddy."

The little guy contemplated what Cooper told him, and Cooper could tell Sam wasn't going to let him get away with that politician's response. The kid wanted an answer to his question. A subject change was needed—*now* before Sam asked another question.

"So, what do you want to see at the zoo first?"

They chatted nonstop until he pulled into Cassie's drive, and Sam ran ahead to find his friend.

"Hey, where does Lucas go to preschool?" the Marine captain asked first thing when he walked in Cassie's front door to pick up her son. He tried to sound nonchalant, but the dark-blonde looked at him suspiciously as he sat down at her kitchen island.

"Outer Limits. They cater to law enforcement and military families. Why?"

"Um, do you think there's any way..."

Cassie smirked. "They're not cheap."

"I'm not worried about the cost."

"Well, your girlfriend probably is."

Cooper sighed. "I'm not, and I will figure out a way to pay for it so she doesn't even know."

"You'll have to sponsor him since you're the one who's military—is she going to be okay with that? And I think there's a waiting list."

"Fuck," he muttered under his breath and looked at her in desperation. "I kind of fired Sam's preschool today."

"You did what?!"

"Cass, it was awful. He was being berated for having an accident in his pants. It broke my heart to hear how sad he sounded telling the dumb bitch he was sorry. She just kept going on and on, making him feel like shit."

The new mom winced. "Oh, Coop, that's awful. I would have done the same thing. Except you kind of fucked Katie over because if she can't find new daycare..."

Just then, Cassie's sister, Brenna walked in through the back patio sliding door.

"You ready to take my favorite niece to the doctor?" the older sister called as she entered the house.

Cassie grinned when her sister appeared in the kitchen and said to Cooper, "If there's anyone who could help you get to the top of the waiting list, it would probably be the Lieutenant General's wife."

Brenna looked at him thoughtfully and smiled. "What do you need?"

Chapter Thirty-Three

Kate

Cooper arrived at her apartment at five fifteen, her son's preschool bag slung over his shoulder and a bag of takeout from Danny's Barbeque in his hand. His expression was sheepish when she met him and Sam on the outside landing on the stairs.

"Hey, kiddo. How was the zoo? Did you guys have fun?"

"We had so much fun!" Her son launched into telling her about the monkeys' antics and how Cooper said the monkeys' names were Lucas and Sam.

She looked over at the blonde man standing by the door in her kitchen and smiled.

"Hi, baby girl," he said timidly and held up the food bag chest high. "I brought dinner for us."

"Oh, I didn't think you wanted to have dinner with us. I was just planning on making Sam his favorite.

"I have a new favorite, Mom," her son said authoritatively as he took off his shoes and lined them up on the mat by the door.

Mom? What happened to Mommy?

"You do, do you? And just what might that be?"

"Barbeque ribs and Danny's macaroni and cheese."

Kate folded her arms, trying to disguise her amusement. "And how do you know it's your new favorite?"

"Because Coopah said it's the best macaroni and cheese in the universe, and I like the way the ribs smelled in the car."

"Well, Cooper has never had my macaroni and cheese," she reminded both of them.

"Is it okay I brought this? I didn't want you to have to cook after your long day, but if you have other plans, this will keep for a few days."

She smiled, "No plans. I wasn't sure what time to expect you guys, so I thought I'd wait to start dinner until he got home."

"Good." Cooper set the bag down on the table and started pulling to-go boxes out of it. "Go change your clothes while Sam and I set the table," he said and kissed her hair.

She narrowed her eyes in confusion. He'd been so hot and cold with her over the last few days, she was surprised he wanted to have dinner after what he'd said last night.

Before she could turn toward the hall, he asked, "What time do you get done with your internship tomorrow?"

"It's my half day, then I have to go to work. Why?"

He didn't answer her question and instead asked, "How late are you at the diner?"

"Ten or so."

"Who's watching Sam?"

"He's going to daycare, then the neighbor girl up the street is coming here. Why?"

"Do you think you could maybe take an hour or so between your internship and work to check out the daycare Lucas goes to?"

"Which daycare?"

"Outer Limits."

246

She sighed and smiled with her mouth closed. "I can't afford Outer Limits, Cooper. Plus, you have to be sponsored by law enforcement."

"Or military," he corrected. "And they have scholarships available. What would it hurt to check it out? I already arranged for him to do a trial day tomorrow with Lucas so he doesn't have to go to Promises, and I'll pick him up so he doesn't have to be with the neighbor girl."

She eyed him suspiciously. "Why did you do that?"

He glanced over his shoulder at Sam to indicate he didn't want to say in front of the boy. "I just thought he'd like to try a new school."

Her stomach fell. He'd witnessed her shitty choice in preschools first hand and was judging her.

"I don't know if that's a good idea, Cooper," she said quietly and motioned him into the hall where she hissed, "I really wish you wouldn't have done that. I can't afford that school. He's going to go there and love it, and I'm going to be the asshole for not letting him go back."

"Katie, just let him go as a guest, and you do a tour tomorrow. If you like it, you can meet with the financial aid people and see what's available."

Sam appeared. "Can I watch TV?"

"Just for a few minutes, baby."

Sam turned on the television and Cooper went for the kill shot. "I don't want him going back to that place. I overheard him being yelled at for pissing his pants. Who the fuck tells a three-year-old he's bad for having an accident?"

Tears immediately welled up in her eyes. Not only was she failing her son, but now the guy she was dating got to witness her failure firsthand.

"Cassie offered to pick him up in the morning and take him with Lucas. The school is expecting you anytime between one and four. I can go with you if you want," he pushed.

She knew he was only looking out for Sam, and she should be grateful, but all her insecurities about being a crappy mom came to the forefront, causing her to feel defensive and lash out.

"You don't get to make those decisions, Cooper. You're not his dad. I'm his parent, not you."

He looked like she just kicked his puppy, and he watched her a long time before responding, "You're right. I think Sam would like the school, but if you decide not to send him, just call Cassie, so she doesn't come tomorrow." He started walking toward the kitchen. "I'm gonna go."

"You're leaving?" That wasn't what she wanted.

"Yeah, I need to take some time to figure things out. I don't think I can keep doing this."

"Doing what?" she accused.

"This," he said gesturing back and forth between them. "With you only half-in." He paused with his hand on the doorknob. "Take the weekend and figure out what you want, but if you're not all in, I'm done."

"So, you're just going to leave. You don't like something, so you're bailing."

He jutted his bottom lip out and cockily shrugged, "Pretty much."

She felt her jaw drop at his arrogance, then defiantly lifted her chin. "Take care."

The Marine was digging in as hard as she was. "Don't forget to call Cassie, but I urge you to at least check it out, for Sam's sake." He opened the door and said, "I'll call you Monday."

Kate snorted. "Don't bother."

He looked at her thoughtfully, and she expected him to realize what an ass he was being and take her in his arms and apologize. Instead, he said quietly, "I'm sorry you feel that way," and hesitated for a brief second before closing the door behind him.

She slumped down at the kitchen table, wondering what the hell just happened. Did they really just break up? It seemed pretty easy for him to walk away like she knew it would be for him. Tears threatened to spill down her cheeks. Frankly, being right about him sucked.

Sam came into the kitchen. "Mommy? Are you we going to eat soon?"

Brushing under her eyes with the tips of her fingers, she produced a big, fake smile.

"Oh, sorry, baby. Yes. Let's eat, this smells delicious."

"Where's Coopah?"

She started opening the containers and scooping the contents on a plate for her son.

"He had to leave, sweetie. He said to tell you he had a fun day."

"Is he picking me up tomorrow from Lucas' school?"

"I don't think so, baby." She put his plate down in front of him, then took the seat across the table. "Hailey is going to come over and babysit you until I'm done with my shift at the diner."

With his mouthful of food, he protested. "I don't want Hailey to babysit me, I want Coopah."

"Cooper is busy, Sam. I'm sorry." His forlorn look broke her heart, so she relented on telling him he couldn't go to school with Lucas. The Marine was right, she owed it to Sam to at least check it out.

Chapter Thirty-Four

Kate

Sam had a terrific day at Outer Limits on Friday, and Miriam Neuman, the director was warm and welcoming when she personally gave Kate a tour of the modern school. Kate kept looking for things to hate as they walked through the brightly colored rooms so as not to be as disappointed when she couldn't afford to enroll her son. Try as she might, she couldn't find anything as the curly, dark-haired woman in the Kelly-green cardigan, khakis, and white tennis shoes walked her around. There was a yoga room for crying out loud, how could she not love it?

They were walking toward the admissions office when the forty-something woman smiled and asked her point blank, "So, what do you think?"

Kate hedged. "Well, it's amazing, but I think it might be out of our reach financially."

The woman ran her fingers along the pearl necklace over her pretty green sweater. "Why is that?"

She decided to set her pride aside and lay her cards on the table. "I'm a waitress going to college with a part-time internship that is paying me in experience for my resume. I can't afford tuition. I'm sorry if I've wasted your time."

"Don't write us off yet. Let's see what Sandy says about the scholarships we have available first, okay?"

They walked into the enrollment counselor's office. A blonde-haired woman about thirty was standing at her desk, shuffling a stack of papers into a new manila folder with

Sam's name already typed on it. She smiled at Miriam and extended her hand to Kate.

"You must be Miss Connelly. Are you ready to get started on your paperwork?" she asked before she even sat down.

Kate didn't want to waste anyone's time, including her own. She was already late for her shift at the diner, and she still needed to take Sam home.

"Look, why don't you give me the paperwork, and I'll take it home and fill it out this weekend, but I'll be honest, I don't see how I can afford tuition." She gathered her things and began to stand.

"Well, we have a scholarship I think Sam would be a perfect fit for," Sandy said enticingly, causing Kate to sit back down. The blonde with the high ponytail opened a tab on her computer screen and starting asking Kate questions about her personal information. Sandy got to a line on the form and asked, "Sponsor?"

Katie was quiet, unsure how to answer.

"This is a school for law enforcement and military families. Who is your military or law enforcement sponsor?'"

The question made her want to cry. Their would-be sponsor no longer wanted anything to do with her. Did that mean Sam's opportunity was gone? She couldn't imagine Cooper would want that.

Miriam interjected after Kate's hesitation became almost uncomfortable. "Brenna Thompson said she and Lieutenant General Thompson would be her sponsor."

"Oh," Sandy said with raised eyebrows, obviously impressed.

Kate wondered if the lieutenant general's wife would still be willing to vouch for her if she knew Kate and Cooper were no longer dating. Part of her wanted to make sure Brenna knew what she was agreeing to, and part of her was afraid to in case that caused the woman to change her mind.

"Start date?" Sandy asked.

"Oh, um. How soon will you know if he's awarded the scholarship?"

"I should know for certain by the end of the day. But, between you and me, I think it's safe to say he'll get it."

"Oh, wow. That soon? Well, I guess if he could start on Monday that would be great."

"You won't need him to come on the weekend?"

"You're open on the weekend?" she asked incredulously.

The director smiled and spoke up to explain. "Law enforcement and military families don't necessarily work Monday through Friday, nine to five. We're open seven days a week from six in the morning until midnight. For those families needing overnight assistance, we have vetted caregivers who are available for hire in their homes."

Sandy added, "The scholarship makes you eligible for forty hours of care a week. You can spread that time out over the seven days, however works for you. If you have a semi-permanent schedule, we'd appreciate knowing when you plan on bringing him. That helps with planning our staffing, but if you don't, that's not a deal breaker."

"I have a pretty consistent schedule right now, but it will change again once school starts."

"Not a problem, just let us know when it changes."

"So, if he's approved, would he be able to start tomorrow?" she asked tentatively. If he could, that would really help her out since Mrs. Neal wasn't due back until late next week, and she was scheduled to work at the diner from three to ten.

"Yes, he should be able to. I will call you later this afternoon once everything has been finalized," Sandy promised.

"Oh, of course. Thank you." Kate and Miriam stood, Kate extending her hand to Sandy and shaking it heartily.

"Let's go find Sam," Miriam said with a wink.

****

Having her heart broken hurt, but having her heart broken while pretending to put on a brave face for her son was devastating, and trying to keep busy, so she didn't have time to think about Captain Cooper Johnson was downright exhausting.

She got home from work Friday night, paid the sitter, and sunk into the couch cushions, still in her uniform. She was thinking about how lucky they were to have found Outer Limits and she really had Cooper to thank for that, when her phone dinged with a text. She practically leapt out of her seat to pull it from her uniform pocket. She'd been constantly checking it throughout her shift, hoping to hear from him.

Unknown number: Hi Katie, it's Cassie Rivas. Hope it's okay Cooper gave me your number. I was just checking in to see how Sam liked Outer Limits and to make sure you had my number.

She realized right then Cooper had never given her Cassie's number in the event she decided not to let Sam go to Outer Limits with Lucas. She plugged Cassie's information into her electronic phone book before responding.

Kate: It went great, thank you. Sam loved it. And Cooper was right—he was eligible for a scholarship. He actually starts tomorrow.

Cassie Rivas: Oh, that's wonderful! Congratulations!

Kate noticed Cassie seemed to be deliberately avoiding any mention of Cooper, both tonight over text and that morning when she had picked Sam up, so she obviously knew what was going on.

Kate: Please let Cooper know if you talk to him and thank him for suggesting it. I also need to send Brenna a thank you card for agreeing to sponsor Sam—that was very generous of her. Do you have her address?

Cassie Rivas: I will send you Bren's address, and I will definitely let Coop know. Although I'm sure he'd love to hear it from you personally.

That made her smile before tears filled her eyes. She let a few fall so she could see again before replying.

Kate: Thank you.

She wasn't going to say anything further. Cassie was Cooper's friend, whatever Kate told her would get back to him. It was better to just be polite and call it a night.

That's not to say she didn't write thirty-six different text messages to him before finally falling asleep, never hitting send once. He never sent her one either. He was probably out tonight and had gone home with some beautiful woman who didn't have kids to worry about hiding him from. The thought made her sob into her pillow. She cried herself to sleep and woke with swollen eyes.

"Are you okay, Mommy?" her son asked when she started his breakfast.

"I'm just tired, baby. You have a fun day ahead of you—it's your first official day at Outer Limits!"

"Lucas isn't going to be there," he solemnly told her.

"I know, but you'll make other friends. Everyone seemed really nice yesterday."

"I can't wait to tell Coopah about my new school."

She feigned a smile, debating when to tell him he wouldn't be seeing Cooper anymore. She decided she didn't have the energy today to answer the questions he'd be sure to have. "I know he'll be excited to hear all about it, baby."

"My new friend, Tyler's daddy is in the Marines like Coopah. I bet they know each other."

"I bet they do, too," she agreed absent-mindedly, lost in thought about who the blonde Marine was probably waking up with this morning.

****

"Ohmygod, do you really think he went out and found someone already?" Carol chastised her that night at the diner as they worked the dinner rush.

With a sigh, she confessed, "No, I don't, but he hasn't tried getting ahold of me, and that would make makes sense why he hasn't. Plus, I like to torture myself."

"Have you reached out to him?"

"No. He said he'd call me on Monday, I'm not contacting him before then."

"Oh, for fuck's sake, Katie. If he said he'd call you Monday, why are you so convinced he's already moved on?"

"I'm not. Not really. I think I'm just preparing myself because he will after we talk on Monday."

Carol scowled. "Why?"

"Because I'm not able to give him what he wants, and he said I was either all in or he was done."

The older redhead looked at her with sympathy in her eyes. "You know I love you and will support you through thick and thin, but I have to tell you, I think you're making a big mistake."

Kate didn't know how to tell her she had her own doubts as well, so she didn't say anything while Carol added, "But it's your mistake to make. Just know I'm here for you, honey."

The younger girl knew that, and it caused her to tear up. Actually, everything seemed to cause her to tear up today. Pulling out of Outer Limit's parking lot, knowing Sam was going to be taken care of—thanks to Cooper. Slamming on her brakes and not rear-ending the car in front of her because her tires weren't bald—thanks to Cooper. Taking the couple's order in the corner booth who couldn't stop staring at each other and realizing she'd never even given him his thank you cookies or blowjob.

He would soon be showering his kindness on someone else who would probably do a better job of showing her gratitude. He'd probably even be a dad someday soon. Or maybe he'd meet another single mom since he'd dated her and gotten a glimpse of what that was like and seemed to enjoy it.

I'm so glad I could pave the way for someone else, she thought bitterly, then reminded herself, *this is your own doing*.

She felt like she'd had a pit in her stomach since he left Thursday night and could hardly bear to eat anything. She'd had a few bites of a sandwich Friday and nibbled on some mashed potatoes one of the cooks at Frank's offered her on Saturday night. Sleep came in fitful waves, and she woke up every few hours.

She was a zombie most of Sunday, simply going through the motions of living for the sake of her son. Nothing brought her joy, and she faked every smile she offered Sam that day.

"Are we going to make cookies today, Mommy?"

"Not today, sweetie. Mommy is tired."

"Is Coopah coming over?" he asked hopefully.

"I don't think so, Sammy. He's been really busy with work."

It was a lame excuse, but one that was easy enough to sell to a three-year-old.

Her son nodded knowingly. "Jax's daddy is overseas. He hasn't seen him since Easter."

She hated that Sam compared Cooper to his new classmate's fathers, but she understood there was a commonality with other kids' dads being in the military. Still, Cooper wasn't his dad and never would be. She'd pretty much guaranteed that.

There was part of her that told her to take the leap, he was worth the risk. That voice got louder as the weekend wore on. She was so miserable without him, and it had only been three days. But could she really go all in with him? Would that be fair to Sam? What about him? She wasn't convinced his affection for her wasn't going to wane once the shine of the newness of their relationship wore off.

Carol's voice sounded in her head. *Take the leap.*

If only it were that easy.

Chapter Thirty-Five

Cooper

He woke up on Cassie's couch Saturday morning, hungover as fuck. He'd shown up there Friday night to play with Lucas and Sofia Claire and try to ease his broken heart. Once the kids went to bed, he'd started drinking and had poured his heart out to Cassie and Luke. He even convinced Cassie to text Katie for him under the guise of finding out if Sam liked the school. He'd hoped maybe it would spur his little kitten to realize she missed him and send him a text. No such luck, so he drank some more.

Cooper knew Sam liked the school. He'd set up the scholarship with Sandy Friday morning and told her he'd sponsor Sam if Kate named him when asked, otherwise Brenna agreed to. So Sandy called him in the afternoon to tell him everything was approved and to finalize his banking information for the monthly tuition payments to be automatically withdrawn. That's when he learned Katie hadn't named him as a sponsor.

Knowing Sam was going to be taken care of at daycare helped his peace of mind a little, but goddammit, he already missed Katie so fucking much. Then came the phone call from General Thompson Saturday morning.

"Hey, Coop, I need to talk to you. How soon can you be on base?"

"Are you at the base right now, sir?"

"No, I'm still at home."

"Well, I'm right next door if that would save you a trip."

His commander chuckled. "Why don't you swing by in fifteen minutes."

Cooper had a feeling what this conversation was pertaining to. He'd successfully avoided going overseas for too long and knew it was just a matter of time before he was called to go. It figures it would happen at the worst possible time in his personal life.

Actually, maybe it was the best time, considering Katie didn't want to give their relationship a fair try, and as tough as he talked, he knew he'd be willing to settle for her scraps if push came to shove. Which his head said was bullshit, but his heart didn't give a damn as long as he was with her.

His head had been winning the last few days, and his heart was definitely feeling it. Going overseas might help him get over the hurdle of having to be with her because he wouldn't have that option.

****

Sunday night found him lying in bed with his thoughts on Katie and Sam. He was shipping out Wednesday and knew he needed to see them before he did, so even though he told her he'd contact her Monday, he found himself composing a text to her.

Cooper: Hi, Kitten. Are you busy?

The three dots showing she was responding appeared immediately.

Katie Connelly: Not too busy, just getting ready for bed. How was your weekend?

Cooper: Fucking lonely as hell. Any chance I can see you tomorrow? We need to talk.

Katie Connelly: I have my internship until noon, then I'm available.

Cooper: Can you meet for lunch without Sam? I need to talk to you about something important.

Katie Connelly: Yes, of course. No problem. One o'clock?

Cooper: Will Barrio downtown work?

Katie Connelly: See you then.

He waited a good five minutes before responding again, mainly because he was at war with himself about sending it. His heart won.

Cooper: I miss you, Kitten.

Katie Connelly: I miss you, too, Cooper.

And she sent those fucking multi-colored hearts again. The ones that made him way happier than they should make a thirty-four-year-old man. Especially when he was fairly certain she was going to be sending black ones when he told her the news about him leaving.

He could hear her now. *This is why I couldn't let Sam get attached to you. I have things to do, something like this is going to sidetrack me. Blah, blah, fucking blah.*

Families dealt with it all the time, they could too if they wanted to.

And therein lies the rub—*if they wanted to.*

****

He saw her walking up the sidewalk to the front door of the restaurant as he waited outside by the fountain, enjoying as much of the San Diego summer weather as possible while he still could. She had dark circles under her eyes, and her face was thinner.

Good, at least she seemed as miserable as he was.

Still, she looked beautiful. Her hair was styled and down around her shoulders, and the navy-blue dress she was wearing hugged every curve like he wanted to. Her pumps were stylish and professional but had a few nicks and scratches. She was definitely due for a new pair of navy heels, maybe he could buy her some for her birthday. That's when he realized, he didn't even know when that was. Or Sam's, for that matter.

He stood to greet her, resisting the urge to wrap his arms around her and press her body against him. *God, this sucks.*

"Hey," she said with a small smile.

"Hi. You look beautiful."

"Oh," she looked down shyly, tucking her hair behind her ear. "Thanks. You look good, too. I've never seen you in your fatigues before."

"Yeah, I'm on my lunch hour. I hope you don't mind?"

She furrowed her eyebrows. "Mind? Of course not."

Cooper put one hand on the small of her back and gestured toward the restaurant with the other. "Shall we?"

She nodded, and they began walking toward the door. "I've never eaten here before," she said as they entered the lobby.

"It's nice," he said and was immediately interrupted with the sound of his name.

He looked up and saw Ben McCallister waving at him. "Come on, let me introduce you to Luke's old roommate."

His mechanic stood and offered his fist to knock knuckles with.

"Hey, man. How have you been? I got a message you wanted to get that Gran Torino in for a tune-up before you ship out on Wednesday."

In his peripheral vision, Cooper saw Katie's head snap in surprise. Ben must have noticed it too because he winced and leaned in to mutter, "Sorry, dude."

"I'm not bringing it now, asshole," he groused through clenched teeth.

He looked at Katie staring at him with wide eyes and admitted, "That's part of why I asked you to lunch."

She looked like a deer caught in the headlights when she murmured, "Oh."

He grabbed her shaking hand. "Come on, baby girl, let's go get a table." He shot Ben a dirty look. "I'll see you tomorrow, dick."

Cooper could tell she was dazed as he steered her through the tables and back to the hostess stand.

"It's a twenty-minute wait," the blonde girl told them, and he directed her back outside to sit on the fountain's edge, all the while without Katie looking at him or saying a word.

"Katie, I'm sorry you found out like this. This wasn't how I wanted to tell you."

"Is that why you gave me the ultimatum last week?"

"What? No. I didn't find out I was leaving until Saturday. That had nothing to do with it."

"Although, it's pretty convenient, huh?" she snarked, scooching away to face him and bending her knee on the cement bench to keep him at a distance.

"Being sent to the Middle East to live in a tent in one hundred degrees heat for months is hardly convenient," he rebuked.

She let out a little gasp. "You're going to the Middle East? For how long?"

"I'm leaving Wednesday afternoon. I'm not sure for how long, but it sounds like at least three or four months."

She had tears in her eyes now. "I'm so sorry."

Cooper shook his head. "Don't be, Katie. This is what I signed up for. Ron says when I get back he wants me to put in for a transfer to Virginia, which would also mean a promotion."

"So I guess it's a good thing you broke up with me when you did," she whispered.

Fuck that. She wasn't pinning this solely on him.

"If you hadn't found out I was leaving Wednesday, what were you going to tell me you decided today?"

"Does it matter?"

He reached for her hands. "Yeah, Katie, it does. If you tell me you were going to be all in, we're going to make this work."

Katie shook her head. "I just don't see how we could..."

"Answer the question. What were you going to tell me you decided?"

"You're going to be gone for months. What am I going to tell Sam?"

"Answer the goddamn question," he snarled.

She stared down at his hands holding hers and ran her thumb over the knuckle of his index finger. "I was going to tell you I couldn't give you what you wanted, but ask you to give me a little more time. I need more time."

He shook his head. "I told you I can't do half-in with you anymore. You need to decide—do you want to be with me or don't you?"

Her expression was sad when she shrugged. "I guess it doesn't really matter, does it? You're leaving."

"I don't have to transfer when I get back," he offered, and she immediately cut him off.

"Oh, no. No, no, no. I'm not stifling my career for anyone and wouldn't dream of letting us hold you back. We just weren't meant to be together in the long run, Cooper."

He stared at her incredulously. "It's that easy, huh?"

Fortunately for his heart, tears were now streaming down her face, letting him know it was anything but easy for her. He dropped her hands and wiped her wet cheeks with his thumbs, staring at her face. The face he was so goddamn in love with.

"No, you know it's not that easy," she whispered.

He cupped her face between his hands and looked into her eyes. "We could make this work, Katie. You just have to trust me."

Her bottom lip trembled, and she shook her head. "I can't, Cooper. You want more than I can give you. And now, with you going away, then transferring, it's just too much."

He realized, at that moment, her mind was made up. Maybe if he were going to be in town, he would have been willing to wait, but unfortunately, that wasn't an option. Dropping his arms to his sides in defeat, he asked, "So, what do we do now? Can I come by tonight or tomorrow night and say goodbye to Sam?"

"Um, yeah sure, I guess. What are you going to tell him?"

"What do you want me to tell him?"

"The truth. That you're going away to protect his country. He doesn't fully understand the concept of country yet, but he does understand having to go to keep us safe. One of his little daycare friend's dad is overseas."

He nodded in understanding. "How does he like Outer Limits?"

"He loves it. Thank you for being so insistent we check it out. It turns out he was eligible for a scholarship after all."

"I'm glad it all worked out." Cooper smiled knowingly. He knew the Ellen Louise Jurden scholarship paid one hundred percent of Sam's tuition since Cooper was the one who created it specifically for Sam. He named it after his late grandma and instructed the school to tell Katie as little about it as possible. Knowing Sam was in a good school was all that mattered, especially now he was going to be out of the country.

"Can I Skype with you and him while I'm gone?"

Her lips parted like she was going to reject that idea, then her shoulders softened. "Just don't promise him anything, okay?"

Promise him anything? Like what?

He took the easier approach and simply replied, "I won't."

Chapter Thirty-Six

Kate

He wanted her to commit to him. How could he still expect that after dropping the bombshell he was leaving to go overseas, then transferring when he came back? She had school to finish, a career to start, a son to raise. She told him from the very beginning, she couldn't get sidetracked from her goals, yet here he was, expecting her to give them up.

"How is he expecting you to give up on your goals?" Carol asked as she put the chocolate shake in front of her. She'd made a beeline to the diner to talk to her friend as soon as they'd finished lunch and ordered a chocolate shake in an attempt to make herself feel better as she poured her heart out from the other side of the counter.

"He wants to try to make this work while he's a million miles away for who knows how long."

"Still not following how that's expecting you to give up on your goals."

"He wants to make this work, then when he gets back, he's going to want me to move with him to Virginia. I won't be done with my degree when he gets back, plus, I'm supposed to just flush away the inroads I've made at my internship so I can move and be with him?"

"How many credits do you need to graduate?"

"Thirty-two."

"So, if you took sixteen credits both semesters next year, you could finish in May a year from now."

"I can't take sixteen credits, Carol," Kate admonished her friend.

"Why not? Sam has a scholarship, so you don't have to worry about paying for daycare and can actually work less and go to school more."

She hadn't thought of that. Still, she wasn't uprooting her and Sam's life and said so. Carol didn't argue, but Kate could tell by her pursed lips, there was censure behind her eyes.

"You should take the leap, Katie Kat," was all her redheaded friend said before going to help her other customers.

She drank her shake and contemplated her friend's advice. Taking the leap would be a lot easier if it was only her heart she had to worry about. She had a little boy whose biological dad had already let him down to think about too.

Leaving a five-dollar bill under her empty glass, she picked up her purse and waved to Carol before heading to get Sam from Outer Limits. Kate hadn't decided if she was going to say anything to her son before Cooper came over tonight. She ended up taking the coward's way out and said nothing except they were baking Cooper cookies. That made her little guy happy.

"Is he coming over, Mommy?"

"Yeah, buddy. He's going to stop by and see you tonight."

"I can't wait to tell him about my new school."

"I'm sure he's going to be thrilled, baby."

His little face turned solemn. "Can we bake some cookies for Connor, too? His daddy has to go away, and he's really sad. I hope Cooper never has to go away, that would make me sad."

This was going to be harder on her kid than she'd originally realized.

"Well, Cooper may have to someday, buddy, it's his job, just like Connor's daddy. But I'm sure if he does, he'll be sad just like I'm sure Connor's daddy is sad. But I'll bet they get to talk on the computer like you sometimes do with grandma and grandpa.

Yeah, her parents lived in the same damn city but only managed to see her son via Skype, and very rarely at that. *Fuck them.* She'd proven she didn't need them, she could make it on her own. Granted, she'd had a lot of help along the way from people like Mrs. Neal, Frank, and Carol, and now, this scholarship, courtesy of Ellen Jurden, but she hadn't needed her parents' help, so yeah, fuck them. She was going to give Sam the best life, all on her own.

Maybe Carol was right about taking sixteen credits next semester. Getting her degree next May would mean she could get started on her career that much sooner. She was going to have to call her adviser, maybe it was actually time to take out a small student loan. It would be worth it if it meant she could start working in finance a whole year ahead of schedule.

It had nothing to do with being ready if Captain Cooper Johnson asked her to move with him. *Nothing.*

****

Sam squealed with delight when Cooper stepped into their kitchen later that night. He'd changed out of his fatigues and was sporting a pair of faded Levi's, a heather-gray Henley, and black leather work boots. It was still chilly in the evenings in San Diego.

Fuck, did he look sexy. *Damn him.*

He knelt down and hugged Sam soundly, then untied his boots, taking them off and lining them up next to hers and Sam's on the mat by the front door.

Damn him for being so considerate.

"We made you cookies!" Sam exclaimed with excitement.

He looked over at her, one eyebrow raised. "Oh, yeah? What kind?"

Sam replied, "Chocolate chips and love. Mommy says we bake our cookies with love," while she simply smiled shyly. She felt awkward around him now, unsure how to act.

The Marine chuckled and glanced at her briefly. "Chocolate chips and love, my favorite kind of cookie."

"Why don't you get the milk out, sweetie, so you two can have some with your cookies."

Her little man was on it the second she suggested it. He was so proud to be sharing cookies with Cooper.

"Do you want chocolate or white milk, Coopah?"

"Oh, definitely chocolate milk." She shot him a look as she reached for the glasses in the cupboard. "I mean, white milk. We both should definitely have white milk. It's good for our bones and makes us strong."

That made her grin involuntarily. *Damn him.*

Cooper asked her, "Are you having some, too, Mommy?"

She debated. Part of her thought she should let them have guy time, and part of her felt like she needed to be there to comfort Sam when Cooper broke the news. He seemed to sense her trepidation.

"I won't.... not without you here."

That was her signal to let them have their time together, so she retreated to her bedroom where she promptly began to cry. Sobbing into the towel from this morning's shower she'd left on her bed, in a hurry to get out the door on time, she decided her fairy godmother really was a bitch. How could she have brought this wonderful man into her life, only to pull him away from her?

This is on you, Katie Kat. He's not being pulled away— he wants to make it work regardless of the distance, you're the one pushing him away.

Fuck you, conscience.

And why the hell did her conscience sound like Carol in her head?

It wasn't supposed to be like this. It was understood from the beginning, it was only going to be a fun one-night stand. She wasn't supposed to fall in love with him, and she sure as hell wasn't supposed to let her son fall in love with him. What an absolute clusterfuck.

Kate took a deep breath. She needed to get her shit together before she went back out there. Sam was going to need her when Cooper broke the news about him heading overseas.

Splashing some cold water on her face before fixing her makeup, she was as good as new when she opened the door and headed back toward the kitchen, except she was sidelined at Sam's bedroom door while she listened to the two play cars.

"Do you know Connor's daddy?" Sam asked into between smashing two cars together.

"As a matter of fact, I do know Connor's daddy."

"He has to go away for work soon. Connor said he's going to be gone until Halloween, maybe even Christmas."

"Yeah. I know his daddy wishes he didn't have to be away from his family for so long."

"Would you be sad if you were away from me and Mommy that long?"

"Yeah, buddy, I will be."

Before Sam could catch Cooper's slip of the verb tense, she stepped in the doorway and looked over at Cooper's sad face. With a nod of her head, she sat down cross-legged on Sam's play rug next to her son and rubbed the small of his back.

"Hey, baby. How were the cookies?"

The little boy stopped playing with his cars long enough to answer her. "Delicious. Coopah says they're the best cookies he's ever tasted."

"We'll have to be sure to send him home with an extra big batch then." She pulled Sam's hands from his toys and tugged him into her lap. "Because we're not going to be able to see him for a while."

Sam leaned back and turned his head to the side to look at her with his brown eyes as huge as saucers. He immediately knew something was amiss.

"Why not?"

Cooper lifted his butt and moved closer to them. "I have to go away for work with Connor's daddy."

Her son immediately stood and hugged him around the neck, howling, "No! I don't want you to go!"

The Marine brought both arms around Sam and cradled his head, letting him cry into his shoulder as tears openly fell down the older man's cheeks. The little man wrapped his legs around Cooper's middle like he was holding on for dear life.

"Please don't go, Coopah," Sam sobbed.

"I have to, Sammy. Connor's daddy needs someone to go with him and make sure he's safe."

"Why can't Connor's daddy just stay home, too?"

"Because our job is to make sure everyone in our country stays safe."

"Like me and Mommy?" the little boy sniffed.

"Yeah, like you and mommy."

Tears continued to well in the kiddo's eyes. "Then why can't you just stay here with us and keep us safe? Why do you have to go away?" he wailed.

The Marine was in a no-win situation. Kate had quickly learned over the years, she couldn't compete with a three-year-old's logic.

"Baby," she said, leaning over and rubbing Sam's back again. "It's Cooper's job to keep everyone safe, not just you and me. Everyone is counting on him. People like Mrs. Neal, and grandma and grandpa, Miss Carol, Mr. Frank, all of your friends at Promises and Outer Limits... they're all counting on military people like Cooper to keep them safe."

"Don't they have Lucas' daddy for that?"

Cooper interjected, stroking the toddler's hair, "Yeah, buddy. Lucas' daddy is a policeman. He's who you'd call if you needed help right now. I..." and he broke off as if unsure how to explain his job to a three-year-old.

"Baby, we need all these people to do their jobs. We're so lucky to know so many brave men and women who are willing to do that for us. Cooper will call you on the computer whenever he can, okay?"

Sam rubbed his eyes and nodded in agreement. "Okay," he sniffled reluctantly, still clinging to the blonde man. "Can we spend the night at Cooper's house before he goes?"

The little shit.

"No, sweetie, we can't. Cooper has a lot of things he needs to do before he leaves."

Kate caught the Marine looking at her. It was obvious he had wanted to tell Sam yes, but they both knew that was a bad idea. Still, the idea of one more night in his arms was enticing.

Cooper squeezed Sam's shoulder. "Tell you what, buddy. I will take you and Lucas to the zoo again when I come back, okay?"

Sam sniffled again. "Okay. Can Mommy come with us next time?"

"Sure she can if she doesn't have to work or go to class."

Her son stifled a yawn, and Kate said, "I think it's time for bed, baby."

"Will Cooper read me a bedtime story?" he whimpered.

This kid is milking it, she thought with a smirk.

Cooper ruffled his hair. "You bet. Why don't you go brush your teeth and put your PJs on, and I'll meet you back here in ten minutes? Think about what book you want to read."

Kate mouthed, "Thank you," then got up to follow Sam into the bathroom.

She was really going to miss him in her life. It wasn't fair.

Fuck you, fairy godmother.

*

Cooper

As he read Sam his bedtime story, he couldn't help thinking, *God I'm going to miss this kid*. Almost as much as his mom. She smiled at Cooper from the other side of Sam as she brushed her son's hair with her fingers while he read *Brown Bear, Brown Bear, What Do You See?* complete with voice changes for each character. He wasn't doing this bedtime reading half-assed, dammit.

He wasn't convinced they were over, this was just temporary. She'd realize it while he was gone.

"Will you come visit again tomorrow, Coopah?" the little man said with a yawn as he fought sleep.

He looked over at Katie. She didn't offer an objection, but he didn't want to say anything until he talked to her.

"I'll see if I can, buddy. I've got a lot I need to do before I leave on Wednesday."

"Pwease?"

It seemed the requisite for having him wrapped around your finger was have the last name Connelly.

"I'll do my best, Sam."

His response caused her to tilt her head.

"Coop, we understand you've got a lot going on. Just tell him no if you can't make it."

That kind of pissed him off. Was she implying he was just telling Sam what he wanted to hear with no regard to actually keeping his word? He was trying to be courteous and not overstep. He rephrased with his eyebrows raised in a deliberate challenge to her.

"What time are you guys available tomorrow? I'll be here."

The corner of one side of her mouth drew up. "I'm at the diner tomorrow from ten to seven."

"I'll bring Danny's Barbeque at seven thirty."

"That place was yummy," Sam chimed in with his little eyes closed.

"Are you sure? I'm sure you've got a ton of stuff you probably need to do."

"Positive."

He had an admin assistant who would do a lot of the office stuff. He had to pack light, so packing wasn't going to take up a lot of time, plus he got a lot done today. The only thing pressing was getting the cars in for an oil change and fluids check so they could sit in his garage for however long he was gone.

Cooper wanted to ask her to spend the night but knew better than to in front of Sam. Besides, he didn't know if his heart could take sleeping with her if she wasn't going to commit to him. Yeah, the irony gods were having a good laugh at his expense lately. He now only wanted a woman in his bed if they were going to be together as a couple. Go figure.

They walked into the living room, both having kissed Sam's sleeping head and her shutting off the light and closing the door.

They stood in awkward silence until he said, "He's such a great kid, Katie." He was trying to keep the conversation neutral.

"I'm really lucky."

Another awkward pause.

"So, can we send you cookies while you're gone?"

"Eventually. Not for at least a month, probably."

She nodded, and another round of uneasiness ensued.

He turned toward the kitchen. "So, I'll see you tomorrow. Do you want anything specific from Danny's?"

"Whatever you brought last time. Sammy loved it. He officially thinks you have brilliant taste."

"I'm in love with his mom, of course, I do."

She looked at the floor and skimmed her toes along one of the wooden planks, not saying anything in response. He decided to let her off the hook and leaned over to kiss her cheek.

"I'll see you tomorrow, Kitten."

Chapter Thirty-Seven

Kate

This was shaping up to be the shittiest week of her life. After being so miserable without Cooper last weekend, she was really hoping he'd give her more time before being *all in*, as he put it. Turned out, he didn't have any more time to give her, he was leaving in thirty hours for God knows how long. Kate especially hated how much it hurt Sam. Her son had already grown attached to the Marine—too attached—which was exactly what she had been hoping to avoid.

Why did the man have to go and be so wonderful and irresistible? To everyone.

She was out of sorts all day at the diner, mixing up orders, dropping things, spilling drinks…

"You're a mess," Carol half-chastised, half-teased as she wiped the counter where Katie dropped a dirty plate that luckily didn't break. "Are you going to be like this the entire time he's gone?"

"I really have no idea," Kate sighed. There was no point denying it, she *was* a mess. "I don't know if I'm upset we broke up or because he's leaving."

"Probably both. I still don't think you should have broken up."

"I don't know, Carol. Part of me thinks it's for the best, and part of me thinks I'm a fool."

"For the record, I'm siding with the part that thinks you're a fool."

She dropped her head on the counter next to the tray of silverware Carol had been rolling into napkins and whimpered, "Thanks a lot."

"So, you're seeing him again tonight, are you going to do naughty things with him?"

"It's tempting, for sure—he's so damn sexy—but I don't think it'd be a good idea."

"Yeah, having amazing farewell sex would just be terrible," Carol said with an eye roll.

"I think it would just make things more complicated."

"Maybe, but I'd file it under closure and bang his brains out. Who knows when the next opportunity will come along; you've proven you're too damn picky in that department."

Kate snorted. "I think I should have pickier."

The older woman put her hand on her hip and raised her eyebrows. "Really? You're going to try to tell me you regret being with him?"

She looked down sheepishly. "No, I'm not. He was nothing but great."

"Which is why I don't understand why you're not willing to take the leap, Katie Kat. He's not done anything to make you think you shouldn't."

"It doesn't matter now, anyway, does it? He's shipping out for at least the next four months, maybe longer."

"And you don't want to wait for him? You have prospects lined up I don't know about?"

"I don't expect you to understand," she snarled then stormed to the kitchen.

Truth was, she didn't necessarily understand it herself. Carol calling her out just brought it front and center.

****

Cooper

He slowly walked up the wooden stairs outside of Katie's apartment, a bag of Danny's Barbeque in one hand and another bag with a new toy for Sam in the other. It was time the kid was introduced to G.I. Joe.

He'd thought about getting Katie flowers, but decided against it, his brain overruling his heart, telling him he needed to stop acting like they were dating. His brain could really be an asshole sometimes.

She looked adorable when she opened her door with her hair piled on her head. She turned around in her yoga pants, and his damn dick moved. It was a good thing his hands were full because he might not have been able to resist the urge to rub her ass otherwise.

Fuuuuuck, he was going to miss her.

Sam came sprinting across the kitchen. "Coopah! You're here!"

He was going to miss this little dude, too. Cooper set the bags on the little kitchen table and knelt down to scoop Sam up, settling him on his hip.

"Hey, buddy! I wouldn't have missed it. How was Outer Limits today?"

Sam clasped his hands around Cooper's neck. "It was really fun. We learned about left and right. Do you know your left and right?"

He chuckled. "Most of the time."

The little boy lifted his right hand up and announced, "I'm right-handed. What are you?"

"I'm right-handed, too."

"Yeah, my teacher said more people are right-handed than left. Did you know Mommy is left-handed?"

He set Sam down and glanced over at her on her tiptoes, reaching for plates in the cupboard with her left hand. "I did know that." The image of her stroking his cock with her left hand while she bobbed her mouth up and down popped into his head.

No! Bad libido!

"What's this?" she asked when she noticed the blue gift bag on the table next to their dinner bag.

"I got Sam something."

The squirt jumped up and down, clapping his hands. With a smile, Katie said, "That was very sweet of you. Sammy, what do you say?"

"Thank you, Coopah!"

He couldn't resist sliding his hand around her waist and whispering in her ear. "I didn't know if it would be okay to get you something."

She leaned into him, that was a good sign, right?

"I'm glad you didn't, Coop. You've done too much as it is. Speaking of..."

She withdrew from his grasp and found her purse, pulling a receipt out and handing it to him.

"You should see the credit on your statement, but I just wanted to make sure you know to look for it."

He looked down and saw it was a Nordstrom's receipt. She'd returned the outfits he bought her.

"I couldn't return one because I'd already worn it."

He was instantly pissed and snarled, "Why did you do that?"

She stammered, "I, um, thought under the circumstances, I shouldn't keep them."

He crumpled the receipt in his hand, mindful that Sam was watching him but couldn't help but growl, "Well, you thought wrong. Those were gifts, Katie. There were no conditions attached to them. There have never been any strings attached to my kindness."

She bit her bottom lip. "Oh. I'm—I'm sorry. I wasn't trying to offend you. I just didn't feel right keeping them. You'd done so much for me already, and given that..." She glanced at Sam. "Since things are the way they are, I thought it would be best to return them."

Cooper chose not to say anything more about it. He wasn't going to have an argument with her in front of her son, but, yeah, he was fucking offended. Cassie would try to calm him down later, telling him, "She's young, Coop. She didn't mean anything by it," but it was still bullshit.

Sam pulled the G.I. Joe doll out of the bag and exclaimed, "Wow! It's an Army man like you!"

He tamped down his ire at being called an Army man; they didn't have any Marine dolls, so this was the best he could do.

"Technically, I'm a Marine. Joe there couldn't get in the Marines, so he settled for the Army."

He heard Katie giggle, and it instantly made him feel lighter. What was it about this woman that drove him crazy and soothed his soul at the same time? How the hell did she capture his heart like she did? He wished more than anything he had the luxury to find out.

He was going to have to win her heart when he got back that's all there was to it.

Provided she doesn't meet someone else while I'm gone.

Whoa! Where did that thought come from? He didn't know, but he didn't like it. It felt like a stab to his chest. He was powerless right now, and it was killing him.

"Are you boys ready to eat?" she asked as she began taking to-go boxes out of the brown bag labeled Danny's BBQ in bold red and yellow lettering on the side.

"I'm starving," he admitted, prompting his little man to agree with him, "Me, too."

Cooper got the feeling if he had said he wanted to wait, Sammy would have parroted that sentiment. Katie must have thought the same thing because the corners of her mouth turned up in a knowing grin as she distributed the plates around the table.

"Sammy, can you get the silverware? Cooper, can you get the serving spoons and a barbeque fork out of the drawer?"

She'd opened the containers and was waiting for the serving utensils when they came back to the table. The two sat down and waited for her to serve their meals. It was all very domesticated and left him with a lump in his throat. This is what his life should be like every goddamn night.

Okay, preferably at his house since he had a dishwasher for cleanup and a hot tub for after Sammy went to bed, in a separate hallway from the master bedroom where there was a bed that actually fit him, but still, he'd take it any way he could get it.

The little guy wanted to be held in Cooper's lap as he settled in for his bedtime story. His thumb in his mouth caused Katie to frown when she walked in the room. She gestured to Sam sucking his thumb.

"He hasn't done that in ages," she said softly.

Cooper knew Sam was taking his going away hard. Hell, it was hard on him, too. He cuddled the boy closer and rocked slightly as he started to read *Goodnight Moon*. That was his favorite from when he was a kid, and he was happy Sam seemed to enjoy it, too.

"Will you read it again?"

"Sure, buddy." Cooper glanced over and saw Katie still in the doorway, watching them with tears in her eyes.

"Hey, Mommy," he addressed Katie, "we can scooch over if you want to sit with us."

She shook her head and wiped her eyes. "That's okay. You two go ahead."

Cooper read the story again and again until Sam fell asleep, nuzzled into his chest. He held the boy close and listened to his gentle breathing in the quiet room. He didn't know when he'd be able to hold the little man again.

God, this sucked. Damn Katie for not trusting him and damn the Taliban for taking him to Afghanistan and away from her and Sammy.

He came out to the kitchen to find her cleaning the kitchen, her eyes red from crying.

"Hey," he said softly to announce his presence. "He's asleep."

She slowly turned around from the sink, avoiding looking at him. "He's going to miss you so much."

Crossing the room in three paces, he was in front of her, tilting her chin with his index finger. "Is he the only one?"

She continued trying to avoid eye contact, but he kept his finger under her chin until she relented and looked back at him.

"No," she whispered as her lip started to tremble and tears filled her eyes.

His brain was telling him, *don't you dare*, but his heart screamed, *do it!* and he leaned over to capture her lips with his.

And it felt like fucking home.

Her arms instantly wrapped around his neck, and he pulled her tight against him as his tongue sought hers out. Angling his mouth, he deepened the kiss, and she moaned into his mouth, the sound going straight to his dick pressed between their bodies.

His lust was fueling images of her waking up in his bed, and his brain finally caught up by reminding him of their reality. He pulled away from her, albeit reluctantly.

"Baby girl," he growled. "We can't do this."

She stepped toward him. "Why?" she asked, running her fingertips on his jawline. "Don't we need closure?"

He didn't need closure. He needed her to realize she loved him as much as he loved her and wanted to give them a chance.

"Not like this, Katie. I can't just fuck you, it will hurt too much to let you go afterward."

She was persistent, he'd give her that. She started to rub his cock over his pants and cooed, "Let's just make each other feel good, Cooper."

"Tell me you're all in, that will make me feel good."

She stubbornly sat silent.

"I can't be with you, Katie, unless you're all in."

She pressed her chest against him. Goddamn her, she knew her tits were his weakness.

"I want to feel your naked body on mine, baby. Don't you want to fuck me?"

He groaned internally. Yeah, he wanted to fuck her—nonstop until he shipped out tomorrow—but he couldn't have meaningless sex with her, and that seemed to be what she was advocating. He grabbed her hand, pulling it off his cock.

"Katie, stop. I'm not having sex with you unless I'm making love to you."

The way she was glaring at him let him know after his rejection of her, the only thing they'd be having was hate sex. He'd bet that would be fucking hot.

As much as it was killing him, he was standing his ground. She wasn't going to cheapen what they'd had so she could feel better. *But fuck, angry sex with Katie... mmm.* And shouldn't he get laid before he left for God knows how long to live in a tent with a bunch of other sweaty men in the middle of the desert?

No. Stop thinking with your dick, asshole.

Those tits though.

Stop it!

He knew he'd regret it, but he wasn't fucking her. Not like this with the way things stood between them. It would only leave him feeling empty.

Did he really just decide to turn down sex because it would leave him feeling empty? He was so fucked over this girl.

"I have to go, Katie." He started toward her front door. "I'll try to get in touch with you in about a month to schedule a time to Skype with you and Sam."

"It won't be with me, it will just be with Sam," she glowered at him as he put his shoes on. "But, yes, let me know, and we'll arrange a time that will work for you and Sam."

Cooper stood at her door, willing himself to leave but his feet wouldn't cooperate.

"I love you, Kitten. We have a lot of unfinished business to tend to when I get back."

"We really don't." She crossed her arms defiantly at her chest, with her jaw set. Suddenly, her face softened, and she uncrossed her arms, reaching out to touch his hand. "Stay safe, Cooper. I know people say it all the time, but thank you for your service."

With a kiss to her forehead, he opened the door and bound down the stairs. He was pulling into his community when he heard his phone ding with a text message. He glanced at his screen.

Katie Connelly: I love you, too. Followed by those fucking multi-colored hearts.

Chapter Thirty-Eight

Kate

Her pride was still stinging at Cooper's rejection. He must not think she's as sexy as she thought. "His loss," she muttered as she washed her face and got ready for bed. She didn't really believe that for a second. She knew damn well it was her loss.

Kate had even surprised herself when she came onto him. It wasn't planned, but as he sat there reading her kid a bedtime story, all she could think was, "What if something happens to him?" which led to an overwhelming desire to just be naked with him. She was shocked as shit when he turned her down. *Asshole.* So, not only did he not want her, but she also felt like a slut for coming onto him at the most inopportune time.

She couldn't get over the fact he didn't want her. He always wanted her. How dare he change his mind about that?

Still, the idea of something happening to him without her having told him she loved him back was too much to bear, and she found herself firing off a text, telling him just that before slipping between her sheets.

He said they had unfinished business when he got back, whenever that was. She wasn't going to count on it. She was staying on track with her goals and wasn't going to worry about anything else. If Cooper Johnson decided to look her up when he returned, she'd cross that bridge when she came to it. For now, she was going to try to mend her broken heart, do a kick-ass job at her internship, and be the best mom she could. It's all she could do at this point.

****

She didn't hear from him again. Part of her was surprised, she thought she'd at least get a goodbye call or text, but nothing. That hurt more than she cared to admit.

Cooper had been gone a month, and she'd settled into her new routine of being single again. She and Sam talked about him every night though, and her son always made sure to include him in his prayers at bedtime. It was the sweetest, most heart-wrenching thing, listening to her little man asking God to be sure to keep *Coopah* safe and bring him home soon so they could go to the zoo.

Still, she'd heard nothing from him—no address where they could send a care package or time when he could set up a Skype chat. Just radio silence.

Because the Marine base was in San Diego, the local news was always really good about covering when servicemen from the area were killed or injured. There'd been no stories about any casualties or injuries, so she felt at ease he was at least safe.

One Monday afternoon she pulled into the Outer Limits parking lot to pick up Sam when she saw Cassie Rivas getting out of her shiny red Lexus. The woman was stunning—she'd just had a baby a little more than two months ago, but you'd never know it by looking at her.

Cassie waved and waited for her so they could walk in together.

"Hey, Katie, how are you doing?"

"I'm okay. Between work and my internship, I'm staying pretty busy this summer."

The blonde woman nodded in understanding. "I don't know how you manage being a single mom on top of it all. I have Luke, a sister and brother-in-law right next door, not to mention my niece who's home from college this summer helping me, and I struggle."

"I'm lucky I have a lot of help, too. They're just not related to me."

The woman tilted her head briefly and looked like she was going to ask a follow-up question, then elected to say nothing more as they walked up the sidewalk. They paused in the courtyard before going inside when Cassie touched her elbow.

"So, I wanted to ask you. Would it be okay if Sam came over for a playdate with Lucas on Wednesday afternoon? I could bring him home with me at five, and you could pick him up whenever. He could even sleep over if you need him to. Cooper is video calling at seven, and I know he'd love to see Sam too."

It felt like the bottom of her stomach dropped out of her body. Cooper was calling Cassie, not her? She tucked her hair behind her ear and looked around before meeting the older woman's eyes.

"Oh, um.... Yeah, that'd be fine, I guess. I can't pick him up until after ten though. I'm working at the diner Wednesday night."

"That's no problem. Do you just want him to spend the night?"

"No, I'll pick him up. We have an interview at a preschool close to campus Thursday morning."

"You're leaving Outer Limits?"

"Yeah, unfortunately, Sam lost his scholarship, and I just can't afford the tuition. Miriam said he could stay until the end of the month though, so I've got a little time to find something."

The pretty dark blonde scowled—and she was still adorable. *So not fair.*

"How did he lose his scholarship?"

"I'm not one hundred percent sure, to be honest. Apparently, there was a problem with the funding source, and the school has been unable to contact the person who created the scholarship. I'm really sad he has to leave, but maybe if we can find something closer to campus and my job, it will be for the best."

"Maybe they'll get the funding figured out before you have to," she murmured.

"That'd be nice, but I'm not getting my hopes up. My internship has a daycare, too, but it's only for their employees on the payroll, so I don't qualify because I'm not actually getting a paycheck. The broker I work for is awesome and is trying to pull a few strings, but I'm not counting on it. I had been planning on going back to school full-time in the fall, but this has taught me not to rely on things I can't control, ya know? So, we're going to look at some places I can afford, and just go back to what works for us."

"Sometimes it's good to rely on other people... You know if you ever need help with Sam, he's always welcome at our house."

"That's really generous of you, and there's not enough shame in my game I won't take you up on that if I need it."

"I wouldn't have offered if I didn't want you to."

That made Kate smile. "Thanks, Cassie. You and your sister have been incredibly generous and supportive of my son, and I really appreciate that. I know things didn't work out with Cooper and me, and I know he's your friend, but I appreciate you haven't held that against Sam."

"Katie, just because you and Cooper aren't technically together right now, doesn't mean I don't consider you a friend, and I know Bren feels the same way. Don't get me wrong, I love Cooper, and if you had done him dirty, this would probably be a different conversation, but I still would never hold it against Sam. But as I understand it, you and Coop's timing just didn't work. It happens. I know you're both going to move on. It will turn out the way it was meant to."

The thought of him moving on with someone else made her sad, but she offered as real a smile as she could muster. "It will. Everything works out the ways it's supposed to, in the end."

****

Cooper

"Hey, Coop!" Cassie was looking back at him from her laptop sitting on her newly remodeled kitchen island.

"Hi, gorgeous. You are a sight for sore eyes. If I never see another hairy man for the rest of my life, I'll be a happy man. How are you?"

"I'm great. How are you?"

"Surviving. It looks like we'll be back around the beginning of October, so that's good news. How are the kids? How's Luke?"

"Sofia is growing like she's supposed to, and Lucas is doing awesome. Luke has been trying not to work so much, but he's not being very successful; luckily, I've got Brenna and Dee next door."

"Have you seen Sam or Katie?"

"Actually, I have a surprise for you. Sam is here and can't wait to talk to you, but I wanted to run something by you before I brought the boys in. Did you cancel Sammy's scholarship?"

He furrowed his brows. "No. Why?"

"Oh, well Katie is pulling him from Outer Limits at the end of this month. They told her the funding for his scholarship stopped, and they couldn't reach the donor to straighten it out."

He rubbed the back of his neck. "Shit, I got a text from the bank my debit card had been compromised, and they were issuing me a new one. I completely forgot that was how I was paying his tuition. Can you talk to Miriam and get it straightened out for me? I don't want him going anywhere else."

Cassie smiled. "I wondered what happened, but I didn't want to overstep in case you had decided to cancel the scholarship."

"Come on, Cass, you know I wouldn't do that. I love that kid."

"I know you do, Cooper."

"So, what aren't you telling me? How's Katie?"

"She seems to be doing good. I talked to her Monday when I asked for Sam to come over so he could video chat with you."

"Uh huh. What'd she say? She obviously was okay with it."

"Yeah, she knew Sam would be excited."

"But...."

"But what?"

"Come on, Cass. What aren't you telling me?"

"Well," she winced. "The gossip about Janet has finally reached Outer Limits. I don't know if it's gotten back to Katie yet, but you know it's only a matter of time."

"How the fuck is my name coming up at a preschool?"

"Well, Sammy talks about *Cooper* all the time like you're his dad or something. I'm sure it didn't take long for someone with an internet connection to look up Ellen Louise Jurden and find her obituary with you listed as her oldest grandson, then make the connection you're the one paying for his schooling, which then gets the tongues wagging of the bitches who know Janet or remember the gossip. Like, why would you pay for Sam and not your own kid?"

He felt his heart quicken. "Fuck, fuck, fuck. God, this is such bullshit. I wish your brother-in-law would have let me nail her ass to the wall in a much more public fashion."

"The rumors still would have hung around."

"Yeah, well, at least there would have an easily searchable paper trail."

"There still is."

"Except she's referred to as *Jane Doe and baby*. Such fucking bullshit."

"It's still out there, clearing your name."

"Then why the hell are the rumors starting?"

"Because that's much juicier. The idea of Captain Johnson, the guy who bailed on his pregnant baby mama is now paying for some other kid's preschool tuition... far more scandalous than, Captain Johnson, the Marine's whose career was almost ruined by a scorned, vindictive bitch, is a great guy in love with a single mom and her kid."

"Fuck. Do you think Katie has heard that shit?"

"Honestly, Coop, I don't know. I tried talking to her a little, but she's a hard one to read. She plays her cards really close to the vest. I will say she was planning on going back to school full-time, but then the thing with the scholarship happened, so she said she realized she couldn't rely on anyone but herself and was just going back to doing things the way she knew worked."

Cooper took a deep sigh. He needed to get his ass back home and take care of shit. "Hopefully, she still goes to school full-time. Promise me you'll talk to Miriam."

"I will. If I have to, I'll cover the tuition for you, and you can pay me back when you get home."

"I would love you forever if you did that."

"You better not love her forever, period," came Luke's gruff voice as he walked in the kitchen with his work gear bag slung over his shoulder.

"Hey, Luke. Just a figure of speech. She only has eyes for you, big guy, don't worry."

"It's not her eyes I'm worried about, devil dog."

"Baby, be nice to him," Cassie cooed, stroking her husband's arm. "He's in the middle of the desert while his girl is here, and he hasn't talked to her since the night before he left."

"And who the fuck's fault is that? Why is he talking to you instead of her?" the SWAT sergeant snarled.

Well shit. Luke kind of had a point. Except, Cooper didn't know what he'd say to her.

The dark blonde reached up and brushed his dark hair with her fingertips. "Because, baby, she's working tonight, and this is the only time he could schedule to call. Go get the boys and tell them he's waiting to talk to them."

He could hear the boys shouts through the monitor and couldn't help but smile when they came barreling in the kitchen.

"Coopah!" Sam squealed at the same time Lucas raised his hands in delight at seeing his image on the computer screen. Talk about an ego boost.

"How are you, Coopah? Are you coming home soon? I miss you!"

"Hey, Sammy. I miss you too. I'm not sure when I'm coming home yet. How's your mommy?"

"She's sad a lot. I don't think she likes having to dress up all the time for work."

That made him chuckle. "Dressing up all the time can be hard work. How's school?"

His face turned sad, and he looked down. "I have to go to a new school soon," he murmured.

"I'll bet things work out that you don't have to, buddy."

"Really?"

"Yeah, I do."

Lucas chimed in, and the two goofballs had him laughing out loud and missing home more than ever. After he hung up, he couldn't stop thinking about what Cassie said. If Katie heard that bullshit, and he didn't have a chance to defend himself... He fucking hated the idea she'd be subject to the gossip too.

Cooper beat the shit out of a lot of punching bags and sparring partners over the next several months. He also didn't call Cassie again. He didn't think his blood pressure could take hearing about how he was the gossip and not being to do a goddamn thing about it.

Chapter Thirty-Nine

Kate

The whisperings started not long after Sam enrolled in school. *Who was the boy that Cooper Johnson sponsored?... Cooper was paying his entire tuition, can you believe that?... Cooper Johnson, wasn't he the one who bribed the commission for his captain promotion after that woman came forward when he denied the baby was his and refused to pay child support?... Didn't the paternity test prove he wasn't?*

There were the women who wouldn't take part in the gossip and even tried to offer refuting facts, but the cackling bitches didn't want to hear it. Fortunately, there didn't seem to be very many, and the only people who took them seriously were their fellow hags.

Ah, it was like when she got pregnant all over again. Except these rumors were false. Kate didn't know which she preferred more—gossip based in lies or fact.

Neither.

Thank God she was busier than a one-armed paper hanger and didn't have time to dwell on it. When Sam's tuition was revoked, she tried to look at it as a blessing and a chance to start over somewhere else. Imagine her surprise when she got a call from Sandy at Outer Limits Thursday morning before she'd even left the house.

"Hi, Kate. I'm sorry to be calling so early, but I am calling with good news. Sam's scholarship mishap has been corrected. His tuition is current and actually paid in advance so there won't be any cause for concern again."

Despite her thinking she wanted to start fresh somewhere else, she knew Sam really loved the school and all the kids in it, and he was always treated wonderfully.

"That's great news, Sandy. May I ask what happened?"

"The donor's bank card was compromised, so the bank canceled the card. We've been given the donor's bank routing information, so there shouldn't be an issue again. And we've guaranteed Sam's tuition by contract for at least a year, so if there is another funding problem, it won't be yours. I'm so sorry we hadn't had that paperwork signed before, and that this happened to you. You have my word, this will never happen again, at least for a year, but the donor was embarrassed and apologetic, so I don't think you have to worry."

This really was a relief. Sam was going to be thrilled he didn't have to leave Outer Limits

"Coopah said I wouldn't have to leave!" the little guy shouted, bouncing on the balls of his feet when she told him the news.

"He did, did he?"

"Yes! He said he knew it would work out and not to worry. He's so smart, Mommy."

At first that struck her as odd, then she realized he was probably just reassuring Sam when he told him he had to find a new school.

"We should celebrate. Let's go have breakfast at Frank's."

"Can I get chocolate chip pancakes?" her son asked as she helped him button his shirt.

"It's a special occasion, I think that would be okay."

"Yay! This is my best day ever!"

It was turning out to be a pretty good week for her too, actually. Sam's preschool scholarship was taken care of, and she'd just gotten her financial aid award saying she'd gotten a grant for her entire full-time college tuition and books— maybe she could actually get ahead a little. And as bittersweet as it was, Sammy had gotten to talk to Cooper. She was happy her son had been able to video chat with his real-life hero, but she was a little jealous Cooper had reached out to Cassie and not her.

It didn't matter she'd told him she wouldn't talk to him if he called, he should have at least tried, dammit.

"Coopah said I'm supposed to give you a hug and a kiss from him, Mommy," Sam said before throwing his arms around her neck and kissing her cheek.

Even though she was still mad at his rejection, Kate missed that Marine more than she wanted to admit to herself. She hoped he continued to be safe and made it home in one piece—and soon. Strictly for Sam's sake, of course, because she certainly didn't dream of him every single night.

Okay, yes she did. Every. Single. Night.

Sometimes they were happy dreams, and sometimes, they replayed their last few days together and how badly things had ended. Not badly like drama and yelling, just badly in that her heart had never hurt that much. Not even when Eric stopped calling her and blocked her number or when her parents rejected her when she'd decided to keep Sam, instead of giving him up for adoption. Those situations hurt, but at the end of the day, she knew she'd be just fine by herself. When Cooper left, she tried telling herself she was going to be just fine, but she hadn't been, not even close.

Her internship was turning out to be an amazing experience, and Jason Ellers, her broker had really taken her and Sam under his wing. They'd been included in pool parties with his family, and he'd even invited her to a cocktail party he and his wife hosted. She hadn't been able to attend the cocktail party because she was working at the diner, but that was probably for the best since she'd probably have felt awkward being there alone.

Jason's wife, Heather had taken a while to warm up to her. Kate didn't know why. The woman was a former model and the mother of his three kids, Kate was hardly a threat. Heather soon realized after her third unannounced visit to the office, she had nothing to worry about when it came to the twenty-five-year-old college student and had been nothing but kind ever since.

Yet there was still this huge missing piece in Kate's life. She wondered if Cooper had changed his mind about them having unfinished business because he'd made no attempt to contact her after the night he'd rejected her. The longer she went without hearing from him, especially once she'd learned he was able to have communication, the more hurt she became. She really was going to find a way to be fine without Cooper Johnson in her life.

****

"The best way to get over a man is to get under another one," Carol advised one late August evening the week before classes started.

"Oh my god, you are impossible."

"Maybe," the older redhead shrugged her shoulders, "but it always worked for me."

"That's not what I want. Hell, I didn't even want to *get under* Cooper if you recall."

"So, are you regretting that decision?"

"Yes and no," Kate sighed. "Our time together was special, and I'm grateful Sam got to spend time with him and have an example of a good man. But my heart hurts, Carol. It literally aches."

Carol gave a sympathetic smile. "I know, sweet girl. I'm sorry."

"On the plus side, I still can't eat, so I'm down another two pounds," she responded with a humorless laugh.

"Don't lose too much weight, Katie Kat. Guys like girls with a little meat on their bones."

"Don't worry," she smirked as she patted her ass, "there's still plenty of meat there."

One of the regulars called from the counter where he was eavesdropping from behind a newspaper, "More cushion for the pushin'."

"Ew, Dwayne."

"I'm just saying," the older guy chuckled as he took a sip of coffee, never taking his eyes away from the newsprint.

"Well, don't." Kate couldn't hide her grin when she stood in front of him with the coffee pot poised to refill his cup when he set it down again. "What would Alice say if she heard you talking like that?" Dwayne had been married to his wife, Alice for at least forty years.

He finally looked up at her. "She'd agree with me!" The salty old man occasionally brought his sweet, diminutive wife for breakfast.

"I don't believe that for a second. You'd be sleeping in the doghouse or at least the couch if she heard you talk like that."

He lowered his newspaper while making his point. "Katie, that woman has been married to me for forty-two years, do you think she would expect anything less from me?"

"Good point," she giggled as she finished topping his coffee off, then laid his check in front of him. "Tell her I said hi, won't you?"

"I sure will. When's your Marine coming back?"

"I know you know he's not *my* Marine, but hopefully, in few months."

"Don't listen to Carol. If you two are meant to be, you shouldn't be getting under anyone except him."

Carol arrived to defend herself. "Well, there's the point, she doesn't think they were meant to be."

"Now, I didn't say that."

"No?" Carol said with raised eyebrows. "What did you say?"

"I—" Kate looked back and forth between the two intently waiting for her response. "I—I think I'll cross that bridge should I ever get to it," she said and retreated to the kitchen where it was safe.

Chapter Forty

"Hey man, welcome back. We want to have a little night out to celebrate your homecoming," Craig's baritone voice came through the other end of his phone.

Cooper had been back over two weeks and avoiding going anywhere, even the grocery store as he acclimated to life in the States again. He'd only been gone a little over four months, but summer in Afghanistan without air conditioning had taken some getting used to. Now, it was taking some getting used to being back in beautiful San Diego.

He hadn't told anyone he was home, but somehow word had spread, and he'd been getting calls and texts daily that had gone unanswered until today when he decided to take the SWAT captain's call.

The Marine had been debating about calling Katie and asking if he could see her, or at least Sammy, but couldn't muster up the nerve. He had no idea how he'd even start the conversation, given how they'd left things the last time he saw her. The fact he was anything but confident was such a fucking anomaly, but damn, that girl had done a number on him, and he had no idea how to proceed.

He had thought about her whenever he had a minute of downtime in his tent in the middle of the desert. He'd lay on his bed and scroll through their text messages, then pictures of her and Sam. Or him and her. Or just her. There was one picture, in particular, that was his go-to whenever he was feeling horny or missing her more than usual. It was taken at his house on his patio—she was sitting at the glass table, leaning forward and laughing at something Sam was doing. The way her body was positioned, her purple blouse had opened, revealing her ample, creamy cleavage and black lacy bra.

Mmm, that bra and those tits... They could end wars. Or start them, which was probably more appropriate, considering where he was.

He'd debated reaching out and seeing if they could arrange a time to video chat, but with the way things stood between them, he wasn't sure if she'd be receptive to it. He didn't think he could handle if she'd rejected him while he was thousands of miles away and unable to do anything about it, so he did nothing. 'Cause, you know, ignorance was bliss.

It was time to join the world again, so he found himself agreeing to Craig's gathering at GolfPlus, the latest attraction in San Diego where people could have driving range competitions, and there were other gaming opportunities for non-golfers. It catered to people of all ages, but more importantly, it served beer, so he agreed to meet on Friday night. He wasn't prepared for the number of people on their private golf deck or the number of women.

"I thought you could use a little welcoming home," his friend said with a grin when Cooper looked around at all the people.

"Welcome home!" he was told in various ways, depending on if the greeter was male or female, single or attached. He'd more tits pressed against him in the last thirty minutes than he could count.

Deciding he needed more beer and their server was taking too long to reappear, he made his way to the lobby bar for another drink. "Sorry, Summer Shandy isn't in season," the bartender told him before Cooper settled on an old-fashioned Miller Light. He walked through the throngs of people with the beer in his hand, musing what a gold mine this place was, appealing to groups of all ages and selling over-priced beer to those willing to stand in line for ten minutes for the privilege.

He started back to the golf deck when he heard a little voice squeal, "Coopah!" and looked around to see Sam running at him in a dead sprint.

He knelt down, and the little dude barreled into him at full speed, immediately wrapping his little arms around his neck in a three-year-old's bear hug. He set his drink on the floor and brought both arms around him, cradling the back of his head while he closed his eyes and breathed in the familiar scent of the little boy he missed so much.

"Hey, buddy, what are you doing here?"

The Marine stood while still holding Sam, and the kid wrapped his legs around him like a spider monkey, refusing to let go.

"I've missed you, Coopah," Sam whispered, completely ignoring his question.

He looked into the huge lobby area to see Katie running frantically through the crowd, searching for her son and slowing up when she realized where he was and who he was with, finally making it to where they stood.

"Hi," Cooper said. "Look who I found."

Katie smiled her fake smile. She'd cut her hair shorter and had it styled to frame her face. He could tell by the way her dark jeans fit her ass she'd lost weight, something he didn't necessarily appreciate, but she still nicely filled out the black sweater she was wearing.

He was immediately lost, just like he'd knew he'd be if he ever saw her in person again.

Sticky fingers held his face in place on both sides, and he was forced to look at Sam. The little man had grown. He'd lost some of his baby face, and Cooper could tell just in the few minutes he'd been holding him, he'd gotten bigger.

"Are you back forever? When are we going to the zoo?"

He looked over at Katie for guidance on how to proceed.

"How long have you been home?" she asked politely.

"About two weeks."

She scowled when she said, "I'm glad you made it back safe."

Sticky fingers touched his face again.

"We pray every night for God to keep you safe," Sam chimed in, and she smiled an embarrassed smile when Cooper tilted his head, silently asking for confirmation what her son shared was true. She didn't respond, which is how he knew it was.

"You look great," he said as he shifted the spider monkey's weight around his middle.

"Thanks. I've been able to take more classes this semester. Sam's daycare scholarship has helped tremendously, and I was able to get a grant for my own tuition costs."

While his primary motivation for Sam's scholarship had been making sure the boy was in a good place, he was happy it was helping her, too. It was great she was able to take more classes so she could finish her degree faster.

"That's great news, Kitten."

With a small smile, she looked down, embarrassed at the use of her pet name

"So, when are we going to the zoo, Coopah?" the little voice demanded just as another, more feminine voice huskily said, "There you are!"

Nicki, one of the women he'd been talking to earlier, materialized at his side. She was platinum blonde, in a tight pink tank top—her nipples poking through since it was now October and too fucking cold to be wearing such a thing—and painted on jeans with high heels. High heels—at a sports complex.

"We're waiting for you," she said and stroked his bicep even though he was still holding Sam.

Katie watched the exchange, tears filling her eyes, but she gave him another fake smile as if conveying she didn't care.

He was about to politely tell Nicki to fuck off and ask if he could tag along with Katie and Sam when a good-looking, dark-haired man with graying temples appeared at his little waitress' side and handed her two tickets.

"We're on Deck Thirty-Six," he told her and was about to turn away when he noticed Cooper holding Sam and Katie's crestfallen face. The man eyed him with suspicion and postured a little, squaring his shoulders and puffing his chest out.

"Jason Ellers," he said and held out his hand.

The Marine shifted Sam again and took the offered hand, gripping it in a firm handshake. "Cooper Johnson."

"Mr. Jason has a name like mine!" Sam exclaimed proudly, then the little shit added, "Mommy is Coopah's favorite friend."

"Is that so?" Jason said with a smirk.

Cooper couldn't help himself, he stared at Katie when he answered, "Yeah. Definitely," causing her to quickly glance at the floor. The man needed to know what kind of shoes he had to fill.

"She's pretty great. I can understand why she would be Cooper's favorite," Jason told Sam.

The man's comment wasn't tinged with jealousy, and that pissed Cooper off even more than if it had been. The bastard shouldn't be so fucking secure in his relationship with her, he wasn't jealous of another alpha male, goddammit.

Nicki brushed her tits against his arm. Cooper wasn't convinced she wasn't purposefully trying to display them for the good-looking, distinguished man opposite him, too.

"Are you ready?" she purred.

He wasn't ready. That would mean he'd have to set Sammy down and walk away again. The last four months of his life had been filled with regret over walking away from the two of them and not insisting they make it work.

Apparently, though, Katie had recovered and moved on. It was probably time for him to do the same.

He eyed the platinum blonde still touching his arm. Craig was right. She was one of the many women at the get-together tonight he wouldn't have a baby with, but she was definitely practice-making-one worthy.

He kissed Sam's forehead, then set him down.

"I love you, buddy. Be good for your mom, okay?"

The little guy's eyes filled with tears, and Cooper almost fucking lost it.

"Will you come visit us?" he whispered.

He glanced over at Katie gnawing her bottom lip like she always did when she was upset.

"I don't think I'll have time, little man." Then threw his arm around Nicki's shoulder.

Sam's bottom lip jutted out and started to quiver, and big fat tears streamed down his cheeks as he whispered, "I don't pee my pants anymore."

And the biggest asshole in the world award goes to... Cooper Johnson.

"I've been a good boy since you left."

Make that the universe.

Katie was at her son's side, kneeling down and wiping his tears away without a second glance at Cooper

"Come on, baby. Greyson and our other new friends are waiting for us." *We don't need that asshole.* She didn't say the last part, but it sure as hell was implied.

Jason also knelt down to comfort Sam, causing Cooper to grit his teeth. Another man was having to give his little guy a pep talk over how Cooper had made him feel.

No. Fuck, no.

He unwrapped his arm from Nicki's shoulder and walked the few steps where the three were huddled together and reached down to swing Sam back into his arms. Sam wrapped his arms around him, burying his head in Cooper's neck, clinging to him while he cried. Katie was shooting daggers at him while Jason just looked on. He turned and stepped away from everyone so only Sam could hear what he said as he whispered in his ear.

"Sammy, you have always been a good boy. I don't care if you *pooped* your pants twenty times a day. I'm sorry I haven't been able to come visit or take you to the zoo."

"But you promised," he choked out on a sob.

Fuuuuck. "I know, Sam. I'm sorry."

"Don't you want to see us?"

"I don't think your mom would like that, buddy. But remember when I told you I would always love and worry about you and be there to help you when you need it?"

Sam sniffled, "Yes."

"That hasn't changed. Just because I don't see you as much doesn't mean I love you or worry about you any less. You are my favorite little man, and you always will be."

He nodded again but continued weeping.

A few tears escaped the corners of Cooper's eyes too.

"Someday, you'll have a daddy, and you'll forget all about me."

Fuck. He shouldn't have said that.

"Will you forget about me when you're a daddy?" the little voice asked.

"Never."

"I don't want anyone else for a daddy. I want you," he said with a shuddering breath.

Katie was going to have his nuts in a vice grip for this.

"I'm sorry, buddy. I wish I could have been. But I will always be your friend. Always."

"So, will you still take me and Lucas to the zoo again?"

That made him chuckle out loud. *Little wheeler-dealer.* "We'll have to make sure it's okay with your mom first." He put his forehead against Sam's and closed his eyes. "I love you, Sam."

"I love you, too, Coopah. Do you love Mommy, too?"

He nodded. "I love your mommy, too," he confirmed.

"Maybe she can go to the zoo with us," the little conspirator suggested.

That was an idea.

"We'll see what she says. She might want to take you herself with Mr. Jason."

Sam shook his head. "She should go with us. Maybe that would help her not be sad all the time."

He glanced over to where Jason was gesturing like he was going to go wait for them on the sports deck, and she smiled at the older man—her genuine smile. Then Cooper looked at the blonde waiting patiently for him. She was no Katie Connelly, and he realized he'd rather fuck his hand than have to deal with the drama she was bound to bring to the table, but his kitten didn't need to know that. He wasn't about to let her know she'd hurt him.

"We'll ask her, okay? But not right now. You need to go join your friends, and I need to go to my friend's party. I promise you, I will call your mom this week and ask her if I can take you to the zoo." He reiterated, "I promise. Okay?"

"Okay," the little boy whispered and kissed his cheek. "I'm glad you're back."

"Me too, buddy. Me too."

He set him down, and Sam ran back to his mom, smiling.

Katie glared at the Marine, and he could tell she was curious what he'd said to Sam to change his mood, but she knelt and greeted her son with a big, animated smile and outstretched arms. He watched her stand and put her hand on Sam's back, looking back at Cooper as he slid his arm around Nicki's waist. Then his kitten did something he never imagined he'd ever see her do.

With the hand that was guiding Sam through the lobby, Katie Connelly flipped him the bird.

He had to suppress his smile. He was going to fucking marry that woman.

*****

The next afternoon, Cooper was lying on a big blanket in the adjoining living room, playing with Sofia Claire while Cassie stood at her kitchen island chopping vegetables.

"You said you'd *what*?"

317

"Take him and Lucas to the zoo again. If his mom said it was okay."

"And what did Katie say?"

He grimaced. "I didn't get a chance to ask her. I didn't want to say anything in front of her date."

Cassie paused her dicing and looked up. "Katie had a date? While Sam was with her?"

"Oh, yeah. *Jason Ellers*. Sam called him *Mister* Jason. Ugh. The kid thinks he's great because Sam's middle name is Jason."

She started laughing out loud, actually setting the knife on the counter and clutching her sides.

"What's so funny?" he snarled.

"Jason Ellers was her boss when she was interning this summer. I'll bet my paycheck they were at his son's birthday party. He's married to like a supermodel and has three kids. She's definitely not dating Jason Ellers, you idiot."

"Oh, God. You're kidding. Fuuuuck."

She narrowed her eyes at him.

"What did you do?"

"Well, there was a blonde at the party..."

She came around the counter and plucked Sofia off the blanket.

"Manwhores don't get to play with my daughter," she chastised and walked back into the kitchen with her, putting her in the high chair.

Cooper followed her and pulled the baby out of the seat.

"I wasn't a manwhore," he corrected as he bounced the little girl in his arms. With a more sheepish tone, he added, "I just might have given Katie the impression I was."

A cucumber slice hit him directly in the face.

"You fucking moron. Oh my God, you're making me swear in front of my kids, you're so stupid. Why, WHY would you do such a thing?"

"Because I'm a fucking moron."

"I—I don't even know how to help you at this point," she sighed, the knife still in her hand as she extended it to her side and shook her head.

"Maybe you could invite her over for a playdate?"

"You want me to help you ambush that poor girl? Uh-uh. Man up, buttercup, and do your own dirty work."

"Oh, come on, Cass..."

She pointed the knife directly at him.

"No way, Cooper Johnson. I like that girl, and I'm not going to have her pissed at me every time I run into her at daycare."

"Well, what should I do? I messed up. I should have fought harder for her."

Mrs. Rivas started slicing a red pepper on the white cutting board, and without looking up at him, suggested, "Why don't you try starting over with her? From the beginning. Hit the reset button. Or just call her and ask to take Sam to the zoo, see where it goes."

He sighed. "I just wonder if I should. I applied for the promotion like Ron suggested. If I get it, I'll have to move to Virginia."

"Would you want her and Sam to go with you?"

"Of course. If she would, but she's got school. Plus, you know, she hates me."

Cassie smiled. "So pour on the Cooper charm and make her not hate you. When do you think you'll have to go?"

"*If* I get it, it could be as early as February, but probably more likely April or May."

"Plenty of time..." his friend said confidently.

"Is it?"

Cassie put the knife down and shifted her weight. "Coop, do you love her? I mean, really love her? Not like the idea of being in love with her, but love *her*."

"Yeah, I do," he said without hesitation.

"Then do something about it. What the hell are you waiting for?"

"Christmas?" he said with a smirk.

"Well, you're in luck, it's right around the corner. Now, get out of my kitchen and go fix your mess."

Chapter Forty-One

Kate

He'd been home for two weeks and was already seeing someone new. *Well, isn't that special? Fuck him.*

Whatever he'd said to Sam had done the trick because her boy was in happy spirits for the rest of the night, not having a care in the world. Exactly how it should be for a four-year-old.

He'd had a birthday two weeks ago, and Kate hadn't been able to afford a big party for him, so she almost declined Jason and Heather's invitation to Greyson's party at GolfPlus. She didn't want it obvious to Sam what she hadn't been able to provide him—yet.

"Next year, I promise," she'd told him on their way home from the party. "We'll have a big birthday party to celebrate you turning five. Mommy will have a new job by then, and we'll be able to afford something like that, baby."

She was going to give him that, no matter what. She would start stashing twenty bucks away every paycheck and make it happen regardless of where she was working next year.

"We can have it anywhere you want. GolfPlus, Chuckie Cheese, the zoo..."

"Coopah is going to take me to the zoo," her son announced, completely ignoring her party planning.

"Sweetie, Cooper is really busy. I don't think he has time to do that."

"But, he promised, Mom."

There was that *Mom* again.

"Sammy, I know, but that was before he had to go away to defend our country and keep us safe. He's really busy now, and we can't hold him to promises he made before he had to go."

"But he promised tonight."

He did what?

She looked at her son through her rearview mirror. "He did? Are you sure?"

"Yeah, he said he promised he'd call you this week to ask if it was okay. It is okay, right, Mommy?"

Ah, there's my Mommy.

"We'll see, Sam."

She wasn't convinced Cooper was actually going to follow through. And if he did, fuck him if he thought she was going to be okay with him taking her child anywhere.

"He said you should go too."

Now, she knew he wasn't going to follow through.

"Baby, Cooper is really busy being a Marine." *And a player.* "I don't want you to be too upset if he can't make it, okay?"

"He'll make it," her son told her confidently from the back seat.

Dammit. If he did, she was going to have to be the bad guy. Suddenly, she was glad she'd never had to deal with Eric and this crap.

"We'll see what happens, baby."

****

Kate juggled the three plates of cookies covered in plastic wrap as she slung her purse over her shoulder and shut the Honda door with her hip.

"Good afternoon," she called as she walked in the staff entrance into the diner's kitchen. She spun around and set a plate in front of the cooks. "New recipe. Butterscotch, peanut butter, and Rice Krispies with melted chocolate on top. Let me know what you think."

She strolled into Frank's office and set another plate down. "Here you go, handsome. New recipe."

Frank looked up from his desk, his reading glasses down on the end of his nose. "Aw, thanks, Katie Bug. I've been craving your cookies."

"Sorry I haven't baked much lately. My heart hasn't been in it."

"Your heart's in it now?"

"Nope, but it's gonna be. Fake it til you make it," she replied with a grin as she whirled around and exited his office.

"I hope you put some weight back on while you're faking it," he called after her.

She was done being sad and miserable over Cooper Johnson. He was back and hadn't wanted to see her... he was dating someone else. It was time to gather her glass slippers and move on. Fuck this turning into a pumpkin shit.

She breezed into the dining room, Carol's plate of Scotcheroos in hand and a smile plastered to her face. She was going to have a great shift, make lots of tips so she could get started on Sam's birthday fund, and just get on with living life.

Her fairy godmother could eat a bag of dicks—Kate was taking over now.

Carol wasn't in the server station, so she must be in the pit rolling silverware in preparation for the dinner rush.

"Look what I brought you... new recipe but still baked with love," she called as she stepped up into the middle of the counter area and almost dropped the plate when she saw who Carol was talking to.

*

Cooper

There she was, her brown hair piled high with wispy curls around her pretty face, light makeup with a just a touch of lip gloss.

"There's my girl," he murmured just loud enough for Carol to hear with a small grin. The redheaded waitress had been giving him the third degree before she'd even tell him if Katie was working tonight.

"So why didn't you get a hold of her once while you were gone?"

"It was really hard to get—"

"Bullshit. Then how were you able to talk to Sam at the one lady's house?"

Jesus, how much did this woman know?

"I didn't know if she'd talk to me. The last thing she said was not to bother. I was pretty much a chicken shit."

That admission seemed to soften Carol because she offered the information Katie was due at the restaurant at four. Just ten more minutes of grilling by this woman... he could do it. Unfortunately, there was only one other customer in the place, so she had plenty of time to devote to his interrogation.

"So how long have you been home?"

"Eighteen days."

"*Eighteen days*?! And you're just now coming to see her? You could have gone to Sam's birthday party. That would have been a wonderful birthday surprise for that little boy."

He closed his eyes and hung his head. He hadn't known when Sam's birthday was. He'd missed it, and he was even home. If he had known.... Cooper hadn't even said anything to him when he saw him last night. Some dad he'd be.

Then came the sweetest voice announcing her arrival with baked goods. She had a smile on her face as she stepped up into the server area between the counters, ready to greet Carol, then she saw him, and her face fell.

Ouch. Not the reaction he was hoping for, although after she gave him the middle finger last night, it was exactly the one he was expecting, and frankly, probably deserved after his stunt with Nicki.

Her uniform was baggy on her now, and her tits were no longer trying to bust out of it. That was a shame. That had been the first thing he'd ever noticed about her.

She kept her distance, setting the plate of brownie-looking things down, and without even looking at him, told Carol, "I tried making Scotcheroos. Let me know what you think. Sam loved them, but Sam would love chocolate covered cardboard, so…" then turned to leave. He called after her.

"Hey, Katie…" She stopped walking but didn't turn around right away, so he tried again. "Kitten, can I talk to you for a second?"

That caused her to whirl around, her eyes flashing as she marched toward him.

"You don't get to call me that anymore. My name is Kate or Miss Connelly or even Miss, but don't you dare call me kitten again."

Was it bad her heaving tits and flushed face made his cock twitch?

Carol made herself scarce while Katie stood there glowering at him, her hand still on her hip as they stared at each other. She really was beautiful, and all he could think about was how much he'd missed touching her. Finally, she stepped away from his direct line of sight and started wiping the counters around him.

"What do you want, Cooper?"

"I was hoping to take you and Sammy to the zoo and maybe take you out to dinner sometime?"

She stopped wiping, and as if on instinct, refilled his empty water glass with a nearby metal pitcher.

"I don't think that's a good idea."

"What's not a good idea? Dinner or the zoo?"

"Both."

"Please, Katie. At least let me take you and Sam to the zoo. I promised him and seeing how I missed his birthday, it's the least I can do."

"How did you know—"

"Carol told me," he interrupted. "I'm so sorry, Katie. I didn't know when his birthday was, I would have been there if I'd known."

That caused her to narrow her eyes, her mouth downturned. "Why?"

"Why?" he repeated.

"Yeah, why? Why would you have been there?"

Is she really asking me why I'd want to be there for Sam's birthday?

"Because it was his birthday, and I care about him and would have liked to help him celebrate turning four."

"You care about him so much you haven't even bothered to call since you've been home? The only reason you've even seen him was by pure coincidence when you were out on your date. So, sorry, I'm not buying it. You don't get to just float in and out of his life when it suits you."

"That's not fair, Katie. The last four months were not by choice."

"Maybe not, but it was your choice not to maintain contact, or you'd know about his birthday. It was your choice not to see or call him when you got home and instead, hook up with your latest conquest."

"Are we talking about Sam or you, Kitten?"

That caused her jaw to drop as she tried to come up with a retort. Finally, she dryly replied, "You can fuck whoever you want, Cooper, that's no longer my business. My son, however, is my business, and I think it's in his best interest if you don't spend time with him."

It was time to put his cards on the table.

"Katie, I didn't fuck Nicki. I didn't even kiss her. She was at a welcome home party for me at GolfPlus, that's all. I went home alone. I don't want anyone but you, baby girl. You and Sam, you're who I want."

She gave him a sad smile. "And yet you couldn't even be bothered to let me know you were okay the whole time you were gone. You managed to let Cassie know, but you couldn't let me know. And when..."

He interrupted, "It's because I wasn't sure if you wanted to hear from me."

She ignored his disruption and talked louder, over him. "And when you get back home, you don't want to see us. You don't invite us to your welcome home party. But I'm supposed to believe we're who you want?"

"It's the truth. I wasn't the one throwing the party. I didn't even want to go."

"But you did."

Fuck! He pinched the bridge of his nose. How could he get through to her? She didn't want to hear anything he had to say.

"Yeah, I did, only so everyone would stop calling me. I was trying to get acclimated to my life again, but they wouldn't stop bothering me."

She gave him her fucking dismissive smile. "You know what? You don't owe me any explanation, and I'm sorry if I've made you feel like you do."

"I do owe you an explanation. I want to see you, Katie. I want to take Sam to the zoo, and I want to spend time with both of you. Please."

He was begging this woman. Fucking Captain Cooper Johnson was begging a woman to spend time with him. What. The. Fuck.

"Who's Janet Wolford?" she hit him with, out of the blue.

He didn't even hesitate with his reply. "Janet Wolford is a woman who tried to shake me down when I was up for my promotion. She said I'd gotten her pregnant, and she wanted child support, and if I didn't pay it, she was going to the promotion committee and tell them. Fortunately, I knew I'd never even slept with her. She had brought me home one night from the bar when I was plastered and dropped me off, but I never fucked her."

"If you were drunk, how do you know you didn't sleep with her?"

"Because my roommate, Sloane was pissed when he came home ten minutes after me and found me passed out in his bed, fully clothed. And not only that, I've been known to suffer from whiskey dick, so even if I could get it up, there was no way I was going to come. You're the only woman I've never had that problem with."

"But still..."

"There was a paternity test, Katie, just to be sure. There is absolutely no chance I am that little girl's father."

"Oh," was all she said.

"How do you even know about Janet?"

"When Sam started Outer Limits..."

He interrupted with a groan. "Goddammit. I'm sorry you two got sucked into the gossip. Thank you for asking me about it and letting me explain the truth."

"I didn't think the rumors were true, given how much of their information about us they had wrong."

He winked with a smile. "That's my girl."

She smiled her fake, dismissive smile again, the one he fucking hated, and he stood up, withdrawing his billfold from his back pocket and tossing a five-dollar bill down on the counter.

"What's that for? You didn't have anything but water."

"I'm hoping you'll sell me one of those Scotch-a-thingys. They look fucking delicious, and I haven't had homemade cookies since you made me chocolate chip ones before I left. You know, I took those to Afghanistan and rationed them out, so they lasted a whole month?"

"I would have sent you more if you would have given me the address," she chastised.

"I know I fucked a lot of things up, Kitten, and I know I have a lot of things to make up to you. So, I'll see you tomorrow, and the next day, and the next, until you agree to at least let me take you and Sam to the zoo. Then I'll be back until you go to dinner with me."

"What if I'm dating someone?" she asked, putting her hand on her hip.

That made his stomach feel like he'd just been punched. "Are you?"

She looked away and began to pick at something on the counter. "Well, no, but..."

"I'll see you tomorrow, Kitten."

"Stop calling me that," she said although it was a lot less defiantly than she had earlier. "And I'm not working tomorrow or Monday."

He wondered what she'd do if he showed up at her apartment.

"So, about that brownie..."

She laughed and walked to the plate covered in plastic wrap, pulling one from the pile. "They're Scotcheroos. And take your money, this one's on the house. Thank you for your service," she said as she handed it to him on a napkin.

He took a bite and smiled. "Oh, no. These are worth at least ten. I think they might be my new favorite." Turning on his heel, without collecting his money, he walked out the front door that jingled to announce his departure.

This wasn't a lost cause, but he definitely had his work cut out for him. Hopefully, she came around before he had to leave again.

Chapter Forty-Two

Kate

How the hell does that man manage to throw me off my high horse every single time?

As he sat at the diner counter, she was properly pissed off at the lack of communication from him, yet somehow, he walked out of Frank's with a Scotcheroo in his hand and a five-dollar bill on the counter while her anger had been abated, and she was actually considering going to the zoo with him. So much for her righteous indignation.

Damn that man and his stupid, handsome face and sexy smile.

"Looks like someone's a smitten kitten, again," Carol teased when she reappeared to help roll silverware.

"I am so pathetic."

"No, you're not. He's a charming, good-looking man, it's easy to fall back under his spell."

"Maybe...."

"Don't beat yourself up, Katie Kat. There are worse things you could do than Cooper Johnson again. But... I am going to help you out and offer you my Sunday shift tomorrow, so you don't say yes to going out with him tomorrow," Carol said with a grin.

"You need me to work for you, tomorrow? What's going on?"

"Ray's company is having a picnic, and he thinks we should go. He's kind of being a stubborn mule about it, actually. I told him I'd see if I could my shift covered, but if not, he'll have to go without me."

"Of course, I'll cover for you. Let me just call Mrs. Neal and see if she's available."

"Thank you. To be honest, I really need to go. The slutty receptionist has been extra-flirty with him lately, so I definitely need to go and stake my claim and let the bitch know what's up."

That made her laugh out loud as she made her way to the break room to call Mrs. Neal.

"Oh, Minette, I am going to stay at Paul's tomorrow for a few days. He's still having a lot of trouble getting around."

"Oh, no! I'm sorry to hear that. Of course, you should go be with him. I can take him to Outer Limits, no problem."

"I'm sorry, Kate."

"Mrs. Neal, don't give it a second thought. Thank you for taking care of him tonight. I hope we're not keeping you from him."

"Not at all, I was never planning on leaving until the morning."

"I'll see you later."

Kate hung up the phone and sat at the old table that had been taken off the dining room floor because it was in such disrepair. Staring at the cracks, scratches, and dents on the fake, wooden linoleum top, she debated making her next phone call. She had lied to Mrs. Neal, Sam couldn't go to Outer Limits tomorrow. His forty hours were already accounted for this week between her classes, mandatory study group, and work.

She did say she wouldn't have offered if she didn't mean it.

Kate scrolled through the digital phonebook on her phone, pausing when *Cassie Rivas* appeared. She traced her hand back and forth over a scuff on the table as she deliberated hitting *send*. Then she thought about how much Carol had done for her over the years, and it became an easy button to push.

****

"Thanks again for doing this, Cassie. I don't normally work Sundays, but they needed me today."

The beautiful blonde waved her hand dismissively. "Please, I'm happy to do it."

"I should only be about six hours. I'll get here as soon as I can."

They started walking toward the front door of Cassie and Luke's beautiful beachfront home.

"It's absolutely no problem. The two boys tire each other out, and Sofia Claire loves to watch them, so it's really a win all the way around for me. I'll talk to you when you get back. I hear you ran into Cooper the other night."

She hesitated in what to disclose. Kate knew where Cassie's loyalties lie. "He says he's going to keep coming until I agree to go out with him again."

Cassie cocked her head and furrowed her brows. "At GolfPlus?"

Kate drew a quick breath. So, Cassie had heard about Friday night. "Oh, no. GolfPlus was awful. No, at the diner."

She turned the doorknob and hesitated when Cassie said, "He was trying to make you jealous, you know. He thought you were there on a date with Jason Ellers."

The waitress burst out laughing. "Oh, I think Heather Ellers would definitely have something to say about that."

"That's what I told him. I'm glad he went to find you at the diner. I'm assuming he tried to apologize and fix it?"

"In a way only Cooper can."

Cassie gave a closed-mouth smile and leaned her head against the frame of her door. "There's a lot more to Cooper than meets the eye. He really does love you, Katie."

Kate frowned. She didn't really want to discuss this with Cassie at all, but especially not right now when she had to leave for work. Still, she couldn't help but add, "Then why did he forget about us for over four months? Even once he got back?"

"He never forgot about you. He's been watching over you from a distance. Didn't you ever wonder who Ellen Jurden was?"

What was Cassie saying? Was the woman named for Sam's scholarship made up?

"I don't understand..."

"Google Ellen Jurden. I think that will explain a lot. I've already said entirely too much."

What the hell was she talking about?

Kate didn't know how she made it to the diner, but the next thing she knew, she was pulling into the parking lot.

She'd never cursed not having a data plan on her phone more than right now.

I wonder if I could just buy like an hour's worth of data?

What did Cassie mean, he's been watching over me from a distance?

Why the fuck isn't T-Mobile's customer service open on Sundays?

She definitely didn't earn her tips that day. Fortunately, most of Sunday's customers were regulars who were willing to cut her a little slack now and then. They knew she was a single mom, going to school full-time, so they were still generous even though she probably didn't deserve it.

Kate had been apprehensive about the prospect of Cooper showing up today. She knew herself and knew she'd blurt out, "Who is Ellen Jurden?" the second she saw him. The young woman had absolutely no finesse when it came to matters that undoubtedly would be better handled with some tact and decorum. Kate was far too impatient for subtlety and restraint. The same impatience that was driving her crazy she couldn't just look it up on her phone.

After she'd finally finished her shift, she sheepishly approached Frank.

"Can I quick look something up on your computer? It will take like two minutes. I promise it's nothing inappropriate."

He eyed her for a second. She'd never once asked to use his internet or computer in all the years she'd worked for him.

"Does it have anything to do with that Marine who keeps spending money here?"

"No, nothing like that," she lied. "It's about Sam's preschool scholarship."

He looked at her skeptically but gestured toward his office. "Two minutes," he growled as he walked in and unlocked this computer screen.

"Two minutes, that's all I need."

The search took all of thirty seconds, but trying to read the information through the tears streaming down her face took way more than two minutes.

She couldn't believe he'd done that for them. That he'd done such a thing and not told her, although she understood why he didn't. She never would have accepted his kindness if he had, and Sam would be in a crappy preschool while she was scraping to make rent on time every month, and she certainly wouldn't be a semester and a half away from graduating with her degree.

"You have to help me," she pleaded when Cassie opened her front door.

Chapter Forty-Three

Cooper

"So, I'm bringing Sam home when I pick Lucas up from daycare tomorrow and have been given permission to let him go to the zoo with you," Cassie told him on the phone Sunday night.

"You are? How'd you swing that?"

"Katie asked if I could help her out. I told her it would be my pleasure."

"Oh yeah? What time are you picking them up?"

"Around one."

"Can I just pick them up from Outer Limits and save you the trip?"

"Wow, that actually would be really helpful. Thank you. I'll leave Lucas' car seat with Miriam for you. When do you think you'll bring them home?"

"Well, after we stop for hamburgers and milkshakes, probably about five thirty. Should I plan on dropping Sam off at Katie's?"

Cassie's pause was too long for his liking. "No, he's spending the night here."

"Why? She doesn't work on Mondays."

"She's got plans..."

"What kind of plans?" he snarled.

"Coop, I don't know. I didn't give her the third degree when she asked if he could sleep over. She said she was going out, and I said he could stay overnight. I asked if she would mind if you took him and Lucas to the zoo because I knew you would appreciate that, and she said that would be alright. It was that simple."

"Maybe she has something for school," he said out loud, in an attempt to find a reason she would be out late that didn't involve her being on a date with another man.

"Maybe." Cassie didn't sound convinced.

"Is there something you're not telling me?"

"What? No! Of course not." Her voice was way too high-pitched to be believable.

"Cassie Sullivan Rivas, I know you're lying to me."

"I am not lying to you, Cooper... whatever-your-middle-name-is Johnson.

He wanted to call bullshit, but she had done him a solid by getting Kate to agree to let him take Sam to the zoo, so he was going to drop it for now. He'd interrogate her tomorrow in person, it would be easier to break her that way.

"I'll see you tomorrow, lady. And you better be ready to 'fess up to whatever you're hiding."

"Have fun at the zoo. I'll let the school know to expect you between twelve-thirty and one."

"Sounds like a plan. If I didn't say it earlier, thanks for doing that, Cass. It means a lot."

"I know you love that little boy."

"I love your kids too, ya know."

"I know you do, but I know you want to be a dad to Sam. And for the record, I think you would be an amazing father."

"Tell that to Katie, would ya?"

"Nope. I'm keeping my mouth shut and minding my own business when it comes to you two."

"Aw, you're no fun," he teased.

"That's not what my husband says."

"Luke's a lucky man, Cass. I hope he knows that."

"He does. This conversation is getting too sappy for me. I'll talk to you tomorrow. Sweet dreams."

Cooper set the phone on his bed and smiled. He really would be an amazing dad. God, he'd love the opportunity. Katie Connelly was going to fall in love with him again, dammit. He was on a mission.

****

"So, what was your favorite part this time?" he asked the two boys in the back seat although he already had an idea.

"Lions!" they shouted in unison.

It was a beautiful autumn day in San Diego, and the lions had been particularly active this visit and had put on quite the show.

"Yeah, me too."

"It's getting kind of late, and I promised Lucas' mom I'd have you home by five-thirty, so no messing around in the play area today guys, sorry."

"That's okay," Sam said. "I'm kind of tired, anyway."

"Yeah, me too."

Cass was going to love him forever for that.

"So, what's your mommy doing tonight, Sam?"

"I don't know. I saw her laying out pretty clothes on her bed, and she had a nightgown with the price things she was cutting off with scissors."

Cooper remembered he'd ruined her sexy one and scowled.

"What color was it, Sam?"

"Red."

Goddammit.

"But you don't know where she's going?"

"Nu-uh. She just said she'd see me tomorrow. She seemed excited though. She kept smiling all night."

This was not good. He was going to grill Cassie when he dropped the two boys off. Cooper knew she knew more than she was letting on.

As luck would have it, or maybe it was purposefully planned, Luke was the only one home when they arrived.

"Where's your wife?" Cooper tried to ask as nonchalantly as he could. Luke already had a tendency to be a bit jealous when it came to Cassie.

"I don't know," the SWAT sergeant said with a sigh. "She put Sofia down for a nap, said she had to run out for a bit, and I couldn't leave because you were bringing the boys home, then took off."

Just then his phone dinged with a text from Craig.

Craig Baxter: Dinner and drinks in thirty at O'Malley's.

Cooper: I'm not home and really should change before heading out.

Craig Baxter: Unless you're coming from the gym or playing basketball, I'm sure you're fine. Your ass better be there.

He gave Sam and Lucas another hug, shook Luke's hand, and headed out the door. He hadn't been to O'Malley's since before he left, and he was a little concerned about what Craig had planned, given the amount of female company he'd had lined up at GolfPlus.

Then again, Katie had an overnight date. And she'd bought new red lingerie. Maybe he'd see where the night took him.

Chapter Forty-Four

Kate

"Luke says he just left, so I'm going to head out," Cassie said as she looked at her phone, then leaned in to hug her. "Good luck." The new mom giggled, "I'm so excited for you two!"

Cassie had picked up Kate and drove her to Cooper's so Kate's car wouldn't be there when Cooper got home. Cassie had a key to Cooper's place to let Kate in, then went around the house helping her 'establish the mood'—lighting candles, putting champagne in the ice bucket, firing up the hot tub, and putting flower petals on the bed. It was by far, the most romantic thing Kate had ever done, and she was nervous as hell.

She'd baked him a batch of Scotcheroos and had them sitting on the counter with a big red bow so they would be the first thing he saw when he walked in the house, followed by her sitting in her new red teddy at his table wearing her sexy, red CFM shoes.

Even though she was relatively certain he still wanted her, putting herself in a position to be rejected was nerve-wracking. She wasn't exactly fond of being vulnerable.

Cassie left, and Katie sat at the kitchen table, adjusting her position every ten seconds, trying to come up with a sexy pose. She held her breath every time a car drove by and even snuck to the front window a few times, but no Cooper.

After ninety minutes, she called Cassie. "Um, he's not here yet?"

"*He's not there yet?!*"

"No, do you think I should call an Uber?"

"No," the older woman commanded. "You stay right there. I'll get back to you in a few minutes."

*

Cooper

Cassie's name showed up on his screen as an incoming call. He knew she was calling to hear about the zoo, but it was too loud in here, and his words would probably be slurring at this point.

"Don't answer that," the redhead purred in his ear as she slid her hand in his.

"Wasn't planning on it," he chuckled and clicked the button to send his friend to voicemail.

His phone immediately began buzzing again. Could the woman not take a hint? He clicked it to voicemail yet again. When she called a third time, he knew something was going on, so he stood and excused himself from the sweet little thing who'd been showering him with attention all night and headed to the front door where it was quieter.

"What's up, Cass?"

"Cooper, where the fuck are you right now?"

"I'm at O'Malley's with friends, why?"

"You need to get your ass home. Right. Now."

He'd imbibed just enough that her bossiness kind of pissed him off.

"I don't need to get my ass anywhere but back to my table and the little redhead waiting for me."

"Cooper. I am telling you, you need to go home. *Alone. Now.*"

"And I'm telling you, *no, I don't.*" He held the phone so he could properly yell into the receiver, then brought it back to his ear. "I know you know Katie's out on a date tonight. Why the fuck shouldn't I be too?"

"Ohmygod, you are such a fucking dimwit. Katie is at your house, waiting for you, you big fucking jarhead moron.

He blinked, the alcohol making his brain fuzzy. Did he hear her right? "Katie's at my house?"

"In a red negligee with candles and champagne, last I knew. But that was *two hours* ago."

"Oh God, Cass," he groaned. "Why didn't you tell me?"

"Because it was supposed to be a surprise, dumbass.

"Fuuuuuuuuck!" he shouted to no one in particular. "I gotta go. I gotta get an Uber. Fuuuuuuck!" he yelled again. "I hope they aren't busy tonight."

"Get on it. I'll do my best to stall Katie and keep her from leaving."

He was on his app, hitting *XL, X, Select, Black Car*, he didn't care as long as it got him home fast. His wallet lucked out, an X was waiting right around the corner. The redhead came out—he'd never caught her name—and snuggled in next to him.

"Are we leaving?"

"I am, sweetheart, but I'm afraid I'm going by myself."

Her eyes flashed, and she took a step back. She was obviously not used to rejection.

"You're leaving?"

"Yeah, I am. I've got some things I need to take care of."

"Are you coming back?"

"Nope. Have a good night."

"You didn't even pay our bill."

Shit. He hadn't. His ride rolled up just then, so Cooper pulled a fifty from his wallet and handed it to her asking, "Can you take care of it?"

"Sure." She snatched the money from him and grinned like the Cheshire cat, then walked toward the parking lot. He was in too much of a hurry to give a shit. He'd text Craig and have him cover it. Just then, his server came running out the door, thinking he was dining and dashing. Which, in a sense, he was.

"Sir, you forgot to pay."

He looked over where red had disappeared and sighed. The only thing left in his pocket was a hundred, so he handed it to the frazzled server with a lame, "I thought she covered it, I'm sorry," then jumped in the back seat of the waiting car.

At least he got an X.

****

Not having his garage door opener, he walked in the front door, and the first thing he noticed was her bag sitting in the entry. She was still there, that was a start. He picked it up and began to walk through the house looking for her, setting it down when he reached his bedroom.

Katie was walking through the sliding glass door in his room—he noted the cover was crooked on his spa—dressed in jeans and a t-shirt, the smell of candle smoke filling the room like she'd just blown them out, and there was a pile of rose petals on the edge of the bed she immediately began sweeping into her hand.

"Hey," he called from the doorway.

She jumped with a gasp and put one hand to her chest. "Oh my goodness, you scared me!"

He looked around at the bedroom. "I fucked this whole thing up, didn't I?"

With a small smile, she squatted and tended to the task of collecting the petals she'd dropped on the floor. "It's my fault, I shouldn't have done something like this."

Cooper crossed the room and knelt down in front of her so he was at an even height with her and grabbed her hands to get her to stop picking up the flowers.

"No, Kitten, this was wonderful. I'm so happy you're here. I'm sorry I didn't get here earlier. Can we start over?"

She gave him that placating fake smile, the one he fucking hated. "I think the mood's lost."

"It doesn't have to be. Come on..." He stood, tugging her up with him, and took the flower petals from her hand, scattering them back across the bed, then went to light the candles. They were burned down and impossible to light. *Shit*, she had waited a long time for him.

"It's okay, Cooper. Really."

He reached for her hand. "Let's have a drink."

"It smells like you've already had quite a few."

"I'm not drunk if that's what you think. Not anymore. Seeing you in my bedroom sobered me right up."

She looked down at the floor and whispered, "I shouldn't have sprung this on you. I'm so sorry. It seemed like a good idea at the time."

The Marine slid his arm around her waist, pulling her into him and bit back a groan. Fuck, he'd missed the feel of her against him. With his other hand, he traced his fingertips along her jawline before lowering his mouth to hers. She reciprocated without hesitation, and he pressed her into his growing cock between them.

Breaking the kiss, Cooper rested his forehead against hers before murmuring, "Katie, this is the best surprise I've ever gotten. I feel terrible for ruining it. Had I known... God, baby, I would have been here hours ago."

"I was still in my red lingerie then," she teased with a wink, "and heels."

This time he didn't disguise his groan. "Ohhhhh fuuuuck, Kitten. Can you... will you?" He gestured to her bag.

She smiled a real smile and grabbed his hand. "Later, I promise. I think we need to talk first."

He sighed and stepped back as his body slouched. "Is this one of those we can still be friends talks? Because if it is, I'd rather not."

"You'd rather not be friends?"

"Only if I'm your lover, too. Katie, I'm so fucking in love with you, I can't be anything else. It would kill me to be anything else."

"What about my son's tuition benefactor?"

Cooper narrowed his eyes. "What do you know about that?"

"Everything," she challenged with her eyebrows raised.

"Define everything." He was thirty-five years old. He'd learned a thing or two over the years, and he wasn't coming clean until he knew for sure what she knew.

"I know you are Ellen Louise Jurden's oldest grandchild, and you have been paying Sam's tuition to go to Outer Limits. Am I missing anything?"

Nope, that about sums it up.

He scrubbed the back of his neck with his hand. "Let me explain."

"No," she shook her head. "You let me talk first."

He nodded his head and folded his arms across his chest as he braced himself for an ass chewing. "Go ahead."

"That was the most wonderful thing you could have ever done for us. Thank you. I wish I had known sooner it was you."

He lowered his arms as he waited for the *but*.

"I don't think you realize how much it's affected both mine and Sam's lives. It's let me go to school full-time, which means I'm going to graduate at least a whole year sooner than I'd planned. It's let Sam be in a great school where he feels cared for and safe, so I'm not a nervous wreck when I have to leave him at daycare. It's let me have enough money at the

349

end of the month, I've actually been able to save a little. Not a lot, but at least I'm not robbing Peter to pay Paul anymore." She wiped the tears from her eyes. "I understand why you didn't want me to know it was you. I probably would have been stubborn and not accepted it had I known."

He was still waiting for the *but* and said out loud, "But...?"

She reached for his hand again. "But I just want you to know, I will be forever in your debt."

Cooper ran his thumb back and forth across her knuckles. "I didn't do it so you'd be in my debt, Katie. I would have preferred you never know for exactly that reason. I want you in my bed forever, not my debt."

"I don't think you understand how much it has meant to us. You have done so much for Sam and me in the little amount of time we've known you. I'm just so grateful."

"How about you put that red nightie and those heels on right now, and bake me cookies once a week, and we'll call it even?"

"I'm serious," she scolded, her hand going to her hip.

He took the hand planted on her hip, brought it to his shoulder, and wrapped her in his embrace.

"I am too," he murmured against her ear. "I love you, Katie. And I love Sam. Making you two happy makes me happy."

"You make me so happy," she murmured against his chest.

"Then my work here is done," he chuckled.

Katie began stroking his cock over his jeans. "Not quite."

"I'm serious about wanting to see you in that nightie and heels," he growled.

Arching back in his arms, she looked up at him with an accusing scowl. "Are you going to rip it off me this time?"

"I can't make any promises other than if I do, I will owe you two," he said as he gave her ass a squeeze, then released his grip on her.

She walked over and picked up her bag before heading toward the bathroom, calling over her shoulder, "I'm going to hold you to that."

"Baby girl, you can hold me to any damn thing you want."

Please do.

Chapter Forty-Five

Kate

Her body was buzzing as she changed *again*. This wasn't the way she'd envisioned the night would go, but it almost seemed fitting that the sexy times she had so carefully planned fell apart, but they still somehow ended up happening.

Prophetic much?

Her high red heels were far from glass slippers, but as she looked at herself in the mirror, she conceded they were probably a fuck of a lot sexier.

She fluffed her hair and reapplied red lipstick before she walked back out into his bedroom. He was on top of the covers with rose petals all around him, a bulge in his gray boxer briefs—just like she expected—and his fingers laced behind his head as he waited patiently for her.

She wished she'd had that drink he'd suggested as she walked toward the bed, his entire focus on her every move. Knowing her luck, she'd trip and fall and ruin the seductive moment. Luckily, she made it without incident, and he let out a low growl when she started crawling up the bed to him.

"Goddamn, Kitten. I swear to God, you get sexier every time I see you."

She smirked as she ran her hand up his inner thigh. She *felt* sexy right now.

"You are sexy all the time," she purred and dipped her head between his legs. His sharp intake of breath as she began to mouth his cock over the fabric of his underwear was exactly what she was hoping for. She breathed hot air onto his dick and moaned as she breathed in his scent.

"Baby, I need to take a shower. I took the boys to the zoo, and I probably smell like a bar."

He definitely didn't smell like a bar. He smelled like a man, and she was surprised at how turned on it was making her. He wasn't dirty or stinky, that would probably be a turnoff, but he just smelled... sexy. Did that make her a freak?

"I like the way you smell," she murmured as she continued tending to his bulge, slipping her hand under the waistband and finding his velvety head already slick with his own arousal. She smeared the precum around the tip with her thumb, then tugged his boxer briefs down until his cock sprang free.

"God, I've missed that," she half-whispered, half-groaned as she took in the sight of his dick.

"He's missed you, too."

Kate closed her eyes as she ran his warm shaft reverently across her cheeks. He was rock hard, yet velvety soft and smooth, and she loved the way he felt against her face.

"I know this is going to make me sound super slutty, but I would love for you to come on my face tonight." His cock jumped in her hand against her cheek. "I've never had a man do that, and it seems like it would be really sexy."

"I've never done that either. It's always seemed like it would be too disrespectful or too intimate, I can't decide."

"It's not disrespectful if I want it, is it?"

"No, it's fucking hot.

"Would it be too intimate?"

353

"Katie, nothing with you would be too intimate. You're the only woman I've ever trusted enough to want to do every kinky fantasy I've ever had with. And I want to fulfill every desire and fantasy you have, so baby girl, if me glazing your face tonight is something you desire, then really, it's my obligation as your man to do that for you. I'm a giver that way," he smirked with a wink.

"You don't think it's too dirty?"

"Fuck no. It's tame compared to what I'm going to do to you—eventually. Not necessarily tonight, but we've got all the time in the world to explore together."

"Good," she muttered as she engulfed his cock all the way to the base.

"Holy fucking shit," he snarled, and she couldn't help but smile. She loved turning him on. It made her feel desired, yet powerful.

She held him in her throat and felt his cock pulse, then withdrew, making his shaft wet and slippery for her to run her hand up and down while she continued sucking him. His moans and gasps provided her all the encouragement she needed.

Cooper dug his fingers in her hair and tugged her lips off him.

"Baby girl, you need to stop."

He was holding her head still, but she continued stroking him although slowing her pace.

"Why?" she teased.

"Katie, it's been over four months. You're killing me, Kitten."

He pulled on her arms until she was flush with his chest, and she captured his mouth with hers, seeking to tangle with his tongue. This being in control thing was addicting. Power was sexy.

As he flipped her over and took the reins, she admitted submitting to Captain Cooper Johnson also had its merits.

Cooper caressed her jawline, looking into her eyes.

"I love you, Katie Connelly. I've been so fucking lost without you. Promise me this is for keeps, that you're all in."

She reached up and mimicked his caress. "I'm all in," she whispered without hesitation. Pulling his head closer so she could whisper in his ear seductively, she lifted her hips suggestively against his, "You need to be all in, baby. Every. Inch."

He grinned at her innuendo and kissed her as he rubbed her slit over her red, satin panties. Kate could feel how wet she was.

"You're so wet for me, Kitten," he praised while slipping a finger under the fabric. She gasped when he slid a digit inside her and spread her legs wider for him.

He tugged on the scraps of her fabric at her hips. "I'm trying really hard not to tear these off, baby girl, but they need to go *now*."

She hooked her thumbs under the miniscule waistband and dispatched the garment in one fell swoop while he looked on with a smirk then spread her with his fingers.

"That's better," he murmured before running his tongue from her from ass to clit. "Goddamn, Katie, you taste fucking delicious."

He continued attending to her pussy with his tongue, then began to flick her clit as he pushed two fingers deep inside her and began to slowly finger fuck her. He took his time licking her, exploring her, in no particular hurry to reach his ultimate destination.

It was sexy as fuck being lavished with his attention while he seemed to be in no rush to do anything but enjoy her. She soon, however, found herself lifting her hips to his mouth, goading him to increase the tempo and pressure.

"Please, Cooper," she begged in frustration.

Kate felt him smile against her folds. "Do you want to come, Kitten?"

"Yes, baby. God, yes. Please," she panted, bucking her hips against him again.

He continued to leisurely finger her, asking, "Whose pussy is this?" as he slammed his fingers in her deeper.

"Yours," she moaned and arched her back.

"My pussy," he reiterated while picking up the pace.

He spread her apart with two fingers and began to lick her faster, matching the speed of his hand. Soon, she felt her toes starting to curl, and her stomach tighten.

"Oh, fuck, Cooper, don't stop," she pleaded.

He growled against her clit, "Not. Stopping," then started to hum.

Hum.

He was fucking humming while eating her pussy. The vibrations caused her to lurch forward.

"Ohhhhhh fuck yesssssssss!" she cried out as her orgasm crashed into her. He kept his tempo, not letting up until she was begging him to stop, pushing his head away while she tried to close her legs.

She lay staring at the ceiling, trying to catch her breath, but Cooper climbed her body and burrowed his face into her neck while he thrust his cock inside, not giving her any respite.

"Ohmygod, you feel so good," she crooned. Her orgasm made his cock inside her feel even more amazing.

"My. Pussy," he snarled through gritted teeth as he banged into her tight entrance. "Mine."

"Yours," she agreed with a breathy whisper.

He leaned back and reached down to pinch her clit while moving in and out of her. He tugged and twisted it like he sometimes did her nipples, and it sent her careening over the edge again.

"That's it, baby girl, come all over my cock," he encouraged as she was happily obliging him. He started to grunt like a caveman and held her hips while slamming deep inside her. His low, feral growl while he found his release was the sexiest sound ever.

Cooper collapsed to the side of her, his cock still buried in her pussy, his arms around her shoulders. After his breathing leveled out, he rolled off her, his hand moved from her shoulder to her breast, and he began to fondle her like her tits soothed him while he stroked her hair with his other hand.

"I didn't come on your face, baby."

"Next time," she murmured, nestling against him as his seed trickled out of her body. She was suddenly exhausted and fell asleep without a care in the world.

*

Cooper

His girl was back in his bed where she belonged. A feeling of contentment was seeping from his pores while he held her sleeping body next to his. If he could, he'd never let her leave his side again, but since that wasn't plausible, he'd settle for holding her tonight and convincing her in the morning that being next to him was where she was meant to be every night.

For the rest of her life. With his baby growing inside her.

Maybe he should start with the moving in thing first.

She came into the kitchen the next morning clad in only one of his t-shirts, her bare ass peeking below the hem, making him have to adjust himself as he cooked breakfast.

"Good morning," she purred in his ear, wrapping an arm around his waist and kissing his cheek. Her breath smelled like the mint of his toothpaste.

He turned from the stove and pulled her into him by her naked bottom. "I like waking up with you in my bed, Kitten."

That brought a small smile to her face as she wrapped her arms around his neck. "Me, too."

He reached up, pulling a rose petal from her hair with a smirk, running it along her cheek.

"God, that was the best thing ever to come home to. I'm really sorry I kept you waiting so long, baby girl. I had no idea." She shrugged as if it wasn't a big deal, but he knew better, so he persisted. "Thank you for giving me a chance to try to make it up to you."

Her grin when she looked up at him through her lashes was contagious. "I'd say it was worth my while."

"I hope you're not too sore."

"The best kind of sore."

"Do you think you'll be feeling less sore by tonight?" he asked hopefully.

"I have to work tonight."

"So, come over afterward."

"Cooper," she sighed pulling away. "I can't keep Sam out that late."

"I'll pick him up from daycare when I get off work."

She scowled and hesitated like she was going to say no, then surprised him when she acquiesced.

"Okay, but do not get him hyped up on sugar, and he has to be in bed by eight o'clock."

"Eight o'clock," he agreed solemnly although inside he wanted to yell, "Fuck yeah!"

"And make sure he..."

"Brushes his teeth and puts his pajamas on." Cooper interrupted with a wink. "I know, Kitten. I got this."

She looked at him skeptically. "Are you sure about this?"

"Positive. He's my little dude. We'll have a blast together."

She took a deep breath. He could tell letting him in like this was hard on her, but he loved she was willing to ease up and at least try.

"What are we going to tell him?"

"That we love each other and are going to be a family someday soon."

The sooner, the better.

"What if he starts asking about you being his dad?"

He lifted her up to set her on the counter, so he was sure she was looking him in the eyes when he told her what he had to say.

"I *want* to be his dad, and the second you say it's okay, I'm telling him that."

"Don't you think we should ease him into the idea?"

"Why? He obviously adores me and would be okay with me being his dad. I love him and personally think I would be a fucking awesome dad, so why should we wait?"

"I just worry that…"

He gripped her hands and bent so his face was inches from hers. "Stop. Worrying. Katie, it's going to be okay. I promise."

She pursed her lips and chewed on her inner cheek, obviously unconvinced. He dropped a kiss on her forehead and pulled her against his chest, reiterating in her hair, "I promise."

Chapter Forty-Six

Kate

She was in new, unchartered territory, and it was scary as hell, but she resolved she was going to take the leap of faith, and there was no one she'd rather jump with than that sexy Marine.

She was so head over heels for the man, it wasn't even funny. Fortunately, he seemed to feel the same about her and her son. It'd been five days since she surprised him at his house, and they'd spent every night together ever since, with only one of those being at her apartment. She knew he was much more comfortable in his bed, and she didn't blame him, so she didn't put up much of a fuss when he'd push for them to go to his house.

He'd left Sammy's room in place even after they'd broken up, which to her, spoke volumes. He hadn't given up on her. God, she was grateful for that. She noticed Sam's drawers had new clothes in them and called him out on it when she opened one after noticing it wasn't closed all the way.

"Have you been buying him clothes?"

He looked up from the area rug he was playing cars on with Sam, unapologetically replying, "Yeah. He needs stuff for when he's here."

"I can just bring a suitcase or backpack when we stay, you know."

"I don't want him living out of a suitcase. Or you either, for that matter."

She knew where he was going with this, but this wasn't a discussion to have in front of Sam.

"When did you buy all that?"

"When we bought my cowboy costume," her son interjected. *Ah, little pitchers.*

Cooper saw the opportunity for a change of subject. "Hey, speaking of which, I thought we should trick-or-treat in this neighborhood if that's okay? I usually try to avoid being home on Halloween, but I am willing to bet it's probably the most kid-friendly subdivision in San Diego County when it comes to trick-or-treaters."

Based on the number of houses in the community decorated for the holiday, she'd be willing to agree with his assessment. Even Cooper and Sam had hung up lights in his front yard, put out scarecrows and witches, hung plastic ghosts from his trees, and bought pumpkins to carve.

"Oh, um, okay? We've never really trick-or-treated before. Mrs. Neal's women's group had a party at the community center last year we went to, and they passed out candy to kids in costumes."

"It'll be fun," he assured her. "Should we dress up, too? We've been invited to a party Saturday night, but that's a grown-up party. You probably will want to wear an entirely different costume to that. Something in the medical field, perhaps." His grin made the meaning behind that unmistakable.

She raised one eyebrow along with one corner of her mouth. "Oh? You don't think I should wear a nurse's costume trick-or-treating?"

"It would probably be uncomfortable traversing the neighborhood in those red heels."

"I think you should be a cowgirl, and Coopah should be a sheriff," her little boy spoke up.

"Yeah, Mommy, you should be a cowgirl, and I can be a sheriff."

She knew just what to say to get Cooper's goat. "Don't you think Cooper should be G.I. Joe, baby? He'd make a good Army man."

Unfortunately, he knew what she was doing and wouldn't take the bait. He pulled her to where he was sitting on the floor and tugged her onto his lap.

"I think I should be a sheriff so I can arrest naughty cowgirls and put them in handcuffs. Or at least lasso them and tie them up," he snarled in her hair as his arms went around her waist.

"Are you guys going to start kissing all the time like Lucas' mommy and daddy?" Sam asked without looking up from pushing his car over the rug.

She felt the Marine chuckle underneath her. "Yeah, buddy, probably. Your mommy's pretty kissable. Sorry."

"It's okay,' the little guy approved. "Lucas told me, daddies are 'sposed to kiss mommies. When you do, that's when I'll know you are going to be my daddy."

She felt Cooper tense under her. She knew he was itching to take on that role and wanted to tell Sam just that but was waiting for her approval.

"Would you like that?" she asked cautiously.

"Yes," her son whispered.

She glanced behind her at Cooper's solemn face and nodded slightly, trying to not do it begrudgingly.

"Sam, come here," the Marine's voice was tender yet authoritative as he adjusted Kate on his lap to make room for the boy. Sam responded immediately, and Cooper situated him on his lap, along with Kate, wrapping his arms around both Connellys.

"I love you and your mom, and nothing would make me happier than to be your daddy someday."

Sam couldn't stop grinning. "I knew you would be. I knew it!"

"Slow down, baby. Cooper said *someday*. Not right now. I need to finish college and find a job before we can really talk about that."

Her son's face fell, and tears filled his eyes. "Can't he be my daddy while you're in school?"

Cooper squeezed her hip and whispered in her ear, "Yeah, Mommy, can't I be his daddy while you're still in school?"

Even though she wasn't looking at Cooper, Kate gave her best fake smile and said in a low, sing-song voice through her teeth with her lips unmoving, "You're not helping," then addressed Sam. "We'll talk about this later. It's time for you to get ready for bed."

"Aw, Mom. I'm not even tired. Can't I stay up a little longer?"

There was that *Mom* again.

*

Cooper

Was it a dick move to put her on the spot in front of Sam? *Maybe.*

Did he care? *Not really.*

Actually, that wasn't true. Of course, he cared, he didn't want her pissed off at him. He just was tired of her dragging her feet for phantom reasons involving her son. He and Sammy were thick as thieves, and Cooper wasn't going anywhere. She needed to lighten the hell up and let the boy see him as his dad. Because that's what he was officially going to be, and soon if he had anything to say about it.

"Come on, little man, let's get your toys picked up and your teeth brushed."

Sam immediately hopped off his lap and into action. Katie shot him a look, and he smiled smugly.

"Hey, people respect my authoritah," he teased, quoting Cartman from Southpark.

She rolled her eyes, but the corners of her mouth curled up.

I'm going to be a great dad, Kitten.

That might have been up for debate later in the week when Katie came to his house after working until seven. Cooper had picked up Sam and Lucas early from daycare and took them for ice cream. When they arrived at the Rivas household, they discovered Luke had brought home a new foster dog. The eleven-month-old Pitbull was grey and white and fucking adorable, and he and Sam bonded immediately. What was Cooper supposed to do?

"Mommy!" Sam shrieked, running full speed at Katie when she walked in the door. She bent down to hug him, and he exclaimed, "Coopah got me a dog!"

Way to throw me under the bus right from the get-go, kid.

Katie stood up straight with her eyebrows raised and looked around. "He did? What does that mean? Like a stuffed one?"

"No, he's outside right now, but Coopah says he can sleep with me if I want him to. Come on, I want you to meet Petey." Sam started tugging on her hand to lead her to the kitchen and the sliding glass door where his new dog was. Katie shot Cooper a bewildered look as she let her son drag her outside.

Petey's butt began to wiggle at the sight of Sam, and when the boy approached the pup, he was greeted with endless kisses.

Katie stood watching, her arms folded and a scowl on her face.

He stood by her and put his hand around her hip.

"What's wrong? You're not upset I got him a Pitbull, are you? They used to be known as nanny dogs before assholes started fighting them and giving them a bad rap."

"No," she shook her head, "I know they're good dogs unless they're raised not to be."

"Then what's wrong?"

"This is really something you should have discussed with me, Cooper. We can't have a dog at Mrs. Neal's, and even if we could, I really don't have time to take care of a dog right now."

"Well, I was planning on keeping him here, and Sam understands a dog is a big responsibility, and he has to be willing to make sure he gets fed every day, twice a day."

She smiled. "So, really, he's your dog."

"No, Petey is not my dog. Petey is Sam's dog. Sam's responsibility. Of course, I will help because that's what dads do, but he's not my dog."

Her scowl was back. "You should have discussed this with me."

Shit. She was right, he should have. But Sam was so in love with the dog and vice versa.

"You're right, baby, I should have. I'm sorry. I don't know what I was thinking."

Well, what he was thinking was this was another reason for them to move in with him. But seeing it from her perspective, he realized he'd been way too rash.

"I'll talk to Luke about finding him another home."

She spun around and looked at him like he'd just said he liked to eat kittens for breakfast.

367

"You can't do that now. Those two are already attached—look at them." She gestured to Sam and his pup running around the backyard.

"Well, I don't want you mad at me, so what am I supposed to do?"

She rubbed her eyes and sighed. "Just promise you'll talk to me before doing anything that's going to need more than a day's worth of our attention."

He brought both arms around her waist and whispered sheepishly in her ear, "I promise. I'm sorry, Kitten. I just got caught up in seeing him so happy."

"He can't always be happy, Cooper, it's not a bad lesson to learn. Sometimes, he's going to be disappointed."

He looked over at the little boy shrieking with joy and shrugged. "Not if I can help it, he won't be."

She shoved at his chest and groaned, "Ohmygod, you are impossible. We're not going to raise a spoiled rotten brat."

He couldn't stop grinning. She'd said *we*. *We're* not going to raise a spoiled rotten brat.

"Can we spoil the sixth one?"

"The *sixth*? Just how many kids do you plan on having?"

"Four more," he said grinning.

"Well, then you better find yourself a baby mama who will do that for you."

"Okay, fine," he sighed. "How many more can we have?"

"Let's see how we're feeling after the next one."

Cooper grinned again, feeling like a sly mother fucker. He'd just gotten Katie to agree to have a baby with him.

Chapter Forty-Seven

Kate

"Teacher says you're 'sposed to check my candy before I can have any," her little cowboy said in Cooper's living room, handing her his bag of trick-or-treating loot.

"If you find any Kit Kats, you probably should let me inspect them," Cooper said, walking into the living room and sitting on the couch directly behind where she was sitting on the floor.

"Sam, put Petey in his crate or let him outside, so he doesn't steal any chocolate and get sick," she said, scratching the Blue Nose's ears. The dog had the nose of a Bloodhound and had been following the candy bag, staying close to whoever had it in their possession.

Her son reluctantly stood and called the dog without luck.

"I promise I won't let her start checking without your supervision," Cooper chuckled. "Try getting a dog treat out of the treat drawer."

The rustling of the imitation bacon bag did the trick, and Petey went to investigate. Cooper took the opportunity of her sitting between his legs to rub her shoulders.

"I've got some candy for you later, little girl," he murmured in her ear.

"I'm not supposed to take candy from strangers."

"I guess I'll have to find something else to entice you with then."

She moaned and rested her head on his knee. "Oh God, keep rubbing my shoulders like that, and I'll gladly get in your white, windowless van for a ride anywhere."

"Anywhere? How about to Pound Town?"

She turned slowly to look at him over her shoulder. "Did you really just say, *Pound Town*?"

He had the mindfulness to at least look embarrassed. "Yeah, I knew it was cheesy as I was saying it."

Sam reappeared and sat next to Kate on the floor, excited and antsy to examine his candy bag's contents. She dumped the bag on the floor and methodically began to inspect the wrappers. He'd gotten a serious haul tonight, people in this neighborhood were legit about their candy.

Kate started from one end of the pile, picking up and dropping the examined piece of candy back into the bag.

"Any Kit Kats in there?" Cooper asked over her shoulder.

Sammy dutifully offered him a red wrapped candy he found in the pile. She was about a quarter way through when she noticed something shiny underneath a Twizzlers package.

"What is that?" she murmured out loud. At first, she thought it was a toy, but when she pulled it closer for further inspection, she realized the diamond ring she was looking at was real. It took her a second to put two and two together. Her immediate thought was it had slipped off the finger of a woman handing out candy, then she noticed her son's intent look and Cooper, who was now at her side on one knee.

He grabbed the hand she had slipped the ring onto above the first knuckle of her index finger and brought it to his lips.

"Katie Connelly, I am so in love with you. I want to start our life together as a family. I want to officially be Sam's dad and have more babies with you. I want to come home every night to my wife and kids and wake up every morning next to you. Please marry me, Kitten. Say you and Sam will be mine forever."

Tears were streaming down her face. Wasn't this too soon? Shouldn't she wait? Then she heard her son whisper, "Say yes, Mommy," and suddenly, the answer was crystal clear.

"Yes," she murmured softly, looking up at the sexy Marine who was staring at her intently, waiting for an answer. "I would love to marry you."

He wrapped his arms around her and kissed her, then drew Sam in for a group hug.

"You're going to be my daddy," Sammy whispered in awe as he leaned his head against the Marine's shoulder. "I'm going to have a daddy."

Cooper planted a long kiss on top of the little boy's head. "I promise I'll be the best daddy in the world, little man."

Kate couldn't stop the tears from flowing, and Cooper turned to wipe her cheeks with his thumbs. "And I promise I'll be the best husband you could ever ask for, Kitten."

"I love you so much," she whimpered, trying not to sob as she said it.

That made him grin. "I love you more, baby girl." Then he squeezed Sam tight. "Both of you."

"Were you surprised, Mommy? Coopah, I mean, Daddy said you would be."

She narrowed her watery eyes at her son and let out a laugh even as she continued crying. "Did you help plan this?"

"Actually, it was his idea," Cooper volunteered. "We went to pick out the ring, and I asked when I should ask you, and he said after trick-or-treating."

"When did you pick out the ring?"

He smiled his toothpaste smile, the one that always melted her panties. "This afternoon."

*

Cooper

She fucking said yes.

Katie Connelly was going to be Katie Johnson, and Sam was going to be...

"I want to adopt Sam right after we get married. You both need to be Johnsons."

"Okay," she murmured against his chest as they laid in bed naked.

Oh, and engagement sex? *Fuck yeah.*

"Do you want a big wedding? How soon can we get married?"

She traced circles on his chest as she seemed to ponder his questions.

"No, I don't want a big wedding, just something small and intimate with our close friends and family. How about in May after I graduate?"

He shook his head. "May is too far away, Kitten. I think my promotion might come as early as January now, and it will just be easier to get your things moved if we're already married."

She sat up like a shot.

"Wait, move? I can't move, Cooper. I don't want to move. My life is here."

"When my promotion comes through, I have to move Katie. At least for a few years."

"You can't commute or something?"

"No, baby girl," he smiled wryly, "it's all the way across the country on the East Coast."

"But doesn't Brenna's husband go back and forth?"

"Ron's job is different. He's only needed in D.C. part of the time, then here the rest of the time. I would be needed on base in Virginia fulltime."

"Maybe we should wait until you come back," she whispered, and that pissed him off.

"No. I'm not waiting, Katie. You're either all in, or you're not."

"So, I'm just supposed to drop everything—school, my plans, my life here—and follow you?"

"First off, I don't expect you to drop school. But if we're married, you'll be able to afford online classes to finish your degree. As far as your future career, there are plenty of investment firms back east, probably more than are on the West Coast so you would have plenty of opportunities. As for your life here, well, I would hope I would be more important than what you have keeping you here and would want to be with me."

"You should have told me this before you asked me to marry you."

"Katie, I told you this back in May. Why would you think that changed?"

"I just…" she looked at the comforter on the bed and tugged at a loose string. "I just thought you might have changed your mind."

He tilted her chin to look at him. "Weren't you the one who told me not to do that? That I needed to pursue this?"

"Just like I need to pursue my plans, Cooper."

"So what are you saying?"

She tugged away from him and looked at the bed again.

"I don't know if I can marry you," she whispered the words so he could barely hear her.

Except he did hear her. This was supposed to be the greatest night of his life so far, and it was turning into one of the shittiest—hands down.

He plumped his pillow and positioned his body to turn his back to her. "You probably should figure that out pretty soon. Whatever you decide, I'll keep paying for Sam to go to Outer Limits whether I'm in San Diego or not. I think it's important he stays there until he starts school." *Or moves to Virginia.*

Cooper clicked off the light, leaving her still sitting up, in the dark.

"So, that's it?" She was obviously pushing for an argument.

He didn't even bother turning back to face her when he said in a low, even voice, "Yeah, Katie, that's it. Either you want to marry me and move to Virginia as my wife, or you don't. There's really no gray area on this one. You know what I hope you decide, but I'm not going to beg you to be with me."

"Unbelievable," she muttered as she flopped down on the bed. He half expected her to get up and leave, but she probably didn't want to disturb Sam at this hour. Seconds later, he did feel her get out of bed and heard her open one of his drawers and rustle around in the dark. When she laid back down, she was wearing clothing of some sort.

Having her in his bed and not hold her was killing him, especially if this was their last night together. He wasn't touching her, but he could sense her body, mere inches from his, and he had to clench his fists to keep from pulling her into his arms. Somehow, sleep kindly overtook him.

He woke up earlier than normal and took Petey for a run. The Pitbull was reluctant to leave Sammy's side but eventually, decided the temptation of the leash was too much. Cooper hoped if Katie decided to stay in San Diego, Mrs. Neal would let her keep the dog. It would be a shame to separate a boy and his dog. Or a boy and his dad, for that matter.

No, Cooper wasn't Sam's biological dad, but he didn't give two shits about the biology factor. That little boy was his. And so was the stubborn woman Sam called Mommy.

Goddammit! His level of frustration was off the charts. Why was she being so damn difficult? He understood she needed to finish school, but he didn't understand why she couldn't do that online. It would only be for one more semester. It wasn't like he was asking her to quit school or give up an established career. He was asking her to compromise in order to be with him.

Maybe she didn't love him enough to do that.

The devil on his shoulder asked, "Do you love her enough to compromise?" *Compromise? Of course.* But would he be willing to forego his promotion to be with her if she wouldn't move?

As his footsteps pounded rhythmically on the pavement in time with the jingling of Petey's tags, he knew the answer. Yeah, he would. He wouldn't like it, but he'd do it if it was the only way to be with her.

Chapter Forty-Eight

Kate

She woke up on November First in Cooper Johnson's bed with Cooper Johnson's ring on her finger, and Cooper Johnson was nowhere to be found.

He'd sprung it on her he was moving to Virginia, and he expected her to just up and marry him so she would move with him. Shouldn't that have been something they talked about before he asked her to marry him?

She'd told him she didn't know if she wanted to marry him now; that was a lie. She wanted nothing more than to marry him, she just wanted to live in San Diego after doing it.

"Do you really expect him to turn down a promotion so you can stay in San Diego, Katie Kat?" Carol asked her as they prepared for the lunch rush after almost ripping Kate's finger off to look at her engagement ring.

"No, of course not. But I would have liked him to not act like it's his way or the highway."

"So you wanted him to pretend there are other options even though there really aren't."

"Precisely."

"You understand he's a captain with the United States Marine Corps, right? He doesn't strike me as the type who's gonna pussyfoot around the obvious."

Kate sighed. *No, he's not.* And in all fairness, that was part of what she loved about him.

"I screwed up, didn't I?"

Carol scrunched her nose and nodded. "Lil' bit."

"How do I fix it?"

The redhead shrugged. "How did you fix it last time?"

Kate blushed. "Scotcheroos and sex."

Carol nodded thoughtfully. "You really can't go wrong with either."

"Any chance you're available to babysit for a while tonight?"

"For true love? Of course."

The young waitress planned what she was going to do tonight. She'd show up at his house in her long winter coat—the closest thing she had to a trench coat—with nothing but her sexy red teddy and heels underneath, a plate of the desserts in hand for him, and a heaping helping of crow for her. If all else failed, there was always groveling.

Kate picked Sam up from daycare, intending to take him home and feed him dinner before dropping him off at Carol's.

"Hey, we're going to make Cooper Scotcheroos," she told him as they drove home.

"You mean Daddy?"

That caused her to smile.

"Yes, we're going to make your daddy Scotcheroos. Then Miss Carol wants you to come over and spend some time with her tonight. She misses you."

"But I want to go with you to give Daddy the Scotcheroos. I have to feed Petey."

She knew it was important for Sam to spend time with Cooper, and she didn't feel right about keeping him from seeing the guy he was now calling dad, but she really needed to make things right with the Marine. She was debating what to do when she pulled up to her apartment and noticed Cooper's BMW parked out front.

Sam noticed it too and was unbuckling his car seat before she'd even put the car in park.

"Coopah, I mean Daddy is here!" The little guy bounced up and down in excitement, sprinting out of the car once Kate opened the rear door.

"Sam, be careful!" she called after him as she grabbed the grocery bags from the back seat, but her words fell on deaf ears—he was already scrambling up the porch steps and rounding the corner to the apartment stairs.

"Dad!" she heard him squeal as she made her way toward her apartment.

Kate wondered what he was doing here, and a sense of panic overtook her. Was he there to officially end things? She adjusted the plastic bags with the Scotcheroos ingredients and let out a puff of air to move the hair out of her eyes while walking up the apartment stairs.

Sitting on the top step with Sam already on his lap was her sexy fiancée, if she could still call him that. She decided she could since she was still wearing the ring he'd given her last night. Then she noticed the dozen red roses in green florist tissue paper and breathed a little easier. Unless he was using them to soften the blow?

"Hey," she murmured when she got two steps below him. "I didn't expect to see you here."

"We're going to make you Scotcheroos," Sam piped up.

"You are? Those are my favorite."

"Mine, too," her son agreed with the man he worshipped. "How's Petey?"

"He misses you and is hoping you come back tonight so he can sleep with you."

"See, Mommy? I can't go to Miss Carol's tonight. Petey needs me."

Cooper raised an eyebrow. "Miss Carol's?"

Sam spoke up for her. "Mommy wanted to bring you Scotcheroos by herself."

The Marine looked at Kate while replying to Sam. "She did, huh?"

"Yeah," she said softly. "I think I owe you an apology."

He looked at her intently for a minute before he spoke again. "Well, I came here to let you know I'll withdraw my promotion application..."

"No!" she burst out and set the grocery bags on the steps in order to grab his hand in hers. "You can't do that. I was wrong to act like that last night. I'm so sorry. You can't withdraw your application, baby, this is important for your future."

"For our future," he corrected and brought his hand behind her neck while leaning his forehead against hers, Sam still in his lap.

"For our future," she whispered in agreement.

****

Cooper

"So, when do you want to get married?" he asked, sitting at her kitchen table while she made the Scotchy brownie-things.

She frowned and hesitated, so he continued, "Let me rephrase. I want to get married before the end of the year. Can we do that?"

"Cooper, that's less than two months."

"I know, Kitten, I just want to be ready for whenever my promotion comes through."

"So, you want me to sign up for online classes even though there's a possibility we won't even move until May?" Her tone suggested she wasn't in love with that idea.

"I think it will definitely happen before May. The rumor mill is saying no later than the end of February."

"How about Valentine's Day then?"

"How about New Year's Eve?" he countered.

"January Eleventh, final offer."

"Why January Eleventh?"

"I dunno," she shrugged as she held the big ceramic bowl, stirring the ingredients with a wooden spoon. "We'll be done with the holidays, I like the idea of all ones in the date, and it's exactly one month after my birthday."

"January eleventh sounds perfect then. What do you think about getting married at our house? Or in the community park and having the reception in our rec center?"

She hesitated, and he knew that wasn't what she wanted.

"Or whatever you want, baby. Cost is not an issue. What's your dream wedding location?"

"I just always thought I'd get married on the beach, barefoot."

"Beach wedding it is."

"A beach wedding in January doesn't sound that appealing, Coop."

"I'm serious about money not being an issue. You want a beach wedding in January? We'll fly to Aruba and make it happen. Whatever you want, Katie."

She set the bowl down and came over to straddle his lap. "I just want to marry you," she murmured before softly kissing his lips.

Cooper squeezed her ass. "Let's get married in Aruba, barefoot on the beach, then I'll knock you up on our honeymoon." He knew he was pushing his luck, but *go big or go home*, right?

"Let me finish my degree first, soldier."

"I'm not a soldier," he corrected. "I'm a Marine. And I want to have a baby with you whenever you're ready."

"Wedding, Sam's adoption, move, degree, *then* a baby—in that order."

He was a sly mother fucker indeed. That was exactly what he wanted, too.

"Let's book the Aruba tickets tonight."

Epilogue

Katie

She'd given up going up by Kate. Everyone Cooper introduced her to called her Katie, and all her friends from work called her Katie, so while her legal name was Kate Allison Connelly Johnson, most people just knew her as Katie Johnson.

And she loved it.

Being Cooper Johnson's wife was everything she could have ever hoped for. They did get married in Aruba in front of a small group of family and friends who made the trek. It had been a weeklong party and the time of her life. True to his word, Coop made Sam's adoption official the day they returned. But his promotion took longer than he'd originally thought, and they didn't end up moving until the end of March, which Katie was glad for since the snow had melted by then. She thought it would be best if they eased into their first winter instead of moving right in the middle of it.

She did her last semester online and finished her degree, and Cooper insisted they all fly back to San Diego so she could walk in the graduation ceremony and spend some time with Mrs. Neal. He'd also been awesome in trying to help her find connections to get her career on track, but she'd decided she was going to forego that for a while.

"Where are the Scotch-a-things?" Cooper asked when he and Sam came in from playing catch.

With furrowed brows, she responded, "I didn't make Scotcheroos."

"Oh. Chocolate chip cookies then?"

She let out a small laugh. "No, I didn't make any sweets."

Now it was his turn to be confused. "You sent me a text that you made me something, I just assumed it was brownies or cookies."

She came around from the kitchen island and wrapped her arms around his waist. "Oh, that's right. I did make you something. It's in the oven."

Cooper smiled a satisfied smile and pulled the oven door down, not releasing his grasp on her ass with his other hand until he realized the oven wasn't on, and there was a note next to the most obnoxious looking bun she could find in the bakery section of the grocery store.

He unwrapped his arms from her and cocked his head, confused until he pulled the cookie sheet out.

It took him a second to put it all together, the note helped.

I made you a daddy again.

*

Cooper

Tears were welling up in his eyes when he put his arms back around her. He was fucking thrilled and upset at the same time.

"Kitten... oh my God. I'm so sorry. Are you okay?"

She frowned and tried to withdraw from his embrace.

"I thought you'd be happy."

"Oh, baby girl, I'm over the moon ecstatic, I just know you wanted to wait until your career was established."

"I've been thinking about it and realized it'd probably be better to just wait to establish my career than start and stop and start again."

He narrowed his eyes. "So you planned this?"

She nodded sheepishly. "I went off the pill before we moved."

"Wouldn't this classify as something that would require more than a day's worth of our attention?" Reminding her of when she'd scolded him about not talking to her first before bringing Petey home.

Katie burst into tears, not at all the reaction he was going for when he started his little teasing.

"Oh baby, don't cry. Shit, I was just kidding."

Her voice was high and squeaky. "I thought it'd be a nice surprise. I thought you'd be happy."

Cooper wrapped her tighter against him. He needed to fix this. The last thing he needed was his pregnant, hormonal wife crying because she thought he wasn't happy about having a baby.

"Baby, I'm so fucking happy. This is one of the best surprises ever. It ranks right up there with red lingerie—probably even better."

She was still crying. *Fuuuuuck!*

"Please don't cry. I swear I was just teasing. You know I've wanted a baby since the first day I met Sofia Claire, which was also the first day I met you. It was destiny you were going to have my baby, Kitten. I'm so fucking happy. I'm just surprised because I thought you wanted to wait."

She wiped her eyes with her fingertips. *Thank fuck she'd stopped crying.*

"Well, you're an old man already, I didn't think we should wait much longer. Otherwise, you'll be fifty when it graduates."

"Baby girl, I'm going to be fifty when *Sam* graduates."

Her eyes widened like she was horrified, then a small smirk formed on her lips, and that's when he knew she was finally teasing him back. He'd take the age insults over her tears any day.

"Thank you, Kitten. I'm so glad you decided you didn't want to wait. I don't want to be on social security when number six graduates."

****

They didn't end up having six kids, which was probably a good thing because Sam and the twins tired him the fuck out. His wife was right—he *was* an old man.

Katie waited until Lily and Logan were in preschool before starting her career, but man, once she got going, she went like gangbusters. She tried to give him the credit, saying people only sought her out because of him.

"It's those fucking tits of yours, Kitten," he snarled in her ear.

"These tits?" she asked as she squeezed them together.

"Those tits," he said, taking over fondling them.

"Will you come on them later?" she whispered in his ear.

"Fuck, yes." She wouldn't have to ask him twice.

He couldn't ask for a better life—a hot as fuck wife who he adored and who liked sex as much as he did, three kids who, as far as he was concerned, were perfect, and a career he loved. He sometimes wondered what would have happened if he hadn't gone to see Cassie when Sofia Claire was born. He never would have gone to the diner, and he never would have met Katie.

"We would have still met," she told him confidently.

"How?"

"At the Marine Ball. The clock would have struck midnight, and I would have lost my shoe on purpose for you to find and return to me."

"So, you're my real-life Cinderella? Does that make me a prince?"

She winked, then kissed his lips softly.

"No, baby, you're a Marine. I'd take that over a prince any day."

Other Works by Tess Summers
Free Book! The Playboy and the SWAT Princess

BookHip.com/SNGBXD Sign up here to receive my
newsletter, and get SWAT Captain Craig Baxter's love story,
exclusively for newsletter subscribers. You'll receive regular
updates (but I won't bombard you with emails, I promise),
and be the first to know about my works-in-progress. (Like
when Ben's story is coming out!)

*She's a badass SWAT rookie, and he's a playboy SWAT
captain... who's taming who?*

Maddie Monroe

Three things you should not do when you're a rookie, and
the only female on the SDPD SWAT Team... 1) Take your
hazing personally, 2) Let them see you sweat, and 3) Fall for
your captain.

Especially, when your captain is the biggest playboy on
the entire police force.

I've managed to follow rules one and two with no
problem... but the third one I'm having a little more trouble
with. Every time he smiles that sinful smile or folds his
muscular arms when explaining a new technique or walks
through the station full of swagger....

All I can think about is how I'd like to give him my V-card,
giftwrapped with a big red bow on it, which is such a bad idea
because out of Rules One, Two, and Three. Breaking the third

one is a sure-fire way to get me kicked off the team and writing parking tickets for the rest of my career.

Apparently my heart—and other body parts—didn't get the memo.

Craig Baxter

The first time I noticed Maddie Monroe, she was wet and covered in soapy suds as she washed SWAT's armored truck as part of her hazing ritual. I've been hard for her ever since.

I can't sleep with a subordinate—it would be career suicide, and I've worked too damn hard to get where I am today. Come to think of it, so has she, and she'd probably have a lot more to lose.

So, nope, not messing around with Maddie Monroe. There are plenty of women for me to choose from who don't work for me.

Apparently my heart—and other body parts—didn't get the memo.

Can two hearts—and other body parts—overcome missed memos and find a way to be together without career-ending consequences?

Operation Sex Kitten

Ava Ericson thought she had her life planned out: graduate with her Ph.D., marry Brad Miller when he finished law school, have 2.5 babies... and mediocre sex for the rest of her days. But when Brad dumps her upon learning he's passed the bar, citing new "opportunities" available, she has to rethink her future.

Believing her lack of experience was the reason Brad broke up with her, she launches Operation Sex Kitten (OSK), a plan to become a vixen in bed and get Brad back. Things might go astray when she meets the notorious attorney, Travis Sterling, the bachelor who she is sure can teach her a thing or two in the bedroom. As she enjoys putting OSK theories into practice, she realizes the real 'operation' will be for the two not to fall in love.

Fun and romantic, *Operation Sex Kitten* turns up the heat with explicit scenes while you root for love to conquer all.

Get it here!

The General's Desire

Ron

I'm a decorated Marine general who doesn't have time for relationships. I've tried—they just don't work out—and I've never lost sleep over it. Then I meet her. Brenna is easily the most beautiful woman I've ever laid eyes on. The first time she blushes under my stare, it's game over. She's going to need to learn that I'm in charge and trust that I always mean what I say because I'm not letting her go.

Brenna

When Ron offers me a drink at the Sterling's wedding reception, I have no idea that he's a military star on the rise, I just know he's the walking definition of masculine—that translates in the bedroom (and couches, counters, tables...) as the best sex I've ever had. The more time we spend together, the more I'm convinced he's hiding something—or someone—and I'm not going down that road again. He can say anything he wants, but actions speak louder than words.

Get your copy here: http://bit.ly/TheGeneralsDesire

Playing Dirty

Cassie

I'm a career woman. I wear success like a second skin, and I'm rarely satisfied with anything less than the best. This includes my love life. If you want to date me, you better bring your A game because I don't play with the B team.

The only type of commitment I'm interested in is the one I have with my career. There is no man strong enough to tame me. Bold enough to rattle me. Or confident enough to win my heart. But then again, I have never met a man like Luke Rivas.

Luke

Cassie is one feisty, fiery, demanding woman who has enough confidence to intimidate even the bravest of men. She's driven, ambitious, and clearly has no interest in anything more than a casual fling.

But here's the thing. I want her, and once I have her, there will be nothing casual about it.

I will crack through that tough exterior she wears so well and bend her into submission. I'll make her break every one of her own damn rules just for me. And in order to accomplish just that...

I'm willing to play dirty.

Get your copy here:
http://bit.ly/PlayingDirtyTessSummers

About the Author

Tess Summers is a former businesswoman and teacher who always loved writing but never seemed to have time to sit down and write a short story, let alone a novel. Now battling MS, her life changed dramatically, and she has finally slowed down enough to start writing all the stories she's been wanting to tell, including the fun and sexy ones!

Married over twenty years with three grown children, Tess is a former dog foster mom who ended up failing and adopting them instead. She and her husband (and their six dogs) split their time between the desert of Arizona and the lakes of Michigan, so she's always in a climate that's not too hot and not too cold, but just right!

Contact Me!

Sign up for my newsletter: BookHip.com/SNGBXD

Email: TessSummersAuthor@yahoo.com

Visit my website: www.TessSummersAuthor.com

Follow me (but be warned, I tend to be a little naughty on social media!)

Facebook: http://facebook.com/TessSummersAuthor

Twitter: http://twitter.com/@mmmTess

Instagram: https://www.instagram.com/tesssummers/

Amazon: https://amzn.to/2MHHhdK

BookBub https://www.bookbub.com/profile/tess-summers

Book+Main: https://bookandmainbites.com/TessSummers

Goodreads - https://www.goodreads.com/TessSummers

Made in the USA
San Bernardino, CA
24 October 2018